MINE EYES HAVE SEEN
THE GLORY

CLINT GOODWIN

MINE EYES HAVE SEEN THE GLORY

U.S. Civil War Horse Perspective: 1861-1865

TATE PUBLISHING
AND ENTERPRISES, LLC

Published by Tate Publishing & Enterprises, LLC
127 E. Trade Center Terrace | Mustang, Oklahoma 73064 USA
1.888.361.9473 | www.tatepublishing.com

Tate Publishing is committed to excellence in the publishing industry. The company reflects the philosophy established by the founders, based on Psalm 68:11,
"The Lord gave the word and great was the company of those who published it."

Published in the United States of America

ISBN: 978-1-63122-144-6
1. Fiction / Historical
2. Fiction / War & Military
14.05.05

DEDICATION

Dedicated to my mother, Betty Jolene Noggle.
She gave me life, wisdom, and unconditional love.
Thank you, mother. Rest in peace.

October 1929 – September 2013

ACKNOWLEDGMENTS

To write a story about the US Civil War from a horse's perspective would have been a daunting task without the support of my family. This project was truly a family affair. I want to thank my wife, Karen, for her unyielding love and encouragement during the writing phase. I want to thank my daughter Allison for providing expert equestrian insights. Her professional knowledge of what horses can and can't do provided realism for this book. I want to thank my editor and sister, Linda Stone, for her limitless energy and encouragement. She knew how to correct my Texas version of the English language. To my son Ryan and his friend Rebecca Calderon for providing professional artistic insights. Our oldest grandson Gavin added his artistic touch to the back cover. I also want to thank our oldest daughter and Gavin's mother Janna, for encouraging him to do his best.

Lastly, I want to thank Ms. Lauren Perkins of Tate Publishing. She was my book's project manager. Her enthusiasm and guidance were invaluable sources of inspiration. I also want to thank Tate Publishing for assigning an expert editor to this book project. Lillian Vistal taught me that I have much to learn about writing still. Thank you!

The Civil War battles referenced in this story are real. The idea behind this book is to simply entertain and at the same time bring attention to a critical period of our American history. To ensure historic accuracy, my friend and Civil War actor Mr. Craig Mastapeter provided invaluable battlefield insights that added realism to the story. I want to thank my friend and mentor—Mr. Tom Henning. Tom's experience in writing and publishing his own books helped guide me through the "book world" with minimum heartache. Thank you, Tom.

I drew inspiration from many professionals who made the Civil War come to life between the covers of their books and on the silvers screen, specifically Ken Burns, whose Civil War documentary made headlines in 1990, and who renewed my interest in American history. Other great Civil War historians inspired me as well, such as Ed Bearss, Mathew Brady, Peter Cozzens, Donald R. Jumana, Shelby Foote, James Longstreet, James M. McPherson, General Edward J. Stockpole, Noah Andre Trudeau, Richard Wheeler, and Jay Winik. Each captured unique perspectives of the Civil War. As I read their books, I concluded that many men died fighting for the belief in freedom. From their works, I also concluded that many horses died in the same name of freedom. This thought encouraged me to write a book that told a story through the fictitious eyes of a horse. I wrote this book to reinforce our Civil War history through a fictitious set of eyes. This book only intends to entertain the minds of people who find historic fictions interesting. I made every effort to capture key Civil War dates, locations, and personalities engaged in those battles. I hope this book reminds its readers that the Civil War was not that long ago. With a dose of imagination, the key book characters saw the same defeats and triumphs the men experienced while fighting for their respective sides—North or South. I know; I fought alongside very brave men and women during Operation Iraqi Freedom. This project gave me an opportunity to express my feelings through the eyes of a horse.

PROLOGUE

A book on a US Civil War from a horse's perspective may be overdue, though it may probably not be on any historian's reading list. That notion is acceptable to me. If I were a historian, I would never consider reading this book either. One cannot help but notice the plethora of the civil war views of a soldier, sailor, general, admiral, politician, or citizen documented by many superb historians. What was missing from the body of literature was a Civil War story told from a horse's perspective.

Historians estimate that over 1.5 million horses died during the Civil War.[1] If they could talk, I am sure the history books would reflect a unique view of our country's past. Thus, I was motivated to write a unique Civil War story that would be interesting for all to read.

I believe a young generation will appreciate a fresh view of the US Civil War. Surely, horses have passed down their stories to their families like humans do. This got me to think—I wonder if horses shared the same sense of loyalty to their "side of the war?" Was there a difference between a Federal and Confederate horse? Did horses carrying riders into battle mourn the loss of a comrade killed on the battlefield?

The names used in this book are for the most part real people who served during antebellum as well as during and after the Civil War. To make this story fictional, I used literary license to develop the book's characters; thus, their actual deeds done during the Civil War were a work of my imagination. The dates associated with the Civil War battles are accurate. The battle locations described in this book are factual. Several maps I used as source material for this story characterize several battlefields that my wife and I actually walked upon as part of my research for this story.

Keep this in mind as you read this literary work: the purpose of this book is threefold. First and foremost, this story is to entertain readers who appreciate historical fiction. Second, it provides a narrative that teaches us about key Civil War events and themes, although not all are inclusive, for there were hundreds of battles fought by over three million soldiers of which over six hundred thousand Americans died. This book honors their sacrifice and the horses that carried them into battle. Lastly, this project gave me an opportunity to express my feelings about war as a combat veteran. I did not need to research the pain and sense of loss and experiences soldiers felt on the Civil War battlefield, as those fields do not change over time. This project gave me an opportunity to express my feelings about going to war and coming home.

IN THE BEGINNING, GOD MADE HORSE

God made man in *his* own image. However, God was smart enough to know man could not cross the rivers, deserts, and mountains without the help of me—a four-legged animal people call the *horse*. Yes, we horses have been around since the beginning, helping mankind fight their wars and win the peace. Thanks to a human, I can now tell our greatest story of how horses helped the United States brave the hottest and coldest days of joy and despair during the American Civil War fought between 1861 and 1865. Of course, there were many other historic American battles where humans rode on our backs to victory, but I will save those stories for another day. The beginning of this story starts with the birth of my great, great-great-great-grandfather called Lucky. I am all that is left of his bloodline. My name is Peace.

I am a three-year-old black thoroughbred stallion, charged with the humbling honor of transporting deceased veterans from their family's hands to the final resting place where heroes sleep—Arlington National Cemetery. How I got here is a long story rooted in the heroics of my bloodline. It all started six generations ago with Lucky who served with courage and commitment to duty during the Civil War. His legacy persists as I stand here in my stall at Fort Meyer waiting for the United States Army's best soldiers to take care of me. Looking around this dark, dusty stable, I wonder how an old horse barn in Alexandria, Virginia became the centerpiece of American history. Many horses have served here longer than me. With that said, there is much tradition and honor here on this hallowed ground.

Looking across the street at Arlington Cemetery, my heart fills with appreciation and gratitude for the United States Army, and of course, all the men and woman who paid the ultimate sacrifice to protect our great nation since the Revolutionary War. For that very reason, I keep working for the United States Army. The Army has provided my family and me a welcome home for over 150 years. On this soil is where my family's story begins.

Six generations of our family have carried or pulled the machines of war since 1861. My dad passed on to me the many wars our family fought and died in. While under fire, my father, Rusty, carried a famous army officer across deep rice paddies during the Vietnam War in 1968. My grandfather, Reckless, carried several brave US Marines across the muddy valleys of Osan during the Korean War in 1950. My great grandfather, Jubal Early, pulled key artillery pieces many times out of the muddy German valleys of the Hürtgen Forest during World War II in 1944. My great-great-grandfather, Tough Guy, pulled artillery in the mud during World War I during the Battle of Passchendaele on the Western Front in 1918. His father, Stonewall, fought Comanches during the Red River War in 1874 and 1875. However, all of my father's fathers recognize and pay homage to the memories of our family monarch that wrote the first chapter of our family's legacy during the US Civil War. His name was Lucky. Our story begins with his heroic deeds. And there is no better place and time to start this story than in 1859!

⌒

Sergeant Sowden brought me my oats and medicine on time this morning. I sure love molasses in my oats. My father, Rusty always said, "Peace, you will never have a sick day in your life if you eat a teaspoon of molasses." I think he was right. I didn't catch a cold during my first five years of life. Standing in the stall next to me was my old friend Blackie who said he knew my great-grandfather back in the big war, World War II.

I got his attention with a big snort. "Blackie, want to hear my family's war stories again?"

Looking through the wooden slats between us, Blackie said, "Go ahead young feller. You sure love to talk. We have time to kill until the next burial. I often think of my days of pulling those caissons and the heroes coming to rest. God bless those veterans. We will miss them."

"Don't worry Blackie, you may be old, but your legs are still strong. I think you are strong enough to stand and listen to me one more time. Here we go."

THE BEGINNING

It was a chilly spring morning in South Carolina, and the date was April 13, 1859. The Magnolia Plantation was expecting their brood mare to give birth—again. Her last foal had unfortunately died from birthing complications. With this past knowledge, Sir Thomas Drayton Jr., the plantation master, was not sure if she could survive another birth. Frankly, he did not expect me to be born alive. I would defy the odds and live to see the *glory of the coming of the Lord*. My name is Lucky. This is my story.

My mother, Sonna, an Irish Draught mare was not old, only a young ten years of age. Sir Tom said my mother had some invisible Irish bug that consumed her energy. I'm not sure what an Irish bug was other than having something to do with her genes. However, she was determined to bring me into the world.

She had done so successfully three times in the past. My three older brothers hauled cotton wagons. Their names were High Fly, Black Hawk, and Rifle. Unfortunately, Sir Tom had to sell all three of them to another plantation owner, old Mr. Lewiston who lived in the big white house two miles from our place. In 1861, the Confederate States of America requisitioned my brothers from Mr. Lewiston. Well, at least I had a family for a time.

Walking with Sir Tom was a black man he addressed as Mr. Joe, a burly thirty-two-year-old man standing about six feet two inches, wearing faded denim overalls and knee-high, brown leather boots. He managed the "plantation help," as Sir Tom liked to refer to those who worked for him, whom he actually owned.

Deep in thought, Sir Tom walked toward the barn with his eyes fixed on the high, hinged doors slightly cracked open. His eyes told the story. Sir Tom said to Mr. Joe, "I sure hope Sonna makes it. I cannot stand the idea of explaining these things to young Allison. She is not quite old enough to understand that our God works in wondrous ways, thought they may not always be to our liking."

"No worries, suh Tom, better thoughts will prevail through him." Mr. Joe saw Sir Tom's face relaxed, thinking the outcome would be less complicated.

Once inside the barn doors, Sir Tom and Mr. Joe opened the right door. It made a loud creaking noise. Closing the door behind them, they walked toward Sonna's stall. With foal still in her, she lay on the ground covered with fresh hay Mr. Joe had put down earlier.

As they walked by several empty horse stalls, Sir Tom whispered to Mr. Joe, "Joe, I sure do miss the boys. Those stallions were three of a kind."

Shaking his head, Mr. Joe replied, "Yea suh, those boys were strong and proud horses. However, times are tougher now, suh. You duz what you had to do."

Unfortunately, Sir Tom had to sell them to keep his planta-tion going. Under his breath, he replied, "The North keeps taxing our cotton exports Joe. This egregious act by the yanks has caused great financial hardships for the Southern states." How Sir Tom wished things would change. Thinking aloud, he said, "Perhaps succeeding from the United States would be best. Maybe our luck will then change. I suppose history will see it was our own manifest destiny or maybe the luck of the draw. We will see."

The sun had risen about halfway over the barn making it two o'clock in the afternoon. Sonna laid for hours on the stall floor sweating and breathing heavily. Mr. Joe spread more fresh hay before her head and wet her mouth with some water. Everyone loved Sonna because she had brought much joy to the Drayton family over the years. Though I was not born yet, I was alive inside listening to her heartbeat. I could tell she was breathing hard, so my heart sped up thinking my moments would be short-lived if she gave up. Mother struggled to keep enough strength in her to give me life. It seemed like forever inside her.

With time passing by, my head was starting to feel funny, so I squirmed my way into the wrong position. Oh, I so wanted to live! Then, within the silence, something physical startled me. I felt something grabbing at my front legs, trying to pull me around inside my mother. Those were strong yet gentle hands clamping down on my front hocks. Within a minute, I heard loud human voices outside again. Mr. Joe exclaimed, "Sir Tom, that foal is breached! You better get in there and turn em' around." I was being shifted around to make my exit. However, I became confused. If Mr. Joe's hands are not grasping on my hooves, I wondered whose hands were on me.

Immediately, Sir Thomas reached inside Sonna and quickly found my front legs pointing in the right direction. He said, "Joe, this foal is not breached!"

"Funny," Mr. Joe replied with a quizzical look. "I could have sworn that foal was turned the wrong way. God must be looking over it."

Before long, Sir Tom and Mr. Joe had pulled me out. Sliding onto the stall floor, I took my first breath of air at about three o'clock in the afternoon. I was finally born. Smiling widely, Sir Tom said to Mr. Joe, "It may have been the dreadful Friday the 13th, and yet, this is the foal's lucky day."

"Sir Tom, the ole girl has barely moved on the stall floor." The hay around her was wet and discolored with red. Both men had an uneasy feeling something was not right with Sonna. They could see it in her eyes that had what appeared to be big human tears running off her snout onto the bed of hay she rested upon.

After opening my eyes and getting my legs straight, Sir Tom put his arms under my belly to help me up. When I felt him pulling me toward the stall gate, I resisted, wanting to go to my mother. He said to me, "You are a strong one. Go to her." I stumbled over to press my nose against my mother's forehead and smelled her breath. She spoke softly to me, saying, "Welcome to our world son. You look so handsome. I am so grateful you made it. Last week, your father told me he had a dream about your destiny, son. God will watch over you every moment of your life."

My mother lay her head back down and looked at the water bucket in the back corner. Her dark brown eyes looked happy, yet I saw teardrops coming down her nose. Sir Tom came over and placed a small rope on my neck to lead me out of the stall. I did not want to leave, but for some reason, I willingly followed. Sir Tom said, "Mr. Joe, you might want to fetch the wagon." Sir Tom took me outside the barn to wash off my coat.

My mother hoped my future would be brighter than her life. She had spent her days as a workhorse on the Magnolia Plantation. Things did not turn out for her as she and Mrs. Drayton had planned. You see, my mom was a top show horse before she retired to be a brood mare. She met my dad on this plantation less than five years ago. Everyone knew my dad was the best working horse around. The whole county knew that he would produce top show horses, and in this case, strong wagon pullers like my dad.

When I first saw my dad, one characteristic stuck out about him. He was a massive black stallion about seventeen hands high with a broad chest and long legs. Sir Tom would say, "Blackie is dark as the night and stubborn as mule." Months before my birth, my dad told my mother that he hoped I would be different, that I wouldn't be as stubborn. Of course, mother knew I would grow up to be the best I could be at whatever I did. All mothers wish the same for their young. She knew my life would take many paths, many journeys filled with joy, and many days fraught with suffering. She knew I would grow into a strong black stallion like my dad. What mother did not know at the time was that unlike most farm animals, my future would be wedded to the names of brave men who would ride me into the greatest battles of the American Civil War. My story would be passed down to many generations of my kind.

I would be remiss not to begin my story with the humans who owned me—my masters—who the local people called the Draytons. They were Southern gentiles who raised cotton, rice, and tobacco sold to countries I would never see. Like most horses during antebellum, my life was to be lived as a "workhorse." This meant spending most days pulling a cart or plow across a land that was not so forgiving during the summer months. Now to most of us horses, this meant spending our evenings grazing and sleeping after working twelve to fourteen hours as day as long as there was daylight. We were not alone. Mr. Joe's family helped guide us, and from my perspective, they worked harder.

I hoped that my future would be different. After all, my father was a descendant of a US revolutionary warhorse owned by George Washington. I do not recollect his name, but he was a famous horse. Someday, I would find out who he was. Perhaps

my master knew his name. If I could talk like a human, I would
ask him.

Sir Thomas Drayton Jr., my owner, was twenty-two years old
when he inherited all of the Magnolia Plantation in 1825 from
his father who died of consumption. Now fifty-seven, my master had changed. His black hair now had streaks of silver running along the sides, and his piercing blue eyes had turned gray.
He sported a set of sideburns that ran alongside his square jaws,
which, as his wife said, "jutted out like a pier." South Carolina
knew him as a gentleman who brought great honor to his family
by helping others less fortunate than him.

Sir Tom's wife was a beautiful young woman from Ireland
whose parents brought her and my mother over to America in
1850 through the Port of Charleston in South Carolina. The
Powers family was from Dublin, Ireland. Like many Irish families
then, they escaped the Great Famine and British rule. The Powers
quickly made a comfortable life for themselves near Charleston.

Nancy Elizabeth Powers, Sir Tom's future wife, was the
daughter of a tobacco farmer. Her favorite horse was my mother
whom she had named Grace. Grace was a three-year-old filly
bred for strength and agility. Her bloodline dated back to the
fifteenth century when the Vikings invaded Ireland. The Celtic
people, indigenous to Northern Ireland, captured several horses
left behind. It was there where my mother would be born on the
Powers farm in 1847. Mr. Powers had said, "This horse is our
future. We will breed her to the best stallion in Dublin." For the
next few years, the Power's dream would become more and more
distant. With the Great Famine and British rule asserted on the
Irish people, the Powers had to make a choice: stay in Ireland to
eventually lose everything or go to America.

My existence can be traced back to a cool Saturday morning where a light fog covered the Irish shipping company. It was
August 17, 1850 when the Powers boarded a two-hundred-foot
merchant ship bound for Charleston, South Carolina. The jour-

ney would be tough. The rough Atlantic Ocean caused great concern for the Powers' safety. The ship's boatswain's mate secured my grandmother, Grace, three decks down in the ship's hull. Getting out on deck was obviously not an option during the trip. The only human contact Grace would have during the long voyage was with the Powers' young daughter Elizabeth. She took care of feeding and cleaning up Grace every day at sea and on land. For three weeks, Grace would not see the sunrise or sunset. Elizabeth came down every day to comfort and reassure Grace as she said, "It will be okay, girl. Once we get to America, you will be able to run as far and fast as you want. I just know you will find a handsome stallion to have little ones with. I hope to meet the same for myself someday. I do pray."

The Powers' Atlantic Ocean journey ended on Friday morning, September 6, 1850. The day was beautiful as the ship approached the South Carolina coast. Looking at the coastline, the Powers' hearts filled with so much hope and joy as they anticipated the start of a new life in the New World. Their life would soon include my father Blackie and Sir Tom. Of course, the jewel of their eyes was not yet born—a beautiful granddaughter named Allison.

Sir Tom said he fell head over heels when he first lay eyes on the Irish beauty he nicknamed Irish Green Eyes. She had long, thick auburn hair that was kept in a bun most of the time. Even though Miss Irish Green Eyes weighed no more than a hundred pounds, she was much stronger than she looked. I remember seeing her throw a fifty-pound ceramic milk churn out the back kitchen door when she got mad for not making the best buttermilk. That Irish temper made her turn red. Those were the days Sir Tom spent more time out in the barn with me.

On the day I was born, Sir Tom was the first human I saw when my eyes finally cleared. He said, "You are going to be something special on the Magnolia plantation." You are a long-legged colt meant for running—not hauling." He took a liking to me and decided I would become a hunting horse. He called me Lucky for "lucky to be alive."

As Sir Tom led me out of the barn, eight-year-old Miss Allison approached me and said, "Papa, he needs his mother. Why are you taking him out of the barn?" At about that moment, my legs gave out on me. I so weak. To get up, I pushed my hind legs up, and then, with all my strength, pushed my front legs into place one at a time. I was a bit wobbly at first, but then my tail whipped in circles to balance my weak legs. Looking back in the barn, I wanted to go back to her. Something was wrong.

Little Miss Allison took the halter from Sir Tom and lead me back to the stall where my mother was. Sir Tom said frantically, "Don't take him to his mother, Allison," but it was too late. Just before Mr. Joe closed the stall door, I saw my mother laying down, drawing very deep breaths. She did not get up. Her head remained against the stall floor. I figured she needed to rest. Sir Tom saw this and, much to my surprise, lead me to a stall at the other end of the barn where Allison had put fresh hay there for me to lie upon.

I was not sure why they separated me from my mother. All I knew was that she had my milk, and I was hungry. Fortunately, little Allison had a bottle of milk ready for me. She lifted my chin. "There boy, everything will be all right. I will take care of you I eagerly took the makeshift nursing bottle and drank every bit of that cow's warm milk. Before long, I fell asleep in my new stall just before noon.

In the late afternoon, I awoke to the sounds of wagon wheels rolling into the barn. I did not know the wagon's purpose. Perhaps Sir Tom had changed his mind about me becoming a hunting horse. Perhaps the wagon was for me to haul. This could not be. I was still too young.

Sir Tom pushed the wagon to my mother's stall. I heard him talk to another man whom I did not know yet. The man looked different. He was not the same skin color as my master. Both grunted and groaned about their task. I heard them struggle and complain greatly as they loaded the wagon with heavy cargo Mr. Joe hooked up a big horse version of me to the wagon. I wondered if the big black horse and I were family. I heard Mr. Joe call him Blackie. The stallion snorted loudly as he stood in place. Blackie raised his head to the rafters and closed his eyes. He had doleful, yet angry eyes. Mr. Joe spoke softly while patting Blackie's withers. "Now, now there, Blackie, you must get this wagon out of here before your son wakes up." Blackie calmed down as he slowly stepped toward the light shining through the open doors. I could feel the wagon wheels strain as it slowly rolled out of the barn.

My nose told me there was a familiar smell to that wagon. Though a brown, oiled tarpaulin covered the back, the smell was pleasant. Not overly concerned and a little weak, I lay back down in my fresh pile of hay. The sound of a breeze passed through the cracked barn doors and hayloft. The air flowed gently across my stall and made me sleepy. I slept the rest of the remaining afternoon.

Early in the evening, I awoke to feel small hands patting my neck and mane. My eyes slowly opened to see a bottle of cow's milk in little Miss Allison's hand. I would rather have had my mother's milk. Yet I was hungry again and needed to eat. My mother was nowhere in sight. Where was she?

During my first night of life, I did not sleep alone as Allison stayed with me, making sure I was not alone. At some point, I went to the bathroom and she even cleaned that up for me. At least I was not so lonely for my mother. I was thinking my mother was already outside waiting for me. As the days went by, it became apparent to me that my mother was not in the barn. Perhaps Sir Tom put her back in the field to work. I would "soldier on" as Sir Tom would say.

Over the next few months, I grew stronger and faster. My legs were not as wobbly. My mane and tail grew longer and

blacker. The tale came in rather handy. As the days became hot-
ter, it seemed every plantation animal was either in a grass field
or in a boarded-up, makeshift pen outside the barn. That long
tail of mine helped swat those pesky flies off my back. I lifted my
head up from grazing and noticed that in the big pasture, several
horses were out playing together. In the corner by himself was
Blackie, whom I had not seen since the day I was born. He was
staring up at the sky away from me. He looked so alone. I noticed
all the other horses stayed away from him. Why, I did not know. I
grazed in a smaller fenced area adjacent to the field where Blackie
stood and called out to say hello. Before I knew it, he was running
toward me as fast as the wind. I did not know what to do. He was
big and I was small.

Why was he in such a hurry? Instinctively, I began to back
away from the wooden crosstie fence that separated us. I thought
Blackie was crazy as it seemed like he was going to run right into
the five-foot-high fence that protected me. Then, like a bird, he
flew over the wooden stake rail fence with such grace and balance and landed less than three feet from me. I stood frozen in
my tracks.

Looking up into his dark eyes, I saw a light twinkle that put
me at ease. He put his long neck over my withers. Snorting, I
understood him to be saying, "Glad to see you son." He was my
family and seemed proud to know me. I had not known that kind
of love since I was born. Over the next year, Blackie was there as
my mentor and teacher. I was so glad to know he was my father.
I can see where I got my colors. He was so black that his skin
reflected a blue sheen in the sunlight. Over the coming months,
he gave me a strong sense of values he called duty, honor, courage,
and faith.

One year later, the day came when seeing my father would not
come to be. Sir Tom had to sell him to the Confederate States
of America (CSA). Not sure exactly what my father would be
doing for the army, I knew one thing: Blackie would do it well.

On the day he left, I whimpered but did not let a tear fall, as my father watched me. He said, "Soldier on, son." I would miss him, but I understood that I had to stand on my own four hooves. My childhood ended the day he left. It was time to grow up to be a stallion and stand tall in the face of adversity.

I grew stronger and faster over the next two years. In the spring of 1860, I experienced the most uncomfortable plantation tradition of what Mr. Joe called branding. Using a hot iron, Mr. Joe pressed the red-hot end of the rod on my left flank. The smell of my flesh burning was horrible. Quickly, Mr. Joe doused my rear with cold water. That felt good. Mr. Joe said, "There you go Lucky, you will forever carry the mark of Magnolia Plantation, like I do, a crescent moon over a palmetto." He let me stand back up. I stared into his dark eyes, turned my head sideways, and wondered why Mr. Joe was branded like me. He did not look like a horse.

In April 1861, a week before my second birthday, Sir Tom decided it was time to "break" me in. "Breaking in" meant it was time for me to learn how to carry a rider without bucking them off. I was not fond of the idea of a 220-pound man and a thirty-pound piece of leather called a saddle sitting on my back. When Tom attempted to put the saddle on, Instinctively, I bucked and jumped for what seemed like hours. Eventually, I gave up and surrendered to Tom's guiding hand, broke but not bent. He then put some metal objects called horseshoes on my hooves. Not sure why, but they sure made walking on the gravel road easier. Looking at those shoe nails, I thought for sure I would bleed to death. I know that the nails driven into my hooves would not cause pain. Though my hooves seemed heavier, the traction gained was amazing. I could now trot on a corduroy road with no trouble. The only problem was the noise made when my shoes connected with the hard surfaced road. I can hardly sneak up on anybody now with those noise makers on my hooves.

For my birthday, Tom tacked me up with a new leather saddle, blanket, and a bridle designed to make my mouth hurt less. The leather was stiff and smelled new. The craftsmanship was impressive. The saddle horn was encased in an engraved nickel silver horn cap that said, "Always faithful." The new bridle was also made of new leather trimmed with engraved nickel silver slotted conchas. I looked impressive thanks to Mr. Joe, Sir Tom's colored friend. Mr. Joe had been working on my new saddle and bridle since I was born in 1859. He was so proud to have given this gift to Sir Tom who said, "Not for me Joe, it is for Miss Allison."

Looking around, I saw the South Carolina morning sun slowly rise above the green pine trees enveloped with white mist that was drifting off the cotton fields. What a beautiful sight to see! I raised my nose to the sky and smelled the crisp honeysuckle fragrance in the breeze. My life was happy. To have a home and owner that provided me love, food, water, and space to run was a blessing—not my right.

With riding tack in place, Tom mounted my back; his heels were on my sides, signaling me to start trotting down the plantation road for about a mile. Running alongside the road was a winding creek the locals called Fish Creek. I was proud to carry my master, considering the alternative of pulling a cart full of rice or cotton.

Sir Tom and I stopped to greet another human on a horse called Red. Sir Tom said, "R.W. Goodwin, what are you doing two hundred miles away from Union County?"

Mr. Goodwin replied, "Heard there was some trouble brewing down here in Charleston, thought I would come down and take a look." While both masters talked, I politely greeted Red with a nose-to-nose sniff. Red was not a mister horse, but a miss horse. Not sure what it was, but my hind legs kicked up a bit. This mare sure smelled good. Perhaps we would become boyfriend and girlfriend. While we horses snorted at one another, my master and the other man yelled loudly with joy. Red and I looked at each other wondering what that noise was. Southern people called their howl the *rebel yell*. The words that followed that yell were, "Fort Sumter surrendered." We were not sure what this place "Fort Sumter" meant.

Fort Sumter, South Carolina was a United States Army fort bombarded by what Southern men referred to as Confederate soldiers. The attack lasted between April 12 and 13, 1861. This attack was the beginning of the US Civil War. Southern folk called it the War of Northern Aggression.

In haste, Sir Tom said goodbye to Mr. Goodwin and we raced back to the plantation barn. Sir Tom quickly jumped off my back to where Mrs. Drayton was standing. She greeted him, saying, "My dear, what is all the commotion about?"

Sir Tom said, "We are going to war to preserve our southern ways, my dear." Our lives would soon take a drastic turn on a red dirt road that had no return. Red and I did not know at the time, that our destinies would cross again in the North, on the battlefield.

Mr. Goodwin and Red moved on down the road toward the city of Charleston. Mr. Goodwin looked down at Red and said, "The city by the sea is known for its grits and shrimp." Red shook her neck side to side. All Mr, Goodwin could think about was how good that shrimp dish would taste with a jar of beer. Red could only think about Lucky. In her mind, she met her lifetime mate. How would she get back to Lucky? She did not know, but knew the Lord would deliver. She had faith.

Red and Mr. Goodwin approached Charleston on a dirt road that was full of potholes and muddy ruts that rolling wagons had left after a rainsquall. Looking ahead, Red noticed hundreds of horses with mounted soldiers wearing gray uniforms. As Mr. Goodwin and Red approached the group, a white horse came up from behind. On his back was a man, wearing the same gray uniform but with more gold. He introduced himself as General Pierre Gustave Toutant Beauregard.

Mr. Goodwin tipped his hat and said, "Good day, sir. My name is R.W. Goodwin of Union County, South Carolina. I understand we gave the Yanks a whipping at Fort Sumpter."

General Beauregard replied, "You bet son. We are looking for more to join us in the cause. You look like an experienced horseman. Interested in riding into battle for honor?"

"Yes sir, my family's plantation needs protection, count me in."

General Beauregard was curious. "Mr. Goodwin, if you do not know, plantation owners who volunteer are given the rank of second lieutenant. Ride on up to the front wagon. Ask for our brigade quartermaster. Give him this note. He will help get you fitted with an officer's uniform and sword."

Now standing tall in the saddle, Lt. Goodwin was sure of the South's victory. He knew where they were going. A young trooper riding behind him asked, "Sir, where are we headed?"

Lt. Goodwin, who had never been north of the Carolinas, replied, "Why Virginia?" The old trooper riding beside Lt. Goodwin asserted in a baritone voice, "Our orders are to report to the commander in the army of Northern Virginia. We are taking the fight to the Yanks. We will train here together for the next month or two. Then once June gets here, we will start our way up north."

Lt. Goodwin, looking perplexed and knowing he should have replied first, said, "Yes, just as the sergeant said."

LUCKY'S NEW OWNER

While carrying my master on a deer hunt in the early morning, a bullet struck Sir Tom's back, almost knocking him off my back. I was familiar with the sound of guns, which is why the sound did not startle me. But that rifle sound was different. It echoed from a distance. I thought I saw a puff of smoke coming from the tree line, but then it could have been the morning mist. Suddenly, Sir Tom dropped the reins and relaxed his leg grip on my sides. I was scared. I did not want him to fall off, so I carefully crossed the field then trotted up to the house where Tom's wife and servants pulled him from the saddle. There were sobs consuming the silent air. I felt very uneasy with the commotion. What had happened to my master? Mrs. Drayton rushed to me and said, "It is all right boy. You did us fine bringing back my beloved Tom."

Mr. Joe pulled Sir Tom off the saddle and carried him to the porch swing. Mrs. Drayton put a pillow under Sir Tom's head saying he was going to be okay. She directed Mr. Joe to get the doctor. He jumped on my back and delivered a strong kick to my sides; we ran a fast as the wind to get the doctor. Eight miles and two hours later, we made it back to the Magnolia Plantation.

Mrs. Drayton knelt down by Sir Tom to pat his head with a wet towel. Poor little Allison was not allowed to be in the presence of death. I noticed she was peeking out the front window, looking so sadly at her father. Her gaze quickly turned away to see the doctor's carriage pull up by the front porch. The doctor stepped out and ran up the steps to fix Sir Tom. In his black bag were bottles of medicine that smelled awful but seemed to make Sir Tom feel better. I almost got sick when I saw the doctor pull out a long probe he gently inserted into the bullet hole in Sir Tom's back. He grimaced but held in what surely was a silent scream. Locating the bullet, the doctor thought he might be able to save Sir Tom. While pulling the bullet out, the red blood flowed more quickly onto the porch deck. Mrs. Drayton desperately hoped that Sir Tom would live now that the bullet was out. The doctor placed a white piece of cloth over the wound. I was thinking that everything was going to be all right. Sir Tom and I would be out in the pines hunting in no time.

What we did not know then was that often times the bullet was not the killer. It was the invisible killer that doctors in the future would call germs. Back then and even until the late nineteenth century, few doctors understood that unclean probes caused infections that ultimately killed the human. This would be the case for Sir Tom. Within six weeks, infections poisoned his blood that would eventually take his life.

On Saturday, June 8, 1861, Mrs. Drayton buried my master next to his father in the family plot west of the main house. Each grave's headstone faced east where the warm sunrise rays glanced across the final resting place for humans. I wondered if they buried horses.

I was sad for Mrs. Drayton and Miss Allison. What would they do? Surely my new life would be wedded to the dreary work of pulling cotton and rice carts to and from the fields; however, I would soldier on. The next few months were trying for the Drayton family. The summer crops needed cutting, hauling, and selling. All the neighboring plantations were hurting financially. It seemed that our country was breaking apart. The South wanted their economic and social freedoms. The North wanted the Southern rebels to give up slavery. The new Confederate army pressured the Southern loyalist for more resources. The Magnolia Plantation would eventually succumb to economic demands required by the Civil War effort. Most of the food grown for the Drayton family were sold to the CSA well below market price.

With little money and food to eat, the Drayton family would have to sell me to the Confederate army. My new owner's name would be Brigadier General Pierre Gustave Toutant Beauregard.[2] His destiny would become mine.

I guess it was around mid-June when the CSA Cavalry came by our plantation. I was so impressed with how determined my fellow horses and their riders moved in unison on the old road by our home. Watching the parade of riders got me thinking about where they were going. All of a sudden, they all stopped. Two riders broke away from the group. I could see them trotting toward the main house. I stayed comfortably safe in my field, watching from a distance. The two riders were wearing gray uniforms. Mr. Joe said, "Lucky, gray uniforms are worn only by white men serving the South. Dayd don't like people like me and most likely want like you boy." One of the men as well as the horse he was riding looked familiar to me. I was not certain for I was a good hundred yards away. Sticking my nose in the air, I detected a familiar aroma; that horse was my Red! Well no fence was going to keep me away from her. Looking at the six-foot-high fence, I figured I would only need fifty yards of running distance to clear it. After making the jump, I ran toward Red who saw me coming. She reared, almost throwing off her rider who I could see now was Mr. Goodwin.

Mrs. Drayton came out of the house holding Miss Allison's hand. I was standing by Red when I heard the other rider say, "Good morning, ma'am. My name is General Beauregard. With me is Lt. Goodwin who I understand is an old friend of your husband, Sir Tom Drayton. As you know, the South has declared war against the North. We are in need of supplies and horses to help further our cause. That black horse there looks strong and spirited. We need more horses like that to pull our cannon wagons. Are you willing to sell him?"

Miss Allison looked at her mom. "No, Mother. We cannot give up Lucky. He brought Daddy back to us!"

With firmness in her eyes, Mrs. Drayton said, "Allison, go back into the house."

"General Beauregard," Mrs. Drayton said in a stern voice, "we at Magnolia Plantation would be glad to help the South's cause. We do not have any crops to share since harvest is not until next month. We do have yams and a few hogs that can go with you. Is the CSA able to provide us a small payment?"

General Beauregard said," We will make payment once our currency has been printed." He went on to say, "With all due respect Mrs. Drayton, the CSA will also need to take that black horse."

Mrs. Drayton looked sadly at me. I looked up at the house and saw Miss Allison looking out of the window. I could see the tears running down her face. I looked back at Mrs. Drayton, and it seemed like hours before she said, "I suspect that would be the right thing to do for the war effort."

She yelled over to Mr. Joe and said, "Bring Lucky's halter over. Lucky is going to leave us for a time."

Looking displeased, Mr. Joe fetched the bridle and placed it on my nose. He whispered to me, "Soldier on, Lucky boy. Sir Tom would expect noth'n else from youza. Da soldier on."

I spent the first years of my young life peacefully smelling the sweet magnolias during Southern misty mornings. Little did I know that the next four years of my life would be spent running through smoke-filled battlefields, where death and suffering would overcome the living. I thought I would never smell the sweet fragrance of freshly cut hay and honeysuckles or watch the morning mist floating over the Magnolia Plantation fields of South Carolina.

As Lt. Goodwin led me away, I looked back at the main house where Mrs. Drayton, Mr. Joe, and little Miss Allison waved goodbye to me. It was funny, because to the left of the house where they buried Sir Tom, I thought I saw him waving too. So I stopped for a moment to stare at the fields one more time. Lt. Goodwin said, "Come on, boy. We need to go north. Lord willing you may be back here someday." I walked behind Red, feeling sorrowful that I may never see my beloved family again. My dad would have said, "It was time to grow up, son." I wished he were with me.

~~~

It was July 18, 1861. It was a Thursday afternoon, and the Confederate military wagon train had clambered through thick brush and air full of smoke and dust for ten hours since reveille. My hooves were tired and sore from the many miles of pulling a wagon loaded up with guns and ammo across Ole Virginny. I overhead the wagon driver, Private Smitty, say, "Men, it won't be long and we will be give'n those yella' Yankees a thrash'n." Where were we going? What was a Yankee? Where was Ole Virginny? Nevertheless, we pushed forward north, hoping the night would bring rest. I had not eaten in two days.

Private Smitty was a scrawny looking man standing five feet ten and weighing about 160 pounds. He was constantly yelling at us, "Get going, you mules." I was insulted for I knew one thing: I was not a mixed breed—half donkey and half horse. I was so glad that with me, five other horses were pulling that wagon burdened with thousands of rounds used by the infantry, or soldiers I referred to as "men marching on the ground."

I felt badly for the soldiers who trudged alongside us. Each of them looked so young and hungry; their clothes were dirty and full of holes. Their eyes, however, told a different story; they burned with hope and determination as they marched on and sang songs to forget about their hunger. Some of those songs reminded of my dear master who would sing the same songs. Now to a horse, the human words don't make much sense. But the words I remembered for the rest of my days would be, "Mine eyes have seen the glory of the coming of the Lord." I liked that song. It motivated us to move forward.

Our brigade had traveled over 480 miles through swamps, muddy roads, and fields when Private Smitty stood up in the wagon seat and said, "Boys and girls, we are going have to take a swim in the Rappahannock River today." He went on to say, "Someday, we will be fighting those blue bellies here in Fredericksburg." He would be right. In December 1862, many men and horses would die on that land.

On Friday morning, the Confederate soldiers rose up from their bivouacs hoping to find something else to eat besides hardtack and lard. One of the soldiers had done some night fishing in the river using only his hands. He swam along the riverbanks, periodically pushing his hands into underwater holes the fish burrowed themselves. The soldier was mighty pleased with his fish. The soldiers called it a catfish that would be fried and served to a brigade of soldiers. After eating that fish, I do not think I had seen the soldiers smile as much as they had since we left South Carolina.

Smitty even brought us a treat—freshly cut hay. He was a very resourceful fellow, though he wasn't very honest. He said we had to live off the land as we traveled through the countryside. "These are General Beauregard's orders," Smitty said in a drunken tone of voice. If other soldiers knew what he did while others slept, I do not think he would be very popular. While in North Carolina, I had seen him get up in the middle of the night and walk over to an empty house to take whatever he could get his fingers on. Not that his stealing concerned me, but in human standards, Smitty should have been shot for stealing from the civilians. He was not my problem—yet.

While standing next to me, Smitty said, "Boy, notice you have been branded much like the rest of them slaves." Running his greasy hands over my left flank, he said, "Boy, I recognize that brand, you be from Magnolia Plantation down in South Carolina. I used to hunt around dem dare parts. Old man, forgot hiz name, kicked me off his property one day. Never did care for dem uppity people thinking them better than us normal folks." I did not like the way he said those words. Something was not right about Smitty.

We all ate well that night. General Beauregard made sure we camped by the river to stay cool. Being in the middle of summer, the feel of the cool breeze coming off the water felt good. Looking up at the stars, I stood tied to the tree wondering where Red was now. How I missed her. When we crossed into Virginia earlier in the week, I had heard Lt. Goodwin make some comment about his company transferring to another cavalry regiment under the command of a colonel named J.E.B. Stuart. All I knew was that one morning Red was there, then the next day she wasn't. She could have told me beforehand. I am beginning to think she does not like me or is simply teasing me.

Our Confederates kept pushing toward a place I had never heard of, a place called Manassas, Virginia, where the first of two big battles would take place during the Civil War.[3] General Beauregard would lead the CSA Army of Northern Virginia during the first Battle of Manassas. It was there at the first Battle of Manassas that my life would take another turn. I would play a key role in the Battle of Manassas. During the battle on July 2, Smitty positioned our wagon behind a grassy hill, not three hundred yards over and down a hill from a house that the men called the Stone House.[4]

Though we were out of sight, the sounds of war were booming. That did not bother me as I was used to the sound of gunfire. I had grown accustomed to it during hunting trips on Magnolia Plantation. However, what I did not care for was the loud explosions of the canons; the soldiers called them twenty-four-pounder howitzers. The amount of smoke produced by those canons made it impossible for soldiers to see on the battlefield. At times, I wondered if my side was losing or winning. It was hard to tell. The rest of the horses were scared and jumpy. However, I remained steadfast and unafraid. It did not take long for the wagon master to recognize that we horses would calm down if he unhitched us and moved us to the tree line below the hill. I continued to remain calm while the shooting and explosions over the hill escalated.

Unfortunately, my friends tied next to me did not remain calm. In fact, the rope line pulled away from the branches, freeing all of us. I saw my friend Bucky from Georgia run to the top of the hill only to come crashing down sideways. Bucky's hooves remained motionless. A red liquid covered his head. I walked to Bucky's left and nudged him, but he did not move. At that very moment, I became afraid of war because I had never seen a friend die that way.

Looking to my left, I found a trail going around the hill where I could get my bearings and a better view of what was happening. Before I could go any further, Private Smitty ran up to me and placed a rope around my neck, trying to lead me back over to the copse of trees. I was confused at first, but then my suspicions gave way to the truth. He was trying to put a halter on me and that meant only one thing: he was going to leave the battlefield. I would differ from his intent. While he was trying to force the bit into my mouth, I closed my front teeth hard on his hand. He let out a shrill scream that was silenced by the cannonades. He looked at me and pulled his revolver from his pocket; I could see he intended to kill me, so I reacted quickly. I reared up on my hind legs and came down hard on his right arm, which loosened his grip on the weapon. Smitty simply snarled those yellow teeth at me, and then he turned and ran like a coward.

Turning back to my left, I galloped over and up the hill to a spot overlooking the battlefield. I stopped and saw a Confederate officer wearing the same gray woolen uniform Private Smitty wore, except he had gold-colored stripes stitched onto the shoulders of his blouse. on his shoulder. I remembered seeing the officer and his horse a few days earlier. I had heard the rider call his chestnut-colored horse Little Sorrel. The man in the dirty gray uniform looked proud and determined. There were silver eagles on his shirt collars and gold-colored markings on his sleeves. A soldier next to him called out, "Colonel! Colonel Jackson, Sir!"

On Little Sorrel, Colonel Jackson rallied his troops to push back the Union flank. He would have nothing to do with defeat. It was why his soldiers gave him the nickname "Stonewall Jackson"; he demonstrated bravery and honor.

Several hours passed, and it was obvious the Union had had enough fighting. The Federals were retreating. To my right toward the east, I could see, what looked like civilians having a picnic just outside the battlefield lines. Those folks looked like they were doing what Sir Tom and Mrs. Drayton did on Magnolia Plantation. I could not believe my eyes. In the corner of my eye, I also thought I saw Private Smitty running toward the Union, waiving a white flag. One word came to mind at that moment: traitor! Glancing back, Colonel Jackson had taken Little Sorrel over to where I had been tied up along the tree line. I followed them, curious about Little Sorrel. This would be a good time to go over and meet Little Sorrel to find out where he came from.

Cautiously, I walked up behind Little Sorrel who reared up and snorted at me. I was surprised how unfriendly he seemed at first. However, after a couple of pawings and head shakings, Little Sorrel accepted my presence. I asked him, "Who is your master?"

"My master is a great, God-fearing man who has no limits in bravery and courage. Like him, I am fearless of the unknowns ahead of us," Little Sorrel replied.

I was struck in awe by his response. "Why do you put your life in Colonel Jackson's hands?"

"Because it is our duty. You should take note to serve your master just as well as I."

"I have no master. He fled our team after removing our tack and securing us to these trees. My friend Bucky over there was shot down by a Yankee bullet."

"Forget about him. You will need another master. You look strong and capable of running fast."

"Yes, I am very fast. Perhaps I would better serve the war by carrying a rider into battle?"

"Yes, we have a group of soldiers that ride horses into battle. They are our cavalry troopers. Those men and horses over there are called the First Regiment Virginia Cavalry led by Colonel J.E.B. Stuart." I had heard that word *cavalry* before. Lt Goodwin and Red were in the Cavalry. Maybe, just maybe I would see my Red again.

After the Battle of Manassas, I was assigned to the First Regiment Virginia Cavalry under the command of Colonel James Ewell Brown (J.E.B.) Stuart.[5] My new master's name would be First Regiment Virginia Cavalry, Company H Loudoun Light Horse Captain Robert W. Carter. I was so glad to be hauling a rider around and not a wagon. My master was young and an experienced horseman. Captain Carter was not afraid of sitting up in the saddle while shooting his rifle. It felt good to run.

After the Battle of Manassas, we followed Colonel Stuart to engage in more than one hundred skirmishes with the Federals throughout Virginia during '61. I was feeling proud and encouraged. My fellow horses were also surprised to see how well the Cavalry fed and cared for us horses and our troopers. Our riders deserved special treatment. Most soldiers assigned to the Confederate Cavalry were experience horsemen from the South. The horsemen knew how to take care of their warhorses. Each gave us a name. Of course, Captain Carter did not know my real name, so he called me Virginia. I was not amused since it sounded like a girl's name and I was a stallion. No matter, Captain Carter and I pushed forward to the next skirmish with the Union.

By the time winter came, my eyes had seen enough glory and death for a lifetime. Thousands of my kind had gone to heaven. Unfortunately, many injured men remained behind on the battlefields. The horse toll was horrifying to me. Undaunted, our hearts remained true to the cause of Southern freedom. This unyielding belief kept us moving forward with little sleep and food in between battles. My horse brothers said it was what made Americans strong and courageous—better than the rest of the world. After all it is said by Winston Churchill, "You do your worst, and we will do our best."

The cold winter of '61 would eventually pass. I did not freeze to death since horses grew winter coats that kept us warm most of the time, except when it snowed. Snow made us look for cover under trees. Our Confederate soldiers had it tough, with just the clothes on their backs and a few woolen blankets. Warmth was rather limited to a campfire and tent. While in winter quarters, our commander, J.E.B. Stewart prepared for spring movements in Virginia. The next battleground for our Confederate brothers would be Williamsburg, Virginia. It was at the Battle of Williamsburg, on May 5, 1862, where I would lose my Captain Carter to a Union sniper's bullet.[6]

Captain R.W. Carter was a very good trooper. During the ten months of fighting together, I got to know him very well. He surely wanted to end the war and go home as soon as possible. I think he missed his old way of living. Being of southern gentry, Captain Carter was accustomed to the better side of things. To maintain his simple pleasures, he sure seemed to have a knack for ensuring that both his and my comforts were taken care of even though others went without. Perhaps his cavalier attitude was from being older and wiser. Captain Carter was not young; he was maybe around twenty-three or twenty-four years old, but he sure seemed popular amongst the rest of the troopers.

It was early Monday morning and time to go to work, so the troopers arose from their bivouacs at around four thirty. As had been the case for the whole year, we quietly picked up and rode out before dusk guided only by the stars. Captain Carter said, "Virginia, look up at the Lord and you will never get lost at night." Looking left and right, I wondered what he meant. He said, "No, Virginia, look up. See the stars formed into a kite pattern. The star at the top of the kite points pretty much north. If you lose me, always remember to follow that star in the opposite direction to go home—south." He was so smart about things like that.

Captain Carter was a good man, though he was not a big man. I would say he weighed about 170 pounds, which made me feel light on my hooves. We made good time on patrols. He also had a good sense of humor and sang every time we crossed a railroad track. I remembered him saying that singing in church made him feel closer to God. One of his songs went something like this:

> Good morning, Captain, when are we going home?
> I said good morning, Captain, we're feeling so alone.
> Good morning, Captain, let this train roll on home.
> Captain says so keep shovel'n, that coal will move us on.
> I said good afternoon, Captain, have we lost our way?
> I said hello, Captain, are we going home to stay?
> He said don't worry, son; the Lord will get us get home today,
> He said don't worry, son; the Lord will get us get home today.

I remembered the sound of a single gunshot first, then the slumping of Captain Carter over the saddle. The reins dropped alongside my face like the time I lost Mr. Drayton. I knew what to do. I took Captain Carter back to the camp where Colonel Stuart was planning his next attack. Colonel Stuart, saddened by the loss of another good officer, removed Captain Carter from my saddle. Interestingly, Colonel Stuart was impressed with my loyalty, and since Colonel Stuart was in need of a horse, he decided to take me and ride into the next battle. I was honored to be chosen, but then according to other horses, Colonel Stuart tended to get shot at often. I was unsure about my new master. However, I remembered the words of Little Sorrel: "Because it is our duty!"

I was given a new saddle and blanket. The saddle had the letters *CSA* embossed on the black leather. I also noticed an interesting mark on the side of the blanket. It was in the shape of a star. The soldiers no longer uttered the word *colonel*. The new title spoken around camp was "General." Colonel Stuart was promoted to Brigadier General J.E.B. Stuart. It was September 24, 1861. I was now serving the CSA Army of the Potomac carrying General Stuart through several more battles for the remaining months of 1861.

Our new commander of the Army of Northern Virginia, General Robert E. Lee, ordered Brig. Gen. J.E.B. Stuart to penetrate Union enemy lines to the north.[7] General Lee would be heralded as one of the greatest military minds the world had ever known.[8] Upon return from Maryland, I got a chance to meet one of the most famous horses during the Civil War. His name was Traveller, and his rider's name was General Robert E. Lee.

When I first met Traveller, the exchange of snorts was much different than that with Little Sorrel. Traveller was in fact a courteous horse that carried much pride and wisdom becoming of a loyal servant to the Confederacy. In fact, Traveler had had the same master for six months since February 1862 when General Lee purchased Traveller from Major Joseph M. Broun, quartermaster of the Third Virginia Infantry. I was impressed with the gray-colored stallion What I did not understand was why Traveller was so nervous and spirited. Traveller said, "I miss my home in Greenbrier County, Virginia. Where is your home?"

"I am from Magnolia Plantation, South Carolina. I miss home and most of all, my mother," I replied.

The spring of '62 was a wet one. It seemed like we were always marching in the mud northward. I was lucky we horses did not get hoof rot like the soldiers. General Stuart and I crossed the Maryland state line in June 1862. This excursion was to be one of our finest moments. General Stuart would circle the Union Army of the Potomac in a three-day raid that supplied General Robert E. Lee with the intelligence necessary to launch his counteroffensive against the Union right wing north of the Chickahominy River. We moved across the Virginia countryside in response to the Union's Peninsula Campaign. The Peninsula Campaign consisted of fifteen different battles between our sides during March to July 1862. [9]

A day after the last Peninsula Campaign Seven Days Battle engagement finished, my luck ran out. We had crossed a rocky creek that caused me to stumble, creating a limp that would have normally required a bullet to solve the problem. However, General Stuart showed mercy. He turned my care over to the quartermaster who wrapped up my hoof with a clean bandage and lard. Whether it was because of the lard or the rest, I was back on my hooves in no time. I was no longer Brigadier General J.E.B. Stuart's horse. He had taken another horse he named Star of the West. I was disappointed I could not ride into battle with the general; perhaps it was fate or simply God's hand that kept me safe. It was not long after the Seven Days Battles that a Union trooper shot down Star of the West from underneath General Stuart.[10] The death toll for the Confederates and Union sides was heavy. General Lee's Army of Northern Virginia suffered about twenty thousand casualties. Union General McClellan reported casualties of about sixteen thousand. Despite our victory, the losses of men and horse stunned the South.[11]

I healed up quickly. My flesh wound fought infection thanks to the care of old Sergeant Delaney from Georgia. The soldiers of Company A called Delaney "Pops." I knew him as an old man who knew his way around the farm and knew how to use old-fashioned remedies to fix us animals. Thanks to him, I would go on to ride into more battles before the war was over.

On the morning of August 3, 1862, near Germantown, Virginia, the sun rose up behind large, gray clouds. The horizon was streamed with brilliant red, blue, purple, and orange colors. Perhaps the colors were a warning of some sorts or maybe a blessing. I had seen a few sunrises from the same spot since we had been encamped there for a few days while awaiting orders from Richmond. I was glad Sergeant Delaney had parked his chuck wagon near a stand of trees that offered much needed shade during the midday. I knew it was going to be another hot one, with thunderclouds building up as usual in the afternoon. I heard my caretaker coming up, breathing hard as usual. Looking behind me, I saw old Sergeant Delaney carrying a bucket of water. Suddenly, out from behind the chuck wagon, there was the commotion.

Like a wet cat, a young Confederate officer rushed by him, knocking the water bucket out of his hand. The young officer did not have a pleasant look on his face, and I could see Sergeant Delaney was unnerved by his rudeness. The trooper was certainly in a hurry for something. Captain Mathew C. Butler was from the Second South Carolina Cavalry and was in need of a new mount.

Sergeant Delaney said, "Sir, how can I help you?"

In a stern, commanding voice, Captain Butler said, "Sergeant, I need that black horse there. Are there any problems with him?"

"No sir."

"Well then, get me a halter. I need a mount for battle. We have to move out of here soon and my other horse has gone lame. Unfortunately I had to shoot the old black stallion."

I could tell this officer meant business. I was not thrilled about the idea of carrying a horse-killer on my back, but then at least I was moving out of here. I knew he had to do what was best for the cause.

My new cavalry regiment was attached to Colonel Hampton's Legion from South Carolina serving under Brigadier General J.E.B. Stuart. We had an important mission ahead of us. According to Captain Butler, our job was to get intelligence on Union positions in the state of Maryland. To get there, we would have to negotiate many creeks, mountains, and of course, the enduring Potomac River during the months of August and September 1862. General Lee wanted us to move toward Northern Virginia and eventually into Maryland. General Lee wanted to go on the offensive.

After crossing the Potomac at White's Ford, we made our way into Maryland. The hours seemed like days; time was slowing down. The mornings could not come quick enough for me to get to the next day. For some reason, I felt uneasy about what lay ahead. Perhaps it was the conversation Captain Butler had with another officer riding next to us on the trail two miles behind.

Captain Butler had said, "Alex, I wish I did not have to do it."

"What you talking about, Matt?" Captain Alexander Hamilton Boykin replied

"Having to put down that black stallion I had for the past year. He served me well. There were times he ran so fast, I could see the wind passing me by. I sure miss that horse but this one seems just as good. We will see."

"As long as I have known you, you never got attached to a horse. You know they are going to be the first in a sharp shooter's sight. Plus, you never take time to groom them. That black horse you're riding looks like a bay with so much dirt on him."

"Yes, I know, but that horse was special. In fact, he had been branded with the crescent moon and palmetto tree."

I thought of home every time I got on his back. The words he spoke—"crescent moon over palmetto"—were familiar words to me. I could not remember what they stood for. I did not know at the time, but Captain Butler would remind me after we crossed back over the Potomac in to Virginia. The war made me forget many things. I guess forgetting was the only way warriors could cope.

On Sunday, September 7, 1862, we made it to a key rendezvous point west of Urbana, Maryland. We were about thirty miles east of Sharpsburg. Our regiment stayed around the Urbana area for about five days during which Brig. Gen. J.E.B. Stuart took time to review strategic plans and build goodwill with the local leaders. I welcomed the rest for it had been a month since we had bivouacked for more than a day in one place. The trees started to turn colors as the fall season neared. Those trees were mighty beautiful. Orange and red colors tinted the edges of the leaves like wood singed by fire. The morning air was light and fresh. I would not mind living up there in the north if it were not for the Yanks.

Over the next few days, Captain Butler and I reconnoitered between Urbana and Frederick located to the northwest of us. The locals called the valley east of South Mountain the Cumberland Valley. To the west of South Mountain lay the Hagerstown Valley. According to Special Orders, No. 191, it was the intent of General Lee to occupy both valleys, giving the Confederates a strategic advantage in the north. Our job was to assess enemy strengths and positions south of Fredericktown (now known as Frederick), Maryland. The only problem was, General Lee was marching up from the south to Sharpsburg located on the west side of South Mountain. How could we get intelligence to General Lee before the Union Corps moved on top of our Divisions?

On September 11, Captain Butler and I observed three Union Corps encamped nearby, and the rest of our regiment moved out quickly from Urbana toward the northwest of South Mountain. The Union would have to cross several mountain gaps to advance toward General Lee's position. Our job was to help turn the Union's right flank towards Lee's chosen field of battle south of Sharpsburg. The place of battle would be known as Antietam.

BATTLE OF ANTIETAM

In 1763, on a plot of land called Joe's Lott, Mr. Joseph Chapline laid out what was to be the first town in Washington County, Maryland. Mr. Chapline named it Sharpsburg in honor of his friend Governor Horatio Sharpe. He chose that site for the town because of the "great spring" of water located there. Like Mr. Chapline, the rest of the Sharpsburg residents in the '60 were primarily of English and German decent. It was there that his son-in-law, Mr. Joseph Poffenburger, settled his family from Germany. Thirty-year-old Joseph was an entrepreneur at heart. He truly believed that America was the land of salvation. As such, he owned a feed store built parallel to the Chesapeake and Ohio Canal, also known as the C&O Canal that ran along the Potomac River. Mr. Poffenburger also owned a nice farm just south of Sharpsburg.

Joe's feed business gave him the ability to take care of his wife and children while trying to get his farm going. He purchased his farm from the estate of his father-in-law, Mr. Joseph Chapline. Between running the feed store and farm, Joseph stayed very busy as most men his age during those days. He had hoped to pass his businesses to his oldest son, Otto, who was very helpful around the farm when he was not getting into mischief.

Typical of teenage boys during that time, Otto amused himself with exploring creeks and the adjacent woods in the area. During the weekday, his father counted on fifteen-year-old Otto to weed the fields and keep the rows turned. However, Otto had other ideas on September 16, 1862. Being a blond German-American, Otto prided himself in being stronger than most of the boys his age in Washington County. In fact, he had been the champion hammer thrower two years running. Life would test his courage and personal resolve on the very next day.

While walking along Antietam Creek, Otto heard distant cannonades from the northeast near South Mountain. His father told him to stay close to home. War was coming, but as a fearless teenager, Otto's unbridled curiosity kept him walking along the creek until it got dark. Realizing that he would get wet from the rainsquall passing over, he decided to stay put under a rock bridge arching over Antietam Creek. Under this bridge, he would sleep during the night and most importantly, stay dry. The rain did not let up that evening. Without a blanket, he could only curl up behind some logs he had fashioned into a lean-to. Otto listened to the roar of distant cannons as the booms got closer and closer to him. He worried about his family and thought he should have listened to his father.

At sunrise, Otto awoke to the sound of horsemen galloping fast along the opposite side of the creek. He could not tell if they were Federal or Confederate troopers. Not wanting to find out, he carefully crawled around the backside of the bridge up to the ridge behind him. To his surprise, standing at the top of the ridge were horse-mounted troops, clearly Confederate. The one officer-looking rider came up to him and said, "Son, you need to get out of here quickly. The hand of God will be upon this place shortly."

Not knowing where to go, Otto ran southwest along Smoketown Road toward high ground to the Dunker Church. From there he could make his way back to the farm, or so he thought. Though Otto was safe for that moment, his curiosity got the best of him. He figured if he hid behind the big oak tree less than three hundred yards to his right, he would be safe and get a firsthand view of a soon-to-be battle between the North and South. A regiment of Confederate infantry came close to Otto. One soldier yelled out, "Get out of here boy. God's fury is coming!" Otto ran as fast as he could to get back toward home along the low areas between rolling hills that provided him some cover. Then a loud screeching sound stopped him in his tracks. The long-range cannonades began. He dropped to the ground, covering his head. Though the explosion was a hundred yards away, he could feel the blast pressure displacing the air around him. He prayed for his life. About halfway to his farm, he stopped and took cover behind Dunker's Church. From thereon, young Otto's life would change forever.

⌒⌒

While Otto was scrambling for his life, I was carrying Captain Butler down the steep embankment along Antietam Creek. I wondered if he was going to fall off my back, or if I would slip into that darn rocky creek. It had been a tough ride the previous night, as we didn't stop for rest or food. I was still shaken up from the South Mountain skirmish the day before. Captain Butler, who had a gunshot wound in the shoulder, said out loud, "Thank the Lord the ball passed through."

I felt a sting in my right rump but thought it was just a sticker. Neither one of us was in good shape. Captain Butler kept saying, "Let us get out of here Lucky. We have to report the Union positions back to General Lee."

I did all I could to keep from stumbling into the creek. The water was rising fast, and at one point, I had to swim to keep Captain Butler on my back. We were cold, miserable, and motivated by fear. Though it was cold, the good news was that most of the red Virginia clay was washed off my coat.

Running forward, I could see the rock bridge he wanted to get to in a hurry. From there, we turned right and climbed up the hill, which seemed to be a mountain since the sun was not up yet.

I struggled to keep my hooves moving as the slope was covered with wet grass and leaves. Finally, at the top, we ran into a small regiment of other Confederate troopers.

Their officer-in-charge was Colonel G.T. Anderson. "Captain, what have you brought us?" he said.

"Sir, General McClellan has three infantry Divisions five miles east of here, marching our way," Captain Butler replied.

"Very good. We will give them a rebel yell. Make your report to General Lee yourself. He is three miles southwest of here. Tell him that the Union numbers are about twenty thousand infantry, coming up to our center and right flank."

I would remember September 17 as one the toughest days during my service. This place and time would be remembered as the Battle of Antietam.[12] It was there that Union and Confederate horses suffered their greatest losses in one day during the Civil War. It was hard to believe that so many soldiers were fighting. During that battle, I received my second bullet wound, or in soldier's terms, graze. Across the creek, Union snipers were waiting for us. Looking around, I saw puffs of smoke bellowing from the tree line above the creek bed. Within seconds, horses were falling and in some cases crushing their riders to death. The creek seemed shallow enough to cross, but something was wrong on the other side. The foot soldiers called it Antietam Creek.

I could hear sounds of many, many wagons moving toward our position. Captain Butler took us over a small stream and then up near the ridge facing northeast. Captain Butler turned me around and kicked my sides hard. He said, "Boy, we have to find another way to get to General Lee and report Union positions and numbers.

Early in the morning, we made our way around the southwest side of Sharpsburg. Somehow, Captain Butler and I got confused between the low area creeks. We had to find high ground again, and we ended up behind a white building that looked like a church. Cautiously approaching, we moved behind it and saw a young boy crouching down with his hands over his ears. "Boy, what are you doing here? You need to get to a safe place. What is your name boy?" Captain Butler asked the boy.

"Otto, Otto Poffenburger," the lad replied. "Our farm is about a half mile that way. I am okay here. The Lord's hand will protect me."

"Don't be scared; be brave and we will get you home to your mother."

"I am not shaking because I am scared. I'm scared of noth'n. I am shaking because I got wet crossing the creek."

"I see," Captain Butler said with a smile.

Captain Butler reached down with his hand and said, "Boy, get on. God's hand is here. Get on. Lucky and I will take you home."

With two riders on my back, we made our way through the west woods to Otto's farm. Holding on to Captain Butler, the boy yelled, "Mister, thank you. Just curious, why is this horse not galloping straight? And why does your horse have that funny looking brand?"

Captain Butler looked to his left around Otto to see markings he was very familiar with. "Boy, this horse moved from left to right since we started running. Not sure why he does it for he sure as heck does not obey me all the time."

Once we got the boy to his farm on high ground again, I could see Confederates and Union cannons exchanging fire, but it was tough figuring out which was which considering the amount of smoke in the air. One dreadful sight I never forgot since First Manassas was the vision of fellow horses lying dead or dying on the battlefield. Hundreds of horses and thousands of men lay dead in the cornfields. Both Federal and Rebel sharpshooters were killing us at will. I learned in the Seven Days Battles that orders were to shoot the horses moving cannons and the officers leading the men. I would soldier on.

Captain Butler was a brave man. He knew the Confederates had to move quickly to protect our right flank. He dismounted and led us to a low-lying area in which we could move slightly northwest. The dirt road we were on led us past two cornfields and a high hill on the left. We felt much safer knowing our soldiers were positioned on a road called Sunken Road below that hill. One of the soldiers yelled, "We are attached to General D.H. Hill's Second North Carolina Regiment. He and General Lee are over there on high ground. It is going to get bloody."

Captain Butler and I made it over to where we also saw General Lee and General Longstreet; both were standing by their horses. Captain Butler approached General Lee's aide, Major Charles T. Cockey.

"Sir"—Captain Butler saluted—"I just came from the northeast of here by a creek the locals call Antietam. Across to the east, twenty to thirty thousand Union troops are moving in to our right, sir."

"General Jackson will be moving in from Harpers Ferry later today," General Longstreet said. "We have to keep the right protected until then."

"Yes, and where is J.E.B. Stuart?" General Lee said. "I need him to harass anything coming in to our left."

The major told Captain Butler, "You look wounded, go over there to the field hospital, and get bandaged up. Your horse could use a little bacon grease on that flesh wound."

"Thank you, sir." Captain Butler saluted and dismounted me. As Captain Butler led me away, Major Cockey yelled, "Captain, General Stuart's cavalry division is positioned over there on Nicodemus Heights. You may want to think about rejoining your regiment by day's end." Captain Butler nodded with affirmation.

We walked along a ridge to the direction of a white tent. Captain Butler took out his field glasses to see how the battle was shaping up. He said, "Lucky, I just saw on the ridge overlooking Sunken Road a hundred Union soldiers cut down by our fellas looking up at the ridge. Those must be green Yanks as their uniforms look new and they are standing up. It is so sad to see all this death."

By midafternoon, thousands of dead soldiers and horses had covered the cornfields. The smell of cannon shot permeated the air all around me. Thankfully, the wind kicked up to give all a clearer view of the battlefield. Captain Butler and I broke camp with the rest of our soldiers to move back into a more defensible position in the southwest.

Union General Hooker had taken Dunker Church and the lands behind it. Hooker would say in later years that "every stalk of corn in the northern and greater part of the field was cut as closely as could have been done with a knife, and the slain lay in rows precisely as they had stood in their ranks a few moments before."[13]

Captain Butler said we would move on to fight another day. Thousands of our troops headed back to Northern Virginia on September 19. With what little energy we had left, we tried to keep our heads up and moving forward. I overheard Captain Butler say, "Lucky, you're a true hero to me, boy; so was your father. I suspect the last stallion I rode was your dad since he had the same brand—crescent moon over a palmetto tree. I want you to know he served our country with great honor and spirit. During the Seven Days Battles, he disobeyed my commands that in the end got me out of a Union crossfire in a small valley we had mistakenly ridden into. He took a ball in the leg and went lame. I tried to remove the ball, but it was buried in the bone. I could not let him suffer, Lucky. I am sorry. I am so sorry I had to put him down.

Horses do not shed tears like humans. I did not know what to feel anymore. I suppose I was sad yet proud, knowing my father was a hero. His blood ran through my veins. I will carry our family honor and determination with me until I die whether on the battlefield or from old age. I hoped it would be the latter. I knew one thing about my father's death; the fear of loss left me empty knowing that we all had a job to do: win.

⌒⌒

Otto and his family hid safely in their cellar hoping cannon shots would not entomb them during the battle. Union soldiers were making their way in and out of the Poffenburger farmhouse throughout the battle, not knowing the residents were hiding beneath the house.

On the morning of September 19, Otto heard banging on the locked door. Men were outside shouting, "Surrender yourselves to the Union. Your army has been defeated."

Otto looked at his mother. "What should we do?"

"Son," she replied, "they will not harm us. We are civilians."

Otto yelled out, "We are farmers. Please do not shoot. We are coming out."

The Union soldiers stood at the cellar door with guns pointing down into the darkness. Once Otto's young face appeared into the light, the Union sergeant said, "Put your weapons down; civilians."

Otto, his mother, and three sisters emerged into the morning sunlight, thirsty and tired. Once their eyes adjusted, the view of the world suddenly darkened. Tears fell from Mrs. Poffenburger's eyes as she fell to the ground on her knees.

"My God," she said, "I can't believe this has happened."

Looking across their cornfields, I could see scorched fields covered with bodies of soldiers wearing blue or gray uniforms soaked in blood. Otto was in shock from what he saw. The sergeant said, "Ma'am, you, and your family need to stay in your house. There may still be some Confederate snipers out there. We will ensure you are provided safety."

Otto was not inclined to stay in the house. He wanted to see if his friend Captain Butler and his horse Lucky were still alive, so he snuck out the kitchen window. Once on the ground, he kept low as he moved across the fields. Though there were hundreds of Union soldiers out there collecting their dead, they paid no attention to Otto. Looking down at Sunken Road, he could see dozens of horses and hundreds of Confederate soldiers lying dead in what he had overheard Union soldiers called Bloody Lane. Walking along the cornfield's edge, Otto found himself stepping over bodies that looked unspeakable. Carefully scanning the fields and high ground for a black horse, he saw none. *Good,* he thought. *Lucky and Captain Butler must have made it out alive. I will always be grateful to them for bringing me home.*

The Battle of Antietam hardened my heart to its core. More men and horses were lost at Antietam on September 17, 1862, than on any other single day of the Civil War. The Union losses amounted to 12,410. Our Confederate losses were 10,700. Neither the Union nor the Confederacy gained a decisive victory. However, General Lee's failure to penetrate the North caused Great Britain to postpone the recognition of the Confederate States of America as government. The Battle of Antietam also gave President Abraham Lincoln the opportunity to issue the Emancipation Proclamation on January 1, 1863, that declared free all slaves in states rebelling against the United States.[14] I had mixed feelings about the proclamation; however, it was right to free Mr. Joe and the tens of thousands of like him. After all, as with me, the masters had branded him with the palmetto and crescent moon.

BATTLE OF FREDERICKSBURG

After fleeing the Manassas battlefield, Smitty was quick to replace his raggedy, bloody Confederate shirt and kepi with Union clothing he had pulled off dead soldiers lying in the field. He pulled out the white handkerchief from the soldier's front pocket and wrapped up his left hand. His left thumb was missing. He thought to himself, "The next time I see that black stallion, I will kill him."

From there, he retreated to Washington DC with the rest of the Union regiments. The numerous civilians returning in droves on carriages and wagons provided him the opportunity to fake an injury, so a city family gladly gave him a ride back to his post. Little did they know that he was a Confederate deserter in disguise.

The oldest man driving the wagon said, "Soldier, who you are attached with?"

"Sir," Smitty replied, "I don't rightly remember with all the explosions. My head sure aches and my memory has been shortened a bit. My unit charged that hill, and the last thing I remember was an explosion knocking me down. My memory is a little shaken, sir."

The old man's wife said, "Oh my dear, you must have a bit of amnesia. Here, take some of our food and spirits. That will help you feel better and perhaps clear your head."

"Yes ma 'me, that might do it," Smitty replied, smiling crookedly.

As the wagon rolled along on the turnpike back to the Capitol, Smitty was thinking, *This is too easy. I am going to lie, steal, and cheat my way into society. Who would have thunk a boy from the backwoods of South Carolina would become an important man? I will show them Yanks.*

Once they were in town, Smitty slid off the back of the wagon where he was able to slip into an alley. He quickly ran toward the back of what appeared to be a boarding house. Looking over the fence, he saw clothes drying on a line stretched between two trees. The dungarees and white shirt looked like they were in his size. Looking carefully at the back windows, he made sure no one was watching. He discarded his Union kepi and shirt in the coal bin near the furnace door, and within seconds, he was wearing civilian clothes. His transformation was not complete without boots since his old worn-out boots were Confederate issue.

Walking down the back alleys of Washington D.C., he did his best to act as if he knew where he was going. In truth, he felt lost in a foreign land, but his quick thinking and desire to survive kept his mind clear. He had to find higher ground to see where he was. Looking to the northwest, he saw a hill that would give him a good vantage point. He had to ensure he made calculated moves that would not expose his safety. Looking to the southwest, he saw several multi-story buildings that looked like boarding houses. Perhaps one of those places would provide him a room for the night in exchange for doing odd jobs. He thought, *I will just tell them I am a Confederate spy planning on assassinating President Lincoln. That would go over well.* He laughed to himself.

After crossing several streets, he made his way to the boarding house on the street that he had a feeling would provide him refuge. Standing at the back door, he saw a plain-looking woman of about thirty or forty years old clearing the kitchen table. He found a tub of rainwater by the woodshed and washed off the dirt from his face and hands. Not smelling the best, he took advantage of the rose bushes growing alongside the fence. Crumbling the rose petals in his hands, he smeared the small amount of oils over his short and neck. "That will work," he said, "I don't smell like an old barn owl anymore." With his shirt tucked in and hair slicked back, he approached the kitchen door. Smitty was not a bad-looking man. His dark hair had just a touch of grey. His high-set brows and deep-seated brown eyes made him look foreign. He firmly knocked on the door three times.

The woman adjusting the kitchen chairs looked up and saw Smitty standing on the back porch. Smitty made eye contact with her and smiled. The woman, Mrs. Mary Surratt, answered the door. With careful diction, Smitty turned on his southern charm. "Ma'am, I am in need of a place to stay for the next week or two. I have an appointment with one of the local congressmen to discuss building wagons for the war effort. I will get monies once these meetings are completed, so would you be so kind to put me up until then? I would gladly help you by making any repairs to your business as I am a skilled carpenter."

"Don't have much need for fixing up around here though I could use some help in my tavern," Mrs. Surratt said. "Sometimes we have too many drunks on Friday nights. What is your name, mister?"

"My name is Gordon Smith. Gordon Isaac Smith. And how shall I address you, madam?"

"You may address me as Mrs. Surratt. My husband, John, passed away a few years back, but I still keep his memory close to my heart."

Smitty thought, *A widow. I can use this woman.*

Since the First Battle of Manassas, deserter Smitty became a fixture of the Washington D.C. red-light district. He no longer identified himself as a Confederate soldier but as a soldier of fortune who took advantage of those less fortunate. How one can betray their country is beyond me. His split personality was confusing to me. Before Manassas, he was going out of his way to find fresh hay for us horses to eat. Then within twelve hours, he was pilfering local homes for family heirlooms. He was like many who failed to believe in the cause. He only looked after himself, and those survivor skills in the end kept him alive at the expense of others.

⌐⌐

After crossing the Potomac, Brig. Gen. J.E.B. Stuart sent our regiment ahead to clear the way of the Union pickets. That was what the Confederate cavalry did the best—ride and fight. The cool October breeze and fall leaves made us feel stronger. There was not much resistance to our movement, so we moved quickly through Loudoun County to Middleburg, Virginia. We were surprised that McClellan did not pursue our corps after the Battle of Antietam. Years later, historians would say the Union could have ended the Civil War if General McClellan had finished the job all the way to Richmond. The south was determined in 1862, and there would be many battles ahead to prove ourselves.

Once in Middleburg, we found good sources of food and forage. I was mostly pleased with the bluegrass growing in the expansive fields around the town. The townsfolk welcomed us with open arms. In fact, many of the Virginia locals supported our cause.

Riding up the hardened road south of town, we came across a wonderful-looking horse farm spanning both sides of the road. The owner marked their property with whitewashed fencing making the bluegrass stand out against the horizon. Aligned with the fences was a single row of oak trees that were standing over sixty feet high. There must have been a hundred of them lined up perfectly on each side of the road.

After riding about a mile, we turned a corner in the road to the left where the red horse barns and white house came into view. The owner had lined the property with rose bushes and Virginia dogwood. Whoever lived here, must be wealthy.

Captain Butler got us to the main house front door where he dismounted. Again, he just let the reins hang free for he knew I was not going anywhere. Or at least that was what he thought. One of these days I was going to just take off and go home with or without you Captain Butler.

The Captain walked up to the big house where a stained oak porch wrapped around the house. The steps rising up to the porch were made of gray rock. The front door was made of oak. It looked like someone had carved intricate designs that looked like roses spreading from the top of the door toward the bottom. The six front windows aligned in perfect order. The engraved rose vines branched out to the left and right of a stained glass window that had a purple colored cross inlaid on the center. I almost thought we were at a church.

Captain Butler looked to the left and right of the door into the windows while he stood in front. He knocked three times. The door opened and standing there was a medium-built man wearing a white smock and black riding boots that covered his gray woolen pants. Standing behind him was a woman who looked like she might be his wife. She was wearing a light gray cotton dress and a white-laced shawl draping over her petite shoulders. By her side were two children who looked like twins, one boy and one girl. The boy was wearing a blue plaid shirt with a pair of dungaree overalls, and the girl was wearing a blue cotton dress that seemed too large for her.

"Good morning, sir," Captain Butler said with a smile. "My name is Captain Butler of the Cavalry Corps of the Confederate States of America. My commanding officer, Brigadier General J.E.B. Stuart, respectfully requests permission to cross over lands owned by the honorable citizens of Virginia. We also provide compensation for any available food and woolen cloth.

The man standing in the center of the doorway replied in a heavy foreign accent. "I understand, sir. My name is Dr. Thomas W. Smith. To my side is my wife Mrs. Avigail Smith. These are our two children, Thomas Jr. and Hannah Lee. Permission is granted, as it is our honor to assist the Confederacy in any way we can.

I also caught a glimpse of a small black girl standing in the window nearest to the left, smiling at me. She reminded me of Mr. Joe's children. Standing next to her was a young black woman holding her hand. Both were wearing plain, off-white cotton dresses and white bonnets. I wondered if they were free.

Dr. Smith gestured to my Captain Butler. "Please. Please join us for lunch. Our servants will prepare another plate for you."

While Captain Butler enjoyed the Smith's generosity, he left me outside to fend for myself. Where was my lunch? It had been a very long ride from Maryland. I looked to the left of the house and saw endless rolling fields of bluegrass. A horse's dream. I looked to the right of the house and saw what looked like a newly constructed red barn with a hayloft. On the right side of the barn was an eight-foot-long watering trough full of fresh spring water that I could smell. I was awful thirsty. Since Captain Butler was going to be a while, I thought I would walk over to the trough to drink and maybe go over to that field and graze for a bit.

On my way over, I stepped on my right rein dragging in the dirt. I wish I did not have to wear this old leather bridle. The bit made my mouth sore. I tried to spit it out. I understood human commands such as left, right, stop, and run. Someday I would be like those stallions freely grazing over there across the road. Captain Butler could trust me.

While quenching my thirst, I heard some fellow horses kicking it up in the barn. Based on the smells, sounds, and pitch, I could tell there were mares in there. Being a lady's man, I thought

I would go right in there and pay a visit. Nearing the open barn door that must have been twenty feet in height, I thought the barn looked very much like the one I lived in back at Magnolia Plantation. Carefully, I stuck my head through the door to make sure the barn was clear of any humans. I did not want to make an entrance then be chased out by a pitchfork. No sense in dying at the hands of a farmer when there was a war going on.

After my eyes adjusted to the low light conditions, I walked in slowly. The mares were heating up the situation. I was a stallion and they were mares. Now I know why Dr. Smith put them in stalls on a beautiful day. I guess they could smell me or maybe there was a mouse in the barn. At this point, I was mighty interested in a familiar smell coming from the end of the barn. Looking intently, I saw a red mare in the stall all the way to the end on the right. She sure looked beautiful. I had a thing for redheads. She reminded me of Red back in South Carolina. That cannot be Red all the way up here.

Taking a few steps forward, I could almost see that maybe it was Red. My heart raced faster as I got closer to the stall. I had to be quiet. Then out of nowhere, I felt a stern tug on my left rein. My head jerked back. I was almost ready to kick the intruder when I saw it was Captain Butler. He said in a stern voice, "What are you doing in here Lucky? I guess it has been a long war even for horses. Come on boy." I relented and obeyed. He was my master and we had serious business ahead of us

Once Lucky cleared the stable doors, Captain Butler shut them hard. The slap awakened a red horse in the stall at the far end of the barn. She had been napping. Red blinked her eyes several times to clear away the dried tears. Red stuck her neck over the stable gate and looked left to the stable doors that were just slammed shut. She was not dreaming. She smelled him and heard him outside neighing. The old mare next to her said, "Red, you looked like you just got stung by a bee." Red replied, "No, I am afraid I the love of my life—Lucky just walked out that door. Someday, someday we will be together. I just know it."

Captain Butler and I walked back over to the main house where Dr. Smith and his wife were standing under the big black walnut tree shading the front steps. Dr. Smith said, "Captain Butler, that stallion you have sure looks strong. How long have you been fighting with him?"

"I picked Lucky up in August of this year just in time to fight in the Battle of Antietam in Maryland. I admit, he is one tough war horse."

Dr. Smith ran his hand over Lucky's neck. "You are welcome to live here with me, boy. You look like a good stallion. I have never seen such a stout and tall horse like you." I snorted, "You bet mister. I am one of a kind now."

Dr. Smith said, "Lucky looks like a cross between a thoroughbred and some other work horse—probably foreign."

"I don't know sir." Captain Butler replied. "He looks like a simple black horse to me." I kicked out my rear legs a little.

Dr. Smith said, "I don't think he appreciated you calling him simple."

Captain Butler gave me the evil eye. "Sir, in any case, I appreciate the offer, but Lucky is not for trade or sale."

"Very well," Dr. Smith said with a frown. "I suspect you need to be moving on. Here, take this sack of food. There are a couple of apples in there for Lucky. Also, let me give Lucky a new horse blanket. The one you have on him is worn and too small. His back will sore up to the point where neither one of you will be riding into battle."

Captain Butler removed the saddle and placed a brand new blanket on my back. It was made of thick wool, double sewn in between thinner-brushed cotton liners on both sides. It was the nicest saddle blanket I had ever seen or felt. Captain Butler threw the old black leather saddle on my back and readjusted the leather girth straps under my belly to account for the extra thick blanket. Captain Butler, after this blanket is broken in, you will need to readjust those straps again. Otherwise, you will be riding underneath and in between my legs.

Captain Butler looked down and saluted. "Thank you, Dr. and Mrs. Smith. I greatly appreciated your generosity. I will report to General Stuart your permission given to pass through these parts. Our horses will feed on the fields and men can drink the fresh water.

"Glad to serve the cause." Dr. Smith replied. "My wife and I came from a place where you had to fight for freedom. We understand the need to sacrifice."

Back on the main road, Captain Butler and I continued moving southeast. We were to rendezvous with another cavalry regiment converging with General Jackson's First Corps. Captain Butler said aloud, "Come on boy. We be headed to Fredericksburg. Winter is coming and General Lee wants us all to be there. I am not sure of his plans, but you know old Granny Lee."

Later in the evening at Dr. Smith's house, the family settled down in the family room after having a warm cooked dinner consisting of sweet potatoes, Cornish game hen, and bread.

Looking at Avigail, Dr. Smith said, "You know dear, those Confederate officers are so polite."

Avigail, looking confused, replied, "What do you mean? They are supposed to be officers and gentlemen."

"Oh, I understand that my darling wife. However, Captain Butler just seemed to be so concerned about our welfare and safety. He truly is an honorable man. Even his horse seemed to carry an 'air' about him. I was surprised to see Lucky was not gelded. Well, I do hope they both survive the war. I hope we all survive the war."

"Dr. Smith, as far as I am concerned, this war is guided by Providence. The end will be the beginning for all of us. My premonition tells me we will see them again someday."

"Darling wife, you always have a way with words. Perhaps you will be right."

"Dr. Smith, I am a woman. We are always right."

Turning his to look at the window, Dr. Smith's smile turned to a frown he did not want his wife to see.

⁓

General Lee moved our Divisions south across the Potomac River to regroup and prepare for winter encampment around a town called Fredericksburg, Virginia. Thinking we were going to settle in for the winter, since no one fights during the winter, the Union would have other ideas about winter campaigns. In fact, United States President Abe Lincoln was so anxious to capture Richmond, Virginia that he quickly replaced the overly cautious Major General George B. McClellan with Major General Ambrose E. Burnside. President Lincoln ordered Burnside to move quickly. Looking back, many historians said Major General McClellan could have ended the Civil War by coming after us on September 19, the day after the fighting had stopped at Antietam. He chose not to do so, much to the displeasure of President Lincoln who relieved M.G. McClellan of his command. President Lincoln put Major General Ambrose Burnside in charge.

General Burnside promised President Lincoln that his three Grand Divisions would defeat Lee's Army of Northern Virginia. Burnside swore he would capture the Confederate capital of Richmond, Virginia by winter's end. However, to do so, General Hooker would have to survive the Battle of Fredericksburg. This battle would be one of the largest and deadliest campaigns fought during the Civil War.[15]

To fight the Confederates, the Union had to cross the wide Rappahannock River about one hundred yards from the Fredericksburg town center. However, we were fortunate enough to cross this river before the winter of '62 set in. That would not be the case for the Union side. The river would present many challenges for the Union. Captain Butler said they would use pontoon boats to cross. He said our snipers would make light work of the Yanks trying to cross over on the narrow pontoon barges latched together into a bridge-like walkway floating on the river.

On the morning of December 8, Captain Butler and I were detached to ride with the North Carolina Seventh Regiment under Brigadier General J.E.B. Stuart's Cavalry Division. Our orders were to carry a message to Major General Jackson who headed the Second Corps positioned just two miles southwest of Fredericksburg. Captain Butler and I encountered thousands of other Confederate horses and troopers patrolling the Fredericksburg countryside.

Throughout the morning, Captain Butler stayed quiet. He was usually singing some song or humming some old southern tune. I think he was lost in thought. I could feel him constantly checking his saddlebag to make sure the message General Stuart gave him was secure. I suppose it was important. He mumbled something about a lost Order Number 191 that would not happen again.

We crossed several creeks and valleys southwest of Fredericksburg to reach Maj. Gen. Jackson's position. Once we emerged from the trees, I looked over an open field and saw white command tents set up on higher ground near a grove of trees. Captain Butler took us over to the center tent where he dismounted and extended his military courtesies to a junior officer before entering the tent. I stood outside looking around with amazement. Soldiers were packing up their haversacks with what looked like one or two day's rations, knowing well and good the sparse food would have to last three to four days of fighting.

I suppose us horses were luckier in that regard. If the grass was alive, we ate it.

Once inside the tent, Captain Butler presented the secret message to General Jackson. "Sir, General Stuart wanted me to deliver this message to you sir."

"Captain, what are its contents?" General Jackson said. "I do not have time to read Jeb's poor handwriting."

"Sir, the contents were sealed, I am sorry I do not know."

Using his knife, General Jackson broke the seal and string. As he read the message, his eyes narrowed and his lips thinned as he breathed out and said, "We must move north of Fredericksburg. General Stuart reports enemy positions across the Rappahannock will be reinforced in one or two days by troops marching in from the Shenandoah Valley." General Jackson said to his aid, "Get this to General Lee. We must move quickly."

Captain Butler emerged from the tent with a worried look on his face. I wondered what he was thinking. He had become so quiet over the last couple of days. We rode over to the chuck wagon so he could get something to eat before it moved out. He said, "Going to need something to eat, Lucky. It will be a while before I have another hot meal. That General Jackson is an impressive soul. He has so much faith, Lucky. He told me, 'God is with us, Captain.'"

As we trotted away from the general's tent, I saw a familiar horse ties up to the oak tree. It was Little Sorrel! Captain Butler had no idea of the importance of that horse, but I did. I remembered what Little Sorrel told me at the First Battle of Manassas: "Because it is our duty." Little Sorrel looked at me and saw the scars on my legs. He slowly bowed his head, pulled his ears back, and then looked away to the north. I think he was saluting me. Why would he be doing that?

To ensure the Union did not overtake us from the north, General Lee positioned his Second Corps, facing northeast along the Rappahannock River just above the town. Always looking for the tactical advantage, General Lee ordered Longstreet's Corps to the high ground where at Marye's Heights and Prospect Hill, the Army of Northern Virginia took defensive positions. By December 11, General Lee had over seventy-eight thousand Confederate troops encamped in and around the town of Fredericksburg. We were ready for battle. General Jackson and General Lee had the advantage. They both took the high ground. The Union would have trouble.

Captain Butler and I made it to Prospect Hill in the late afternoon. Looking toward the river, we could see that the Union troops were positioned to the north, center, and south of the Rappahannock. According to our intelligence, there were over a hundred thousand soldiers under the command of General Burnside. Lincoln again was pushing his Union general to capture Richmond at all hazards. Burnside would have to get through us to do so.

Our intelligence reported indicated that Burnside's strategy consisted of establishing three Grand Divisions which were divided equally into three positions across the Rappahannock River. Position one was to south just across the river from Prospect Hill. The second position was located directly across the river facing the center of Fredericksburg, and the third position was located a couple of miles north of Fredericksburg. The biggest problem the Union faced was trying to figure out where to cross the river. That effort would require hundreds of pontoon barges. Once the bridges were in place, the troops would be able to march over the river. The Union also looked like they were staging themselves across the river north of the town center. We did not worry for our sharpshooters would dispatch of them quickly. How brave those Federal pontoon engineers must have been to build barges while they were exposed to our snipers setting up in the trees across from them. Many of those engineers would give their lives to ensure their army was able to cross that river.

Captain Butler and I stayed with the general's staff on Prospect Hill throughout most of the first day of battle on December 11. We heard the Union engineers marching over those river pontoons in the early morning under the cover of darkness. However, our snipers were making good aim and light work of the Yanks that seemed to keep coming. Hundreds of Union soldiers died from our sniper's bullets on those pontoon bridges. However, they kept coming. The Union soldiers coming marching over those pontoons would just step over the lifeless bodies of their comrades. They kept coming.

About midday, the Union was able to push out a few regiments we had positioned downtown. Our soldiers were not in a good position in downtown Fredericksburg. The number of Union soldiers coming over would soon overwhelm us. We did not retreat. Our soldiers simply moved to higher ground while leaving behind well-placed snipers hidden in the top floors of the houses along the main streets. It was rumored that one South Carolina sniper killed thirty Union soldiers in one day. After the war, his recovered rifle had forty-two notches carved in the rifle stock.

Our soldier's retreat from the town center was no accident. The move was planned in advance. General Lee wanted to give some resistance, which in the end would give Burnside a false sense of security. General Lee knew the Union soldiers would have to stage themselves in the streets of Fredericksburg. From there, the Union would have to cross over a large open field called the Fairgrounds to reach our positions.

By the morning of December 12, the Union had moved about twenty thousand troops across the Rappahannock River. We did not retreat. Our soldiers simply repositioned to a stronger defensive positions at Prospect Hill and Marye's Heights. General Jackson positioned our right flank behind Prospect Hill located off Telegraph Road south of Fredericksburg. We would stand our ground.

Marye's Heights was located about a mile west of the town center. The Heights was a low ridge rising about fifty feet above the Fairgrounds. Located midway up Marye's Heights was a four-foot-high rock wall, which ran parallel to the ridge along a muddy ditch the soldiers called Sunken Lane. Our artillery commanders took full advantage of that wall, where Major General Lafayette McLaws positioned about two thousand Confederate troops and a dozen cannons on the heights by the evening of Friday, December 12.

Author's picture of "The Wall"

Captain Butler was ordered to assist the artillery by positioning Napoleon cannons on Marye's Heights. The strain of hauling the caissons full of powder and grapeshot reminded me of the wagon I pulled to the first Battle of Manassas. I wondered what happened to that Confederate traitor, son-of-a-gun Private Smitty.

Orders were orders. We departed Chancellorsville in midafternoon. It would only take us a couple of hours to get to Fredericksburg. As we road across the countryside, I became overwhelmed with the thought of going into battle again. My fear of dying became my strength. I suppose fear was what had kept me alive. Captain Butler was quiet most of the way. I could tell the war was wearing him down as well. I had hoped he would be my last trooper.

We approached Marye's Heights from the southwest, staying close to the tree lines. Captain Butler wanted to keep us under cover until we reached the top of the heights, which was about four hundred feet uphill. To get up to Marye's Heights, we had to cross over another cold and iced over stream I was not really looking forward to getting wet again or climbing the backside of Marye's Heights. The steep incline would pretty much put Captain Butler lying on my neck. However, as Sir Tom had told me years ago, "Soldier on, Lucky."

The uphill gallop took a good five minutes, and Captain Butler almost fell off my back because the girth strap securing the saddle to me was too loose. I wished he took the time to check the tack before riding me. Maybe a good fall off my back would remind him for future considerations.

Just when we got close to the ridge, I had no choice but to duck under a low hanging tree limb. I made it, but Captain Butler did not. To keep my balance on the hill, I stopped and turned sideways parallel to the hill. Looking down, I could see Captain Butler slowly getting up, mumbling imprecations I had never heard before. I wasn't sure if he was mad at me, the tree, or himself. Maybe he felt a little of all three. Captain Butler grabbed my reins and said with a huff, "Come on, Lucky. We are walking the rest of the way up."

At the top of the ridge, we could see hundreds of Union camp-fires across the river. "Lucky," Captain Butler said in a low voice, "We have a fight on our hands. Let us get over to our men's position." Colonel J.B. Walton's Louisiana battalion had bivouacked about a hundred yards in front of us. They were preparing what little rations had been given to them two days before. Water and food were running low but few complained.

The winter's darkness came and again blanketed the grass with frost. Not too many men slept comfortably. I stayed warm by standing behind a small clump of bushes near a house that smelled like gingerbread and candy. On the previous day, General McLaws had ordered the homeowner, Mr. Ebert, to abandon his house and seek refuge elsewhere. Mrs. Ebert said they would go to her brother's house several miles west of town. After the battle, the Eberts returned to find their home still standing though damaged by hundreds of bullet holes.

When dawn came on December 13, the soldiers were up and positioned behind the wall. Their breakfast was again a small portion of hard tack and dried ham. I could see the soldier's faces were worn and tired, yet their eyes were full of determination. They had loaded their rifles and primed the cannons. The soldiers' canteens provided the only source of water on Marye's Heights. Each soldier would have to manage his own consumption. Every Confederate soldier was given enough shot to last throughout the day. Once they ran out ammunition, another regiment would replace the worn out shooters. Our cannons were primed with grapeshot. For the next eight hours, the carnage of war would resume its deadly march.

The heavy fog started to lift above the town at around ten o'clock in the morning. Looking toward the river, I could see the Union soldiers approaching toward Marye's Heights. To get within shot of our positions, the Yanks had to cross the open

Fairgrounds. The only protection they would have was a narrow swale that ran parallel three hundred yards from our wall. There, the Union soldiers would lie down to avoid our bullets. First, they would have to cross over low, wooden fences that would delay their advance.

I saw the Union soldiers' faces as they struggled to stay low on the ground. Their faces wore the same determined look as our soldiers. The only difference was the Yanks were marching in the open field while our soldiers took position safely behind a rock wall. At about ten thirty, gunfire exchanges and cannonades from both sides began to escalate. The sound of incoming rounds was horrible. The speed of which cannonballs moved through the air caused a crackling noise that ended with a loud excruciating explosion. My ears would ring for minutes afterwards. Captain Butler had to kick my sides to signal movement forward as I could not always hear his commands.

During the battle, we stood away from the wall but close enough where I could see them coming. The Yanks' blue uniforms, shiny black leather belts and boots, and clean kepis meant they were new enlistees, young and willing to follow orders to their deaths. Looking toward the center, I noticed regiment after regiment dropping to the ground in a small ditch that ran running along the field. Reserve soldiers had to lie down upon their dead to find cover in that ditch. Our sharpshooters would reload and wait for a blue kepi to rise above the line. Death soon followed. Occasionally, a Union soldier would shoot and kill one of our men. Soon thereafter, our side fired three shots to silence the gun. I think it was at this moment I decided that no war was worth the loss of life no matter whose life it was. The killing was merciless. By the end of the day, thousands of men and hundreds of horses lay dead across the Fairgrounds.

As the sun started to drop behind us, my eyes could not believe what I saw Looking over the Fairgrounds, I was reminded of the courage and bravery of the many men and horses that charged us while carrying their regiment's colors. Most likely, some family member back home sewed each Union regiment flag. Like the regimental flags our soldiers carried into battle, I was sure their regimental flags lying on top of those dead bodies represented honor, courage, and heritage. Most men from both sides carrying their regimental colors would die.

At that point, my throat was so dry and coated with smoke I wished water was nearby. Shaking my head up and down, Captain Butler saw that I was almost choking.

Before he dismounted, a soldier came up to us, saying, "Captain, let me give your horse some water. The cold air and smoke zips the moisture out of all of us."

"Thank you Sergeant. What is your name and whose unit are you with?"

"Sir, my name is Sergeant Richard Rowland Kirkland from the Second South Carolina Volunteers."

During the next day, Sergeant Kirkland's selfish acts would earn him the title "Angel of Marye's Heights." History would call him a man with compassion and Christ-like mercy. What he did was heroic and selfless. The wounded Union soldiers were crying for water in the field. He could not stand the cries and did something about it. He gathered all the canteens he could and walked out into the line of fire. Once he made it to the first Union soldier to give him water, the Union commanders gave orders to stop shooting. Sergeant Kirkland demonstrated that there was a time for killing and a time for healing. I hoped the war would spare his life.

On the morning of December 14, the Lord again masked our positions from the enemy with a thick fog that shrouded Fredericksburg. A soldier next to us said the fog was collecting souls. I was not sure what he meant by that, but I am sure it was related to the sound of wounded soldiers' cries breaking the morning silence. The Union had suffered devastating losses. I felt sorrow for the Union horses that had also laid down their lives on the battlefield. Their cries were not heard for each was surely dead.

As evening approached, we were amazed to see colorful lights settling on the northern horizon. Captain Butler said to me, "Look, Lucky, the sky is alight with magnificent colors of red and orange dancing on the northern horizon. God is watching over us." Captain Butler said the aurora borealis were a sign from God that the South would win the war. Look how well we pushed back the Union forces over the last few days. I think he was right. We stood watching the lights as they eventually faded away into the night sky. When the lights were gone, my heart felt saddened as I thought what if it was a sign from God that the Union was going to win.

Captain Butler and I moved to the far right position on Sunken Lane. The cold air had frozen the mud and blood beneath my hooves. I could not help but wonder about the cracking sound of my footsteps. Fear of the enemy hearing me ran along my back. I suspect Captain Butler felt the same. Fatigued from the months of battle we shared together, he whispered to me, "It will be okay Lucky. This battle will end, and you and I will move south toward home. I miss my wife and kids. I bet you miss your family as well." I did indeed. I missed my Red.

In position with the rest of the regiment, we stood fast waiting for our orders to push the Union back across the river. General Lee saw that he had the advantage and he took the offensive knowing the Union's General Burnside was not a known risk-taker. Burnside still maintained his reserve forces in the rear. With this knowledge, our divisions pushed toward the river. Realizing the large number of Union losses, Major General Burnside ordered his men to move back across the Rappahannock to take a stand and protect the Union capitol. He was more concerned about protecting Washington D.C. than taking Richmond.

It was a glorious day for our side! The Confederates clearly won that battle, leaving Captain Butler and I to live to see another day and another battle. I was hopeful that we would get some rest and relaxation time, but that was just wishful thinking. The commanding general ordered our regiment to penetrate enemy territory to do what we did best in the cavalry—gather intelligence. Riding under the command of Stewart, Captain Butler and I would travel several hundreds of miles through enemy territory in the states of Maryland and Pennsylvania.

My final thoughts of the Battle of Fredericksburg were that both Union and Confederate troops fought in the streets the Civil War's first urban combat engagement. With nearly two hundred thousand combatants, no other Civil War battle featured a larger concentration of soldiers. I was glad to put that one behind me. I so looked forward to running with our regiment behind enemy lines. Ironically, skirmishes were easy compared to the battles. Captain Butler and I thought we were seeing victory, yet in my heart, something was not right.

Today, a marker sits at the gateway to the Fredericksburg National Cemetery. It commemorates the thousands of Union and Confederate soldiers who paid the supreme sacrifice during the battle. A poem by Theodore O'Hara is inscribed on it and a portion of it reads as follows:

> On fame's eternal camping-ground
> Their silent tents are spread,
> And glory guards, with solemn round
> The bivouac of the dead.

GETTYSBURG'S
FIELDS OF SORROW

Once we crossed into Pennsylvania in June '63, I knew the land was privileged. The many miles of golden wheat fields and hundreds of fruit orchards represented prosperity and comfort. In fact, the most beautiful farms were near a town called Gettysburg. God truly blessed that part of the country. Maybe it would be a good place to settle down, if I could not go home with Red.

Mrs. Drayton and little Allison woke up on June 8, 1863, wondering where Lucky was and if he was still alive. They often missed their beloved horse since he was the one who brought back the injured Sir Tom back in '61. It had been over a year since Mrs. Drayton's life changed from bad to worse. Without her husband, she had worked tirelessly trying to keep Magnolia Plantation. The one blessing she counted on was Mr. Joe and his family who elected to stay and help her and little Allison keep the Magnolia Plantation spirit alive.

The morning would be the same it had been since Tom passed on. She would awake alone in her bed wishing he was near her. Looking at the ceiling, she felt so alone and worried about the future. She would lie in bed thinking about the war. On one hand, she was glad Tom did not have to suffer through the battles, but on the other, she thought he might have survived and come home when the war was over. *Oh*, she thought, *when will this retched war be over?* The war was taking its toll on the south.

She had heard of the Confederate victories from passing neighbors who said, "General Lee will take us to the Promised Land." Mrs. Drayton thought, *I hope the neighbors meant a promise land here on earth, not in heaven.*

The morning was cool that day. The hot summer months were still ahead, so she and Allison enjoyed making the trip to the barn as she had done every day since Lucky had left. Holding Allison's hand in one hand and a bucket of feed, Mrs. Drayton and Allison would go feed the chickens that now lived in the stalls where their once great horses lived.

"Mother, where do you think Lucky is today?" Allison said.

"He is probably up on some horse farm grazing on the green alfalfa grass they grow up there. I am sure he is loving life," Mrs. Drayton replied.

"Oh, I do hope so mother. He was such a beautiful horse. He never made me feel nervous, not like his old dad Blackie."

"Now be careful what you say Miss Allison," Mrs. Drayton said in a concerned voice. "Blackie was the reason why we were able to keep this farm. Besides, without Blackie we would not have had a Lucky." A thousand miles north, Lucky was thinking about home, Red, and the Drayton's.

⌒

Captain Butler and I continued the daily patrols around Culpepper County, Virginia on June 7, 1863. Our regiment had orders to keep the Union cavalry away from General Lee's divisions bivouacked in and around the county which lay at the foothills of the Blue Ridge Mountains. To the southeast of Culpeper County was Fredericksburg, a place I called "winter's hell." I never wanted to see that forsaken place again in my life.

In preparation for the next battle, General Lee continued positioning and repositioning our divisions near the Rappahannock
River. He did so in response to our intelligence, which indicated
that the Union had maintained their positions across the river
to the northeast. Communications between Lee and President
Jefferson Davis laid the groundwork for the next move into
the north.

General Lee was preparing to take the fight to the Union by
moving north into Pennsylvania. The plan was for us to move
north above Baltimore, Maryland, then circle to the right and
down south to threaten the Union capitol. The idea of moving
north again caused me great concern as I remembered Antietam.
Captain Butler and I had experienced great pains during that
battle. I hoped not to repeat that experience. However, I trusted
General Lee and of course, the horse that carried him into battle,
my friend Traveler.

In midmorning, General Stuart made an impromptu decision to provide General Lee with a military parade in the afternoon. Captain Butler muttered, "No time for pomp and circumstance. We need to move out on patrols." We prepared for the
event by cleaning up our gear. The best part was finally getting
the red Virginia mud brushed off of me. While the parade cha-
rade was going on, we had no idea that on the other side of the
Rappahannock, eleven thousand Union troopers of the Cavalry
Corps of the Army of the Potomac had assembled by the orders
of Major General Alfred Pleasanton.[16]

Well, unfortunately, General Lee was not able to make the
Stuart cavalry parade. No worries, General Stuart had us do it
again on June 8. Captain Butler mumbled imprecations again,
knowing we should be resting for the next battle. On June 9,
Captain Butler's suspicions would be right. We rode into the
largest cavalry engagement of the Civil War known as the Battle
of Brandy Station in Virginia.

June 9 came quickly. After all that parading around the day before, I was hopeful we would get some rest and relaxation. However, the Union had other ideas. General Stuart should not have been surprised, yet we all were when the Union Cavalry came across the Rappahannock.

General Stuart positioned his command on high ground called Fleetwood Hill. From there, General Stuart could observe the Union's movements across the river. At first, he was not concerned until he saw about three thousand Union troopers ride across the river. General Stuart said, "I am impressed. Those Yanks are staying in their saddles."

The Union did not have an organized cavalry like we did with our experienced southern horsemen, yet those troopers rode with confidence. When I looked over the valley, I saw determined Union troopers moving quickly toward our position. Captain Butler kicked me in the sides and that was the signal. We were going into battle. Though the low fog masked full view of the river, we could still detect them with our ears. We heard thousands of horses moving across the river.

Our patrol moved quickly to a line of trees just north of the Union crossing point on the river. Captain Butler yelled to his men, "Dismount gentlemen. We will make light work of these yanks while they are in the river." We horses stayed just inside the trees while our riders positioned themselves behind a row of blackberry bushes and dogwoods. Once the smoke cleared the barrels, the Union troopers took notice and moved toward our position. Captain Butler said with urgency, "Men, mount up. Let us take them further north." While pursued by what seemed like two hundred Union troopers, the remaining Confederate and Union cavalry engaged in the open fields near Fleetwood Hill.

We galloped at top speed. Our troopers returned fire as we carried our men to a safer area. I heard the familiar sound of Spencer carbine .50 caliber bullets zipping by, striking the ground and throwing up dirt. I knew what to do. Like Antietam, I zigzagged instinctively taking care not to lose Captain Butler. Looking to my left and right, I could see my fellow horses were taking note and doing the same. This made us a hard target to hit. Once we had made it to a ridge overlooking the Rappahannock, the Union troopers split up into two groups. Captain Butler said, "Lucky, it looks like they are going to try and encircle us. Not a chance." Waving his arm, he said, "Come on men. They won't expect us to cross over the river to their side." My ears perked up knowing this is a risky idea.

Our patrol split up into two groups. Captain Butler took forty men across a bend in the river toward a stand of cedar trees throwing dark shadows on the river. He told the rest of the men to cross a thousand yards north of our position and to regroup on the ridge above the river's bend. After we got over the river, the cedar trees provided a welcome hiding place where we could observe the Yanks across the river. Our trooper dismounted and made all of us lie down on the ground behind the trees. Once the Yanks decided to move north where our other men had crossed, Captain Butler ordered everyone up and back across the river. I then saw what he wanted to do. We were going to come up on the Yanks' rear to put them in a crossfire situation. It did not take long for the Yanks to figure out the shooting was coming from across the river and up from behind them. Before it was over, several Union troopers were down on the ground, wounded or dead. Captain Butler whistled toward the river to wave the rest of his men to come back across. The Yanks would be regrouping soon.

Evidently, the regrouping did not take place. The Yanks looked as if they were returning to Fleetwood Hill. Captain Butler knew he had to stop them before they threatened General Stuart's position. With my reins tightly wrapped in his hands, we ran like the wind. Our regiment reformed once we broke the tree line less than a mile north from Fleetwood Hill. The Union did not know what hit them. They must have thought we ran, but that was not the case. Our troopers were firing while we raced across that field.

I imagine the rifle smoke and dust our hooves kicked up was a sight to fear. The Union troopers did not run that time. We all met in the middle of that field. Troopers and horses met head on.

When the battle was over, over a thousand men lay dead on the fields in and around Brandy Station. Perhaps six to seven hundred horses were killed or wounded. Of the 9,500 Confederates who fought, 523 men died. The Union lost 907 men of the 11,000 troopers that battled. Captain Butler and I were spared death again, yet both of us were wounded. A Yankee trooper struck Captain Butler with a saber across his left shoulder. The Union trooper attempted to slash Captain Butler again but missed and cut me. That attack left a one-inch gash in my withers. Using a battlefield remedy, Captain Butler stuffed chewed tobacco into my wound to stop the bleeding and prevent infection. We would live to fight another day.[17]

The Battle of Brandy Station gave us an important advantage that day, distracting General Alfred Pleasonton, Commander of the Union Cavalry Corps of the Army of the Potomac, from discovering General Lee's position not ten miles away from Fleetwood Hill. We were lucky.

On June 10, Captain Butler woke up moaning. My neck was feeling a little sore as well. I hoped that we would have some time to heal. Standing by the smoldering fire, Captain Butler brushed off the dirt from his uniform. I pawed at some hay he had left for me the night before and thought some water would be good. By the time we had shaken off sleep, a young lieutenant had approached Captain Butler. His uniform was clean, so I figured he was one of Brig. Gen. Stuart's aides.

The lieutenant saluted and said, "Captain Butler. The General would like to meet with all regimental commanders at 0800."

"Lieutenant, I am not the regimental commander," Captain Butler said. "Colonel Solomon Williams is the man you want to see."

"Captain Butler, Colonel Williams died this morning. General Stuart has meritoriously promoted you to the rank of colonel. You are now in charge of the Second North Carolina Cavalry, sir."

Our regiment stayed in garrison for one more week. We sure needed the time to rest and plan our next movements. I could sense change in the air. Something bad was coming. General Lee ordered Brigadier General Stuart to take his cavalry and penetrate the northern lines by way of Harper's Ferry where the Confederates maintained control near the confluence of the Shenandoah and Potomac rivers. Our orders were to cross into Maryland and Pennsylvania to disrupt supply and communication lines and gather intelligence on Union forces. The timeline was tight so we quickly pulled up stakes on June 22, 1863. The crossroads ahead of us were familiar. The song's lyrics may be the same but the melody would be different, a song of sorrow.

Recently promoted by General Stuart, Colonel Butler proudly wore his eagles on his collar. It was an honor to have been part of his heroic efforts at Antietam, Fredericksburg, and now Brandy Station. I was grateful for such a skilled horseman and officer riding on my back in the fields of battle. Colonel Butler, like many others serving in the CSA, believed the South would win its independence and freedom. I was still not clear why war was the only remedy but in the words of Mr. Joe: "It is what it is."

General Lee's orders were to screen for General Ewell's division, which would be moving north from Winchester just east of the Bull Run Mountains. Colonel Butler said, "Old Granny Lee wants to take the fight again to the Yanks up north of the Mason Dixon Line. This time we would have the advantage and will press the enemy to our choice of field."

I was thinking we better not be heading to another Antietam. Remembering how hard that battle was fought, I also wondered how young Otto was doing. He was a brave young man. Perhaps he was still there.

From Brandy Station, we headed northwest of a little town called Aldie, Virginia, not far from a place called Upperville. There, we staged our regiments on the high ground below the Bull Run Mountains to prevent Union forces from getting through Snicker's Gap. General Stuart was ordered to collect intelligence and provide screening of Old Granny Lee's divisions moving north in the Shenandoah Valley, just west of the Blue Ridge Mountains. In any case, our assignment, together with Colonel Thomas Munford's Second and Third Virginia Cavalry, was to screen for General Ewell's division which was moving north through Loudoun Valley to eventually cross the Potomac River.

Colonel Butler said our mission would not be difficult as the Yanks scampered back to protect the Union's capitol city. All we had to do was stay on high ground to prevent the Union cavalry from gathering intelligence on our movements. Colonel Butler was not worried since the Union cavalry leader was General Pleasonton who had failed at Brandy Stations and would fail again. Unfortunately, General Pleasonton, known to many as "Kill-Cavalry," would drink some misguided courage again. He dispatched his cavalry, led by Brig. Gen. Judson Kilpatrick's brigade, to break through our positions.

June 17 was another hot summer day in Northern Virginia. To avoid the sun, Colonel Butler let me stand under a large oak tree for needed shade to keep us cooled down. I was already lathering up under the saddle and knew the day would not get better. Little air moved around our camp inside the trees. I could smell water running down in the exposed valley below. However, we had orders. Colonel Butler had ordered his men to stay put and out of sight.

I found some blackberry bushes near some small dogwood bushes growing along the ridge. Growing in the sun, those berries looked blackish-blue in color and smelled awfully good. Except for the prickly and thorny vines they clung to, they weren't a bad desert. There were other horses getting a few bites in themselves. The taste of those wild blackberries was like taking a bite out of heaven. I chewed up the leaves and stems, thorns and all. If I only had some molasses then all would have been good.

Standing on the other side of the bushes was an old brown warhorse, battle-worn and trodden. Judging by the scars on his neck and graying forelock, he appeared much older than me. He had been staring at me for the longest time. Out of curiosity, I walked around to where he was standing.

"Excuse me, sir. Any particular reason you have been staring at me? What is your name?"

"Son, my given name is Star, but my rider calls me Old Virginia."

"Why, might I ask, have you been staring at me?"

"I was looking at the brand on ya backside boy."

"That mark represents my home in South Carolina, the Magnolia Plantation. "

"Now, calm down, boy. I mean no offense to your privacy, but I have ridden with a horse who looked just like you, but older. He had the same brand. His rider called him Rifle."

"That must be one of my older brothers. My master gave him that name. Old Virginia, where did you see him last?"

"Son, I think I saw him during the Battle of Chancellorsville back in early May when I was attached to General Ewell's division. That was when our dear General Stonewall Jackson was mortally wounded."

"I am very sorry about his passing, but surely my brother must still be alive then! He was just like my dad. Rifle is brave and tough as nails."

"Son, you're pretty tough and brave yourself. I have heard how you protected your trooper during the Battle of Antietam. Umm, if that horse is your brother, Lord willing, you will see him again."

"Well, "I…I really didn't see him or my other two brothers. My mother told me about them. Our masters had to sell them to the CSA."

"I understand. That is what happened to me," Old Virginia replied.

Before I could get another question off, one of the soldiers yelled, "Look there yonder Colonel!" We all raised our heads and looked southeast: clouds of red dust were swirling up along the pike. The men yelled, "Riders com'n."

I was ready to go into battle that time. My heart filled with hope, knowing one of my brothers was still alive. When I almost felt no hope of seeing my family again, God's hand delivered me the desire to keep fighting. No one was going to stop me from finding him. Not a yank bullet or a saber!

Our troopers mounted up, and we galloped quickly down to the valley below. I was waiting on Colonel Butler who was coordinating with Colonel Munford. The Union had hauled more firepower in the form of big guns with them. This battle was going to be interesting. Turning away from the blackberry bushes, I made my way back over to the big oak. The screeching noise of cannons made me a little nervous. We had artillery teams getting rounds off less than thirty feet from me. Then I remembered Fredericksburg. I wasn't sure who shot first, but explosions were hitting all around us inside the tree line. By the time Colonel Butler got near my tree, a shell had landed not fifteen feet away near the ammunition caisson on my left.

The explosion was deafening. The oak tree no longer stood upright. The shell split it in two. I no longer stood tall. Colonel Butler rushed to my side, thinking I was dead. While lying there on the ground, I could hear him yell, "Damn it. I need another horse." So much for loyalty. I just could not breathe. For a minute that seemed like eternity, the lump in my lungs relaxed. I was finally able to breath. After seeing my sides move up and down, Colonel Butler said with a solemn voice, "Come on and get up, mister, we got a battle to fight." I saw a small teardrop in the corner of his eye, but no. That man never showed his emotions. He showed none at Antietam, Fredericksburg, or at Brandy Station.

Once more, Colonel Butler and I raced down into the valley. Riding over a small rise in the field, Union troopers greeted us with rifles firing and sabers slashing the air. The ground beneath my hooves was hard clay with small chunks of granite strewn from left to right. I was glad he had the blacksmith back in Culpeper put new horseshoes on me. Stepping on sharp granite rocks protruding from the ground felt so darn bad that my eyes watered.

Moving down into the valley, the troopers were loud, yapping it up with the rebel yell. Energy was in the air. With my ears back, we raced like the wind toward the enemy, perhaps designed by rank for he always steered me toward an officer riding a mount that looked as scared as the trooper. I just kept running and changing left or right depending upon which spur Colonel Butler stuck me with. Once we passed through the first round slashing of sabers with the Yank captain, Colonel Butler would turn me around and go for it again, trying to pick off another union trooper. This carried on for about forty-five minutes. Colonel Butler was relentless in his pursuit of victory.

The battle ended in midafternoon. I was too tired to feel the pain from the saber cuts on my withers. Colonel Butler's right arm was, as he said, "just a nick." He just tied a bandanna around the wound and forgot about it. Though this battle was small, it was still costly for both sides. The Union lost over three hundred troopers, while we only lost about a hundred. The Union retreated toward the town of Middleburg. Colonel Butler said we would go after them the next day. Until then, we would encamp by the blackberry bushes and oak trees that remained. After we collected our dead from the field, we buried our comrades on the hillside where the blackberry bushes grew beneath the one remaining oak tree. Their personal effects were given to the quartermaster who would make sure they were delivered back to the soldiers' families.

On June 18, we repositioned ourselves near a familiar town called Middleburg. Intelligence reports indicated that Union reinforcements were moving up from the south of Middleburg. Our job was to provide a deterrent. As we rode along the pike, Colonel Butler said aloud, "Lucky, do you remember land? We came through here last fall on our way to Fredericksburg. I remember Dr. Smith and his family treated us pretty darn good. I hope they are okay. I remember how kind Dr. Smith's His wife was so kind to give this saddle blanket to us…I mean…you. That blanket sure help made these rides a bit more comfortable. Do you remember ole boy?" Yes, I do remember and no kidding, I like that cotton blanket between me and…well, you are not caring a 200 pound man on your back Colonel.

As we got closer to Middleburg, I felt a sense of déjà vu. With that said, a faint memory came back to me. I remembered. This was the place I thought I had smelled the scent of my girl Red. Oh, how I wish I had just one more chance to see her! As I started to pick up the pace, Colonel Butler said, "Slow down, Lucky. We need to stay quiet on the road. I should take those damn horseshoes off you. They make a heck of a noise on the road." I slowed down and could not help but hope my Red was still there in that barn.

While patrolling down that familiar road toward the Smith Farm, the trees looked much different. There was no color in them. The gold and reds had turned green and, in some cases, brown. There were no flowers alongside the dirt road. In fact, all the grass looked brown. I kept my head high as my eyes scanned the horizon for that red barn on the left. It was early in the summer and already the temperatures were in the high nineties. My saddle blanket felt drenched with sweat. Dried sweat turned white on my chest. The creek running beside the road was barren as an empty chicken nest. Suddenly, my wondering thoughts about water were misplaced by the clopping sounds of many horse hooves traveling at a high rate of speed toward us.

Peering over the horizon, we saw a large cloud of dust coming up with the familiar sound of horses double-timing with their riders on back. Raising his right hand high, Colonel Butler commanded all troopers to halt. Realizing that the oncoming riders were not wearing grey, he silently commanded us to split into two groups along the tree lines where a small draw ran alongside the field. From there, he ordered everyone to dismount and put the horses down. With his left arm, Colonel Butler tugged my reins downward, forcing me to lie on my left side. The troopers pulled the rest of the horses down the same way. Colonel Butler whispered, "It is okay, boy. We want them to pass without seeing us. We will then give them enough distance before we push them into a cross fire with Colonel Munford's men back at Snicker's Gap."

Two hours later, that Union patrol did not know what hit them. As Colonel Butler predicted, we got the Yanks positioned into lethal crossfire. No man survived the hail of bullets. Forty Union troopers lay dead on the ground along with two dozen or so horses. Our trooper roped the surviving Yankee horses and put them into the rear. I often wondered about the horses captured after a battle. What was their story? Were the horses sold by their masters, or worse, were they stolen by a thief like old Private Smitty? Looking across those fields, I thought better them than us. Whoever had owned those horses would be proud to know they had died on the battlefield with honor.

We bivouacked at Snicker's Gap that night. Tired from the previous days' battles, both men and horses lay down on the cool evening grass, giving no thought to the day and hoping to make it through one more night. Maybe war did that to a man. Perhaps it was just pure survival, but one thing was for sure: we all had to stuff the bad memories into the back of our minds in order for the next day to make sense. Thinking about what went wrong did nothing for anybody during war.

The next morning, our troopers packed up their haversacks, fed us horses, and moved north along Ashby's Gap Turnpike. Our ultimate destination was unknown at the time. We only knew that we were to move north, parallel to Lee's Division. As always, we screened and collected intelligence. While patrolling, we engaged smaller Union patrols, or pickets quickly dispatched by our sharpshooters. Colonel Butler said at some point that we had to start making our way across the Potomac River again. If I remembered correctly, he said with an upbeat voice, "Lucky, we are going swimming at Edward's Ferry just east of Leesburg, Virginia."

On June 26, late Friday morning, we crossed over Maryland's Blue Ridge Mountains located just west of a town called Frederick. From there, we continued riding east toward a town called Rockville, southwest of Baltimore. A messenger from General Stuart's staff intercepted us before we made five miles outside of Rockville. The messenger told Colonel Butler that General Stuart wanted our regiment to circle north of Baltimore to draw attention away from Stuart's true self-imposed mission. I wasn't sure if I heard correctly, but Colonel Butler was not real happy about Stuart's mission of capturing wagons and supplies. Nevertheless, our cavalry pressed forward into enemy territory.

We encountered a few Union patrols along the pike north of Baltimore but did not engage. Colonel Butler thought it strange that we didn't see any signs of Union infantry divisions along the way. "Where did they go, Lucky?" Colonel Butler asked with disdain. He stopped us on a hill to look west. With his deep voice, Colonel Butler bellowed, "Looks like I spoke to soon." Kicked-up dust slowly rose over the horizon. He kicked my sides and said, "This could be trouble." Not wasting a moment, our trooper moved northwest to stay just out of reach of whatever it was kicking up all that dust on the horizon. I had heard that sound in Antietam; it meant thousands of marching soldiers.

We continued traveling north toward the Pennsylvania border to a rendezvous point with General Jenkins's cavalry. We would then reconnoiter the defenses of Harrisburg, Pennsylvania. To get there, we stayed out of sight just inside the tree lines along the pike. By the end of the day, we were standing by a river that defined the southern Pennsylvania border just four miles south of Harrisburg, Pennsylvania. The river was the Great Susquehanna.

Before I could even see the river, I could smell fresh water breaking the heat in the air. Looking to my left and right, the view of the Susquehanna was breathtaking. That river looked a hundred feet deep and a mile wide up and down for as far as I could see. Fortunately, we would not be swimming across it that day. Colonel Butler decided to just stop and encamp by the river to rest our men and us horses.

Walking carefully on the sandy beach, Colonel Butler let me test the water. The sand gave way to my hooves, and I was not sure if I liked that feeling. While I was shaking my head up and down, Colonel Butler asked, 'What's the matter of boy? That water is no different than what you went through in the Potomac, Rappahannock, Rapidan, and hundreds of creeks we have crossed over." He obviously could not see that big old snapping turtle I saw on the bottom. With my front hooves, I pawed at the water causing it to splash up underneath my chest. That was the trick; no more turtle.

The cool water flowing underneath me was the most wonderful feeling I had had in such a long time. I looked to my right back at Colonel Butler who said, "Come on boy. Let us get over to those bushes and get that tack off. We are all in need of a bath. You need one in the worst way." I looked back at him and snorted, "Well, you don't smell like rose water either."

Colonel Butler removed my bridle, saddle, and blanket and placed them on a stiff bush on top of the riverbank. He knew

I would not run. With his left hand, he pointed and said, "Go enjoy the water, Lucky. You deserve it." Looking at the river beach, I cautiously walked down to make sure all was clear. I suppose a Yank could not hit us from across the river since it was a good mile. Taking my time, I walked into the river to make sure there was no sudden drop-off. With two front legs in, the water came up to me knees. The cool water running over my sore knees felt tingly. It felt as if the Lord suddenly removed a hot stove off my back. Then all of a sudden, my ears could finally hear silence. There seemed to be only the sound of water flowing over rocks and broken trees that refused to yield to the current.

After an hour of cooling down, Colonel Butler said, "Come on, men. Grab your horses and get back into your uniforms. We need to make camp for a couple of nights." After Colonel Butler brushed me down, he saddled me up for an evening ride. The sun was going down and it was hard to believe a war was going on. This spot of land in Pennsylvania was so peaceful. Little did I know that hell's furry would soon show its wrath in a place called Gettysburg just twenty-five miles south of our bivouac.

Before closing our eyes for the night, the men sang a song I had not heard before. Sitting around the fire, the smoke flowed across the worn faces of men who had seen much battle since 1861. The smell of smoke and coffee filled my nose with memories of what had been a long road from home. Within a few minutes, Sergeant Wilson started humming a song that slowly pierced the crackling sound of the campfire. Before long, the rest of the troopers joined in with pure harmony. The words seemed so sad yet gracefully showed their longing to be home. At the top of the melody, Sergeant Wilson sang:

> Take me home—where I belong
> Where my love—waits for me long
> Take this gun—from my beating chest
> The good Lord knows what is best
> Take me home where I belong

On this road so hard and long
I keep my eyes and hands on my steed
Away from this place from which I bleed
Now I am home where my love awaits
The good Lord has carried me
To that place where I belong
To this place which I call home.

The morning of June 30, 1863 came quick. The sun's heat was already reflecting across the backwaters of the Susquehanna. Our troopers packed up the haversacks at around seven o'clock in the morning. I recalled that late the previous night, a young confederate officer rode into camp looking for Colonel Butler. My eyes were half-open but open enough to see the officer present to Colonel Butler a rolled-up piece of paper. Colonel Butler confirmed the message had the waxed CSA seal. The orders were from General Stuart. Colonel Butler read them in silence.

He took a deep breath and said to Sergeant Wilson, "Make sure the men clean their weapons and brush, water, and feed the horses. Tomorrow is shaping up to be a tough ride. We are to rendezvous with the rest of General Stuart's Division at a place northwest of Gettysburg, Pennsylvania."

"Yes, suh. I will get the men in order."

Two columns of horses and men rode silently along the riverbank. Looking to the right, the Susquehanna River glistened in the morning sun. The smell of water was like perfume in the air. The trees cast their cool shadows across our path. Wild flowers accented the black berry vines crawled beneath the oak trees. Colonel Butler showed a soft side that I thought he didn't have. He whispered, "Lucky, see those purple-looking flowers. My wife called them Gayfeathers. You see those yellow flowers? They are black-eyed Susans. You only see those up here in the north."

It was such a beautiful morning for one to behold. I had not felt any sense of peace for so long. I suspect the troopers had the same sentiments, or perhaps their silent thoughts knew where we were going. I was not sure. My fellow horses did not waver from left to right. We all walked in line. I looked back and saw a hundred men and horse bringing up the rear. I could not see their faces hidden beneath the shadows of their hats. Some could have been getting a few winks in; some may have been praying. I started to feel somewhat uneasy knowing these men may be fighting for their lives before long.

On July 2, the summer sun was exceptionally bright and hot that day. My eyes watered. Briefly, my thoughts about living up there after the war faded with every degree of heat; so much for cool summer breezes of the north. As we approached Gettysburg, booming cannonades miles away captured our attention. Drawing closer, we could feel the ground vibrate. The gray and black smoke rose high into the sky making the clouds look darker. Sticking my nose up, I could smell trouble. Colonel Butler picked up the pace for our patrol moved briskly alongside the Table Rock pike that ran parallel with the South Mountain Range to our right. My battle memories from the other side of those mountains broke my concentration on the road ahead. Antietam was not far from there. I blinked my eyes to get back. We had to move fast. Colonel Butler needed to rendezvous with Brig. Gen. J.E.B. Stuart just three miles northwest of Gettysburg. I wondered how it would come to pass. I learned to take it day-by-day in that war. No future was real, only the present.

At about two o'clock in the afternoon, Brig. Gen. J.E.B. Stuart finally made its presence known to General Lee. General Lee was not pleased with his timing. General Stewart did not expect the kind of reception he got considering the bounty he took from the Yanks.

Looking ahead on the pike, I could see our Confederate troopers escorting hundreds of wagons that had USA markings on the sides. Colonel Butler guided me over to a captain whose uniform looked worn and dirty. I thought they must have been in a fight. Evidently, according to the young officer, they were coming from

Carlisle, Pennsylvania, where the Yanks had put up a fight with General Ewell's division.

He said, "By General Ewell's orders, we burned down the Yank's Carlisle Barracks. The captain said over one hundred and fifty wagons were captured by General Stuart just outside Rockville. It took three days to pull those wagons back to General Lee. With raised eyebrows, Colonel Butler mumbled some imprecation I could not understand, something like, "That SOB should have been screening for Granny Lee. Where has Stuart been?"

Once we had merged with main cavalry, we moved quickly toward the southwest of Gettysburg to rendezvous with General Lee. General Stuart ordered Colonel Butler to keep our regiment to the rear to prevent the Union General Buford's cavalry from getting in behind us. Colonel Stuart said Buford was ten times more skilled as a general than the Pleasonton who pressed us back at Brandy Station. That was not what I wanted to hear during a hot afternoon.

Standing on the edge of Gettysburg, my eyes filled with sorrow again. There were so many dead men and horses lying on the battlefields. Colonel Butler halted our regiment on some high ground to study his pocket map. Looking southeast, he pointed out to Sergeant Wilson, "There. That is Little Round Top and just south is Round Top. Looks like the Yanks are well entrenched in those defenses. I see our men over there to the right on high ground…wait…looks like the map says Seminary Ridge. We are going to need God's help in this one." The smoke drifting across the fields hid the fact that many more had died.

Before he could get another word out, a rider approached us from the west. Major Andrew Venable stopped his horse just short of colliding with me. Colonel Butler replied to the major's salute, "How can I help you major?" Major Venable, trying to catch his breath, said, "Sir, General Stuart needs your regiment to reconnoiter northeast two miles from here. Do not engage the enemy."

Colonel Butler turned around and yelled loudly to Sergeant Wilson, "Let's work our way north of them Yanks and give them something else to think about. Maybe we can turn their right flank." General Stuart's major kicked his horse and said while riding away, "Colonel, tomorrow we are moving northeast to get behind the Union lines. Your orders are to protect General Ewell's left flank throughout the night."

Once evening came, we rode northwest for a couple of miles to bed down on the safe side of Cress Ridge. That night, not too many men slept since the booming sounds of cannonades between artilleries persisted until midnight. The shooting stopped for moments to reload. During the long silence, both sides respectfully stopped shooting for the removal of the dead. As the cannons slept, the wounded men's screams pierced the night air. For me, I could hear the gasp of horses taking their last breath on this earth.

At sunrise on July 3, we woke up to a hazy light filtered by the smoke swirling in the air and a bloodred fog looming over the fields of Gettysburg. Across Seminary Ridge facing east, I could see hundreds of confederate cannons lined up on the ridge, their Napoleon brass barrels glistening in the morning sun that broke through with the rising fog. The time for battle was near. The men sensed it. We horses…well, we could hear death as easily as smell it. It was moments like this that, as one human had said, "Defines who we are."

Colonel Butler said that General Picket's brigades were to make an offensive charge after the cannons softened up the federal targets on Cemetery Ridge and Culp's Hill. There was a sense of urgency building up within the men. By the time we reached the top of Cress Ridge north of Culp's Hill, our scouts had returned and reported that Union patrols were east of us on the intersection of Low Dutch and Hanover roads. They knew we were coming. Colonel Butler said, "Lucky, we have lost the element of surprise." Reports indicated between four thousand

and five thousand Union troopers were in blocking positions. With a tightened fist on the reins, Colonel Butler spoke aloud, "Lord, grant us victory." He did not know that the Cavalry ahead of us had repeating Spencer rifles. Our victory would be allusive.

We double-timed across the York Pike along the Low Dutch Road to conceal our movements near peach orchards until we reached Cress Ridge. Our place of choice for battle was the East Cavalry Field. To me it was just another open wheat field lined with oak trees, which defined the order of battle. General Stuart spotted a couple of Union horse regiments coming and ordered artillery to fire. Unfortunately, our artillery alerted Union Cavalry commanders Brigadier General David McMurtrie Gregg and Brigadier George Armstrong Custer. Both would bring an additional two thousand troopers to the fight.

We crossed over the rolling fields of shining bright gold wheat reflecting from the sun and turned right to engage the Yanks. At that moment, a sense of peace came over me, yet I knew it was just an illusion. With his saber in one hand and a pistol in the other, Colonel Butler pushed us to an uncertain destiny. To our left and right over the horizon were six thousand Confederate troopers plus our three-inch guns, but that would not be enough firepower. The Union had positioned additional cannons in front of us. Their numerical advantage in artillery would in the end push us back.

Colonel Butler said, "Lucky, we need to move farther north to get behind them. After putting his saber back, he called up ten men saying, "Gentlemen. You know we may not come back, but we must turn their artilleries' attention away north. The grapeshot is killing us and our horses."

The men replied, "Remember, Dixieland awaits us!" A rebel yell ensued as the troopers put boot and spur to our sides.

Once in position north of East Cavalry Field, Colonel Butler spotted a lone Union scout. The horse the scout was riding looked familiar; in fact, the he looked just like me. Before I could sniff the air, Colonel Butler kicked my sides giving me the signal to run at full speed. I could hear Colonel Butler cock back the rifle's hammer. While running, my mind wondered about the black horse in front of us and closing in a hundred yards away. Just then, a familiar scent hit me. I knew Colonel Butler was going to shoot that horse first, but before he could pull the trigger, I cut sharply to the right causing the shot to go wide. Colonel Butler yelled, "What are you doing Lucky?" He could not have known. He cocked the trigger back again, but this time the Union scout had turned around and headed for the tree line. Blazoned on the horse's left rear was a symbol that confirmed what I knew—the Magnolia brand. The black stallion was my family, but I just did not know which brother he was.

The scout obviously made it back because a hundred troopers or more emerged from the tree line firing their repeating rifles at us and forcing our regiment back. For two hours, our cavalries fought amongst artillery duels and in some cases, hand-to-hand dismounted troopers. Fortunately, Colonel Butler and I survived. Perhaps it was fate, but I am certain we would not have survived that battle if not by providence. Too many died that day. Yes, we had survived many battles before; however, none were more vicious as that one.

I could not believe my eyes. By the time the sun had set on July 3, there were tens of thousands of soldiers and countless horses lying dead on the battlefield. It was Fredericksburg all over again—but with our grays lying out there instead of the Yanks. Colonel Butler said, "Don't worry Lucky, this is not our day. We must move back into position northwest to ensure the Yanks do not circle in on General Lee." With his right hand, he pulled me back from a sight I will never forget.

"Come on, men," Colonel Butler yelled. "We need to get to the rear and do our jobs. Maybe we can find a way to circle around them blue bellies."

The history of the Battle of Gettysburg history will be retold
many times by many humans. The story I pass down to my children will be different. Yes, tens of thousands of men lay dead
or wounded on those fields and hills surrounding the town of
Gettysburg and beside them were my brothers and sisters. The
first casualty on any cavalry battle was a horse. We paid the ultimate sacrifice just as well.

Our regiment tried to get into the Union's flank that day and
engage the Union's General Buford northeast of Gettysburg, but
we turned back due to overwhelming forces that were simply
impenetrable. Colonel Butler said, "Lucky, we will live to fight
another day on the battleground of our choosing closer to home."
I hoped he was right.

Gettysburg would be remembered for the fifty-one thousand
men and countless of my kind that would lie dead or wounded on
the battlefield or go missing. I overhead a foot soldier looking at
a field map and saying, "Looks like those Yanks held their ground
on Cemetery Ridge, fighting at Devil's Den, Little Round Top,
the Wheatfield, Peach Orchard, Culp's Hill, and East Cemetery
Hill." For the first time in the War of Northern Aggression I
questioned if all the death was worth it. The Union's President
did not think so. A few months later, President Abraham Lincoln
made his own history from the blood spilled at Gettysburg.

On Thursday, November 19, 1863, he delivered at Gettysburg
what would be called the Gettysburg Address, which he began
with "Four score and seven years ago…"

On Independence Day, the Lord delivered a heavy rain that
made the fields look like rivers of blood. The dead were everywhere. Both Confederate and Union ambulances and litter-bear-
ers attended the wounded and dead. General Lee had even sent a
white flag of truce to General Meade, requesting the exchange of
prisoners. General Meade denied his request, instead offering the
good care of General Longstreet. General Lee laughed, knowing
General Longstreet was standing safely nearby.[18]

Our remaining Army of Northern Virginia pulled out of Gettysburg to go home. General Lee lost that one. The Union had an opportunity to come after us and end the war. However, the Yanks' General Meade was like the rest of them, overly cautious and unwilling to bear the burden of more bloodshed on his hands. I remembered what happened in '62, that if General McClellan had pursued us after the Battle of Antietam, the war would have ended sooner. The Battle of Gettysburg was another missed opportunity for peace between nations.

We crossed over the Potomac River just below Williamsport on July 14. A few weeks earlier, the Federals had destroyed our pontoon bridge we used to cross into Maryland at Williamsport. However, General Lee was not the slightest deterred. The men, using southern know-how, dismantled several barns, sheds, and fences to make a useable pontoon bridge to get our men safely over to Virginia. Colonel Butler and I even helped. He and I pulled a couple of railroad ties to the riverbank for the engineers. The corporal said, "Thank you, sir. We will secure those heavy pieces to the bank."

The darkness of the early morning concealed our infantry movements across the makeshift bridge over the Potomac. Our regiment brought up the rear to prevent any flanking attack by the Federals on the move to intercept us before we could cross over. Once on Virginia soil, General Lee's divisions would continue toward Richmond via the Blue Ridge Mountains. Stuart's troopers would stay east and to the rear, providing screening security. Colonel Butler received orders to perform advance patrols down toward Leesburg, Virginia.

On July 18, the morning sun rose with a heated vengeance. It was going to be a hot day. Looking behind me, I saw only the hat covers of men who were hanging their heads down to block the bright sun. I think they were sleeping. Though the trees along the trail provided much needed shade, the humidity was merciless. Looking at my friend's eyes, I could see they were tired and simply shell-shocked. I noticed that even some horses were missing, but we weren't sure who. We moved southeast, staying close to the river to observe any possible Federal movements on the other side in Maryland. Luckily, there were no Union patrols. We were not in good shape to carry on another fight.

Our regiment made it to Loudoun County during midday. We pressed forward on a trail that took us to a turnpike leading south toward Leesburg. General Stuart pinpointed Leesburg as the rendezvous point where he and his staff would set up a field headquarters to plan and rethink an attack strategy based upon General Lee's most recent orders.

Within only ten miles between us and Leesburg, Colonel Butler decided to bivouac the troopers in a small valley that provided fresh water, cool water, and summer wheat fields. I liked the place. A small stream ran between the valley hills that provided a secure place to rest.

Colonel Butler said, "Lucky, I saw a spotter on the hill just above us. I think he is our welcoming party and the local militiaman called by his fellow county citizens as Major John Singleton Mosby." Evidently, the Union Army gave him the nickname Gray Ghost. Major Mosby and his Raiders would do hit-and-run raids on the Federals that most officers considered cowardly. As such, Colonel Butler did not care for the man. He said, "Mosby is just another wannabe trooper who does not understand the professionalism and restraint required by military officers." Colonel Butler called him a gorilla, meaning he fought like a coward, hitting and running without looking at his enemy in the eyes. I think this Mosby must have been on to something. At least his men did not march out in an open field where the only protection a soldier had between a bullet and his person was the dead body of the man in front of him.

After pitching lean-tos against the cross fence, the men made quick work of getting the fire started and coffee boiling. The last couple of weeks had gone by so quickly that it wasn't until later that I noticed a dozen of our men and horses had not come back with us. Their last resting place was the fields of sorrow in Gettysburg, Pennsylvania. I wondered about my friend Old Buster. Shaking my head clear, my thoughts wondered back to how Buster and I chewed up so much fat over the last few months. I respected that old horse. Buster was the trusted older brother that I never knew. I would never see him again.

We spent the next couple of days near Leesburg, taking the time needed to mend tack and uniforms while the medical folks stitched up wounds. Along those lines, Colonel Butler noticed my rear left leg was limping a bit, though I never noticed it. Some say the fog of war blocks the pain. Well, that fog had been hanging over me for some time. In any case, Colonel Butler said, "Lucky, we need to get you to a farrier. I think I got enough greenbacks to get you a new shoe or two." He left the men, saying, "Gentlemen, get yourselves and your horses cleaned up and rested. I will return before sunset."

On our way toward Leesburg, we came upon a local famer who said there was a fellow down the road who built carriages. Surely, he would have some tools, shoes, and nails. The farmer said, "His name is Mr. Norris. Tell him I sent you."

"What might be your name sir?" Colonel Butler said.

"My name is James Garnett Sr. My son, Private J.C. Garnett, is attached to the Fifth Regiment of the Virginia Cavalry. Have you seen him?"

"Sir I have not, but if I do, I will be sure he gets word to you."

"Thank you kindly, Colonel. I do appreciate the consideration. I miss my boy."

"Sir, if your son fought in battle, he is an honorable man now, not a boy."

Grinning, the man replied, "He will always be my baby boy."

After leaving Mr. Garnett, it took us bout thirty minutes to get to Mr. Norris's workshop. The property was marked with a sign worded Norris and Sons Wagon and Coach Repairs.

Colonel Butler said to me, "Lucky, we must be in the right place." He reined me to the right on to a path leading toward the main house on the left and a workshop on the right. As we got closer to the shed, we saw an older, one-armed man leaning against a rail extending from the right corner of the shed. Colonel Butler raised his right hand, gesturing a hello.

"Good morning, Colonel. How can I help you?" the man asked.

Both shook hands. Colonel Butler replied, "Sir, sure would appreciate your assistance in getting my horse a new shoe."

The man tipped his hat forward. "Be glad to help. Bring him on over here." Holding my reins in his right hand, Colonel Butler led me over to the shed.

I noticed the man was wearing an old set of blue dungarees and a faded red plaid shirt. He said, "My name is Mr. Bill Norris. Colonel, come over here by the side of the shed. I need to measure those hooves to make sure I got some shoes big enough to fit 'em. That is one big horse. What kind is he?"

"I rightly don't know. I think Lucky is part thoroughbred and, looking at his muscular chest, he must have some Irish Warmblood in him. He sure has an Irish attitude."

Mr. Norris laughed. "Aye, me wife can be a demanding Irish redhead herself, you know what I mean?"

"Sir, I only have enough money for one shoe."

"Well, that don't matter," Norris replied with a crooked smile. "We will fix Lucky up all the way around. Besides, it is for our cause."

"Thank you, sir. You are most kind. I will send money back to you."

"No need. You just need do a good deed for someone else yourself."

"So be it. Thank you."

Mr. Norris continued on. "I sure wish I could be riding alongside ya to fight 'em Yanks. However, this bum arm kept me out of service. So I am a one-arm hammer swinger, but deadly accurate."

"Mr. Norris, we sure could have used you back in Gettysburg. One arm is better than no arm."

"I can swing a hammer. Say, heard things got a bit dicey up there. I heard many were killed."

Colonel Butler remained silent. Looking at Colonel Butler's eyes, Mt. Norris knew not to press forward with any more questions about Gettysburg.

After my new shoes were nailed in place, Colonel Butler slowly walked me around the shed to see how I looked. They felt fine to me. My limp seemed to go away. I guess I must have thrown a shoe running back in East Cavalry Field. I had never paid attention to it since my eyes had caught the sight of my older brother. I was glad Colonel Butler's aim went wide. Then out of nowhere, like he knew what I was thinking, Colonel Butler stopped me, tugged me around to where I was no more than six inches from his face. Looking intently into my eyes, Colonel Butler said, "Lucky, thank you. I know how hard this war has been on you…and well…on me too. I know you saw that black stallion with your home brand back there in Gettysburg. I was not going to shoot him. My bullet would have found its mark on the Yank." I pulled back and neighed loudly as my way of saying "Thank you."

Colonel Butler gave Mr. Norris a couple of greenbacks.

"Much obliged, sir."

"Colonel, come in and have some lunch. My wife, Orla, made some ham and beans last night. She even has a few pieces of cornbread to soak up them beans. Aye, they taste real good cold."

"No, thank you, sir. I need to get back to my regiment camped up the road there yonder. I need to get my men packed up and start making our way back south."

Colonel Butler mounted back up and turned to wave good-bye to Mr. Norris. As we approached the road, Mr. Norris yelled, "Ya'll take care of yourselves hear now. Don't forget to tell my son, should you run into him, that I would appreciate a letter."

"You bet, sir. I will do so."

Back on the hard, rutted dirt road, we headed north back to the camp. No more than a mile down the road, we heard a horse and rider closing in on us. The rider was a young Confederate officer waving his gloved hand and motioning for Colonel Butler to stop. The officer stopped beside us, then saluted Colonel Butler.

"Are you Colonel Butler, sir?"

"Yes Captain, it is I."

"Sir," the captain said in a respectful tone, "General Stuart would like to see you at his headquarters located about five miles from here, just this side of Leesburg."

"Captain, what is the reason for this request?"

"Sir, he did not share that with me. My orders were to locate you and redirect your regiment to his location."

In an irritated voice, Colonel Butler replied, "Go ahead, tell the general my men and I need an hour to pack up camp. We should be there soon as practical."

The captain saluted, quickly jerked his horse around, and galloped back toward town.

Colonel Butler said to me, "Lucky, what does General Stuart want from me? How does he know me?"

After getting our regiment packed up and back in the saddle, it took us about an hour to reach the Leesburg home designated as General Stuart's field headquarters. Just a hundred yards or so from the house, we found a shaded spot of grass under a few large maple trees near a small stream that provided much-needed fresh water. Colonel Butler let me graze while he went over to meet with the general. I thought it odd that he wanted to walk. I guess he needed some time to think about what he was going to say to the general. Well, instead of grazing, I followed Colonel Butler to the house. Thinking I was being sneaky, without warning he whirled around so fast, but I quickly pretended I was eating grass. Satisfied I was okay, he turned around and kept walking toward the house. I resumed trailing him.

Once he was on the creaky porch, Colonel Butler approached the front door and knocked three times, calling out, "Colonel Butler, Confederate States of America, present. Permission to enter?"

General Stuart replied, "Please, please come in Colonel Butler. We have been waiting for you."

When standing in front of a superior officer, the junior ranking officer must stand at attention until told otherwise. Colonel Butler did so. General Stuart said, "At ease, mister. Come on in. We have much to talk about."

"General, sir, forgive me. I am not sure why you ordered me here."

"Colonel, I have heard from Major General Fits Lee about your bravery and courage on the battlefields at Antietam, Fredericksburg, and back north at Gettysburg. I understand you have been shot twice and have countless saber cuts."

"Well sir, as you know it comes with the job. Might I add things would have been worse if not for the skills of my war horse, Lucky." General Stuart looked around Colonel Butler's right side and saw me peeking through the window.

"Mr. Butler, I see your horse shows great concern for you."

"What do you mean, General?"

Laughing, General Stuart said, "Why, he is standing right outside that window looking in at us."

Raising his hand, Colonel Butler looked around at me and silently mouthed, "Go back." I guessed he did not need a quick escape from the general, so I turned around and headed back to the stream.

General Stuart and Colonel Butler discussed upcoming operations in Northern Virginia. General Lee wanted to reorganize the Confederate cavalry into two divisions with three brigades in each division.

"Colonel Butler, I need to merge your regiment into the First Division Cavalry," General Stuart said.

"Yes, sir. I will tell my men."

The wrinkles on General Stuart's forehead became more emphasized as he said, "Well, Colonel, that is what I want to talk to you about. I need to promote other colonels who are senior to you. Though several of your peers were killed back in Gettysburg, I will not have enough cavalry brigades to position you or them for a command. Therefore, since you are more junior in rank, but have distinguished yourself with honor on the battlefield, I need to assign you to CSA headquarters back in Richmond. Your job will be to assist the secretary of war's staff in strategic planning with members of General Lee's staff. Once in Richmond, you will first report to the secretary of war, the Honorable James A. Seddon. He wants a brief regarding your encampment on the Susquehanna River."

A quizzical look on his face, Colonel Butler replied, "Why the Susquehanna?"

"Not sure Colonel. I believe a local up there talked with one of your men without your knowledge. He wants a better under-standing of who that soldier was and why he was talking to an unnamed civilian. I expect you to devote much energy during this assignment. The needs of the Confederate leadership always come first. As a gesture of my appreciation, I am authoriz-ing you a six-month medical furlough upon completion of the Richmond assignment."

Colonel Butler showed no emotion for two seconds before his face turned red. Confused, Colonel Butler replied, "What do you mean, General, sir? Six months is a long time from the battle lines, sir."

General Stuart, glancing back at his aides-de-camp, looked back to Colonel Butler and said, "I hear you are talking to your-self or your horse."

Colonel Butler replied with a smile. "Sir, I talk to that horse because I have no one else to talk to while I am on the trail. No harm meant by it."

General Stuart said, "I see. I suppose I talk to Highfly on the trail when I am thinking about my wife."

Colonel Butler did not know if that was an insult or a by-the-way offering. In any case, Colonel Butler stood at attention. He looked at General Stuart and saluted, saying, "Thank you, sir. I request permission to leave, sir?"

General Stuart nodded with a yes.

Colonel Butler had been gone for about an hour. I had already returned to my grazing under the shade of an old oak tree, while being serenaded by the locust. Colonel Butler approached me from the left, grabbed my halter, and said, "Lucky, looks like you and me are headed to Richmond. We leave first thing tomorrow morning, by ourselves."

He walked me over to the stream where he sat down to wash his face in a small eddy of water. He cupped his hands to keep the water from escaping while he drank. Then he stopped drinking and stared into the pool for a good minute. I could see his reflection and wondered what he was thinking. His mind must have been lost in a bale of cotton. I understood him. War makes one break down to the core and rebuilds to discover or rediscover who they are. I knew Colonel Butler had seen and done much in that war. I would never know what it felt like to take the life of another living thing.

Months later, I thought about General Stuart, a young and brave Confederate officer who at thirty-two would command the new Cavalry Corps on September 9, 1863. During the fall, he fought the Union on northern Virginia soil in the Bristoe Campaign around the town of Warrenton and Manassas Junction. During the winter of "63, General Stuart stayed north of Richmond to provide early warning of any Union advances to capture the South's seat of democracy. General Stuart was also well aware that the Union had replaced General Meade with a herald officer whose victories in the west made him almost indestructible in the eyes of the Union leadership. His name was

General Ulysses S. Grant. Reports indicated he was intending on making an offensive attack on Richmond as part of what newspapers called the Overland Campaign. These battles would occur during the spring of '64, not far from Fredericksburg and Chancellorsville in northern Virginia, just north of Richmond.

In a town called Yellow Tavern, General Stuart's future would take a turn for the worst. Riding with the First Virginia, he waved his pistol in the air, yelling to encourage his troopers on horseback to go after the retreating Fifth Michigan Cavalry. During the retreat, an old Union private heard the commotion, looked back, and noticed a Confederate general charging in front of his men, yelling and waving at his troopers to follow him and go after the retreating Union Cavalry. Seeing a target of opportunity, the Union private stopped his horse, dismounted, took careful aim, and killed General Stuart with a revolver. It was May 9, 1864. On May 12, Brigadier General James Ewell Brown Stuart died from loss of blood and infection caused by the gunshot. According to the surgeons who worked on General Stuart, the bullet struck his left side and excited his back, barely missing his spine. General Lee was deeply saddened with the loss of the cavalry commander. The previous spring, it was General Jackson; that spring, it was General Stuart's time to go home to the Lord.[19]

July 9 would be the last time I would see those parts for some time to come. Colonel Butler turned his command over to one of General Stuart's aides-de-camp who as a colonel looked like he had not fought at all in the war. His uniform was too clean and without blemish. His boots were too shiny. As I carried Colonel Butler down between two perfectly aligned rows of horses and men, the troopers all took off their hats and cheered three times for an officer who loved his country and his men.

TEMPORARY DUTY

The losses at Gettysburg and Vicksburg weighed heavily on our hearts and minds as Colonel Butler and I traveled to Richmond. It was evident that General Lee wanted time for his men to recoup and refit, thus authorizing generous rest and recuperation for his general staff. General Stuart ordered some of his general officers to take themselves home for rest and recuperation. I was a little confused, thinking at first chance we would go back into battle right after Gettysburg, but it did not take me long to figure out Colonel Butler would eventually go back to his home in North Carolina. I hoped I would be the horse taking him home after the Richmond assignment was completed. Six months getting healthy and maybe, just maybe, going back to Magnolia Plantation would be a blessing.

We meandered through northern Virginia with one goal in mind: get safely to Richmond. Union troopers were scouring the countryside for our old friend, Major Mosby and his Raiders, so we just stayed cleared of the east and out of sight. Along the way, we noticed the Federal troopers had been patrolling along the turnpikes not too many days ago. Riding along the Richmond, Fredericksburg, and Potomac Railroad, we discovered sections of track torn up by patrols. Piles of wooden track crossties were burned to ashes. Like we had done to the Union rail lines, the Yanks bent the iron rails around trees.

Colonel Butler said, "Lucky, we need to make sure someone back in Richmond gets these tracks repaired. Those rails provide transportation for troops and supplies between Richmond and the Potomac. On our way to Richmond, we will be passing through Middleburg where Dr. Smith and his family lived. He and his family were so kind to us back in the fall of '62 after Antietam."

The road we traveled was indeed familiar. However, I shook my head as some of the countryside seemed out of place. The corn and wheat fields were either brown or black. Colonel Butler said, "Lucky, looks like the Yanks moved through here not long ago as well. I figure they mean to starve us out if that can't beat us." Turning my head back to look again, I thought maybe you can eat other grub, but I need that belly-deep grass.

We were in no hurry to get to Richmond. Colonel Butler's temporary duty orders were to report no later than September 6. Therefore, the colonel and I would frequently stop so he could make notes on a pocket map. He said it was important to note any indications of Federal movements that may indicate future Union battle lines. I did not mind, as the hot summer days made those shade trees a welcome sight. While he annotated field observations on his pocket maps, I caught up on my grazing. Periodically, I looked up and around to sniff the air for any familiar smell. The scents were not recognizable, as much had changed in a year because of the war. The Yanks tore up the roads. Many of the cross-fences lining the fields last year were broken apart, much like the railroad tracks we tore up in the north. Many of the side trails felt like the rutted roads I hauled war wagons on back in May of '61. Funny, I was so much younger then. Then a thought occurred to me about that wagon master Private Smitty. I never should have let him get away from the Battle of Manassas. I wondered what that traitor was doing.

Downtown Washington, D.C. was filled with celebration and hope for victory against the South. The news of Gettysburg and Vicksburg Union victories gave many people a reason to drink and carry on. People of all kinds were walking down the main streets. Rich and poor alike shared a common belief that the war's end was near. However, the victories at Gettysburg and Vicksburg were but a small step on a long journey toward peace. Many more would have to die. Many more would emerge as reconstruction businessmen who had ill intent, such as the likes of Private Smitty.

Smitty woke up late in the morning after another night of drinking and gambling. The bed he had lain in had not changed. It was stuffed with hay and cotton remnants making it uncomfortable; however, Smitty was just glad not to be sleeping on the hard streets. Someday he would have his own featherbed like the big-shot politicians. The midday sun shining through his lone window drew attention to his trousers lying on the floor. Smitty thought, *Why are my britches laying on the floor? I know I hang 'em on the door knob every night.*

Trying to clear his head, he sat on the edge of the bed, rubbing his eyes and thinking the sun was too bright for his liking. When he stood up, Smitty realized he had one heck of a headache. Dragging his feet, he stumbled over to the window to cover the blinding sun that made his eyes water. Looking at the paint peeling off the window seal, he thought, *I should suggest to Miss Surratt that I would be glad to scrape and paint those window seals in exchange for a couple of months' rent.* However, there was one thing Smitty knew he needed and that was a hot cup of coffee. Surely, Miss Mary would have the coffeepot going down stairs in the kitchen.

After he got dressed, Smitty thought, *What am I doing? Steeling and upping people for small change. I am smarter and better than this. There has to be a better way.* Looking behind him, he saw the new brogan boots he had won at a poker game the previous week. Though the boots were a little big in the toe, he would put a couple pair of socks on and they would fit perfectly. Cold water was what he needed on his face. To the left of the window was the washbowl, which had some brown water in it. He picked it up, went down to the common bath, and got some fresh water. The commons was open so he went in and closed the door. *Good*, he thought, *I can have some privacy.*

Looking into the mirror, he realized he needed to shave. Thinking out loud, Smitty said, "If I am to start new, I need a clean-cut look that would not alarm a would-be business partner." While shaving his throat, he heard people suddenly yelling outside. *Oops.* The dull blade nicked his neck. A small trickle of blood ran down. Wiping off the blood, Smitty wondered what all the commotion was about. The crowd was yelling something about Gettysburg.

That reminded him. Smitty checked his front pockets. There was a piece of paper a dark-haired man had given him at the corner bar the previous night. It was the fifth message he had received over the last few months. Smitty knew what to do with that sealed note. He had been getting those sealed orders at least once a week since Antietam.

After returning to his room, he looked under his pillow and found his Colt pocket revolver. After securing his shoulder holster, Smitty picked up his gun to make sure it was loaded. He cocked backed the trigger and spun the cylinder. He loved the clicking noise made when the cylinder spun smoothly around. The sound was reassuring to Smitty. He then carefully inserted it into his holster. Smitty usually never wore an overcoat, but that day, he wore his gray sack coat and put a little shine on those brogans. He grabbed his blue slouch hat and closed the door behind him.

Smitty walked down the second floor hallway toward the stairs, stopped, then looked into the mirror on wall. He looked younger, though the crow's feet around his eyes were getting deeper with time. Smitty looked and said aloud, "Look out. Here I come to take your money."

At the bottom of the stairs, one of the tenants, Mr. Ethan Beranger, said in a thick English accent, "Good day to you, ole chap. You look like a different man. Where might you be going that requires a proper look?"

Smitty replied in a mocking English accent. "My good man, I am on my way to a party of which"—he switched to an American accent—"is none of your damn business."

"Oh my," the older man replied. "Just trying to be friendly."

Smitty kept walking forward with a crooked grin, mouthing, "You have no idea."

Smitty walked into the kitchen, grabbed a blue ceramic mug, and filled it with hot, black coffee before walking into the back yard. The rose bushes smelled good that morning. His mother had always said, "Stop and smell the roses, son." Smitty reflected and realized she was right. Looking back, Private Smitty was no longer the poor farmer who had betrayed his country. For the past two years, he had learned to survive in the city, read, and write. He had even picked up on math by counting the monies he had stolen from unsuspecting victims on the street. Educated, the country boy was moving up but not at the speed he wanted. He knew his heart burned with desires and ambition for riches and respect. How was he to get respect? The small business venture on the side paid okay money, but Smitty wanted more.

Looking out the backyard, Smitty was amazed at how happy the Washington citizens were. People everywhere on the streets were yelling "hip hip hurray" for Meade and Grant. Smitty rejected the idea that the Union's victory at Gettysburg and Vicksburg would be the turning points in the war. The Union politicians and newspapers believed peace would soon follow. Sensing opportunity, Smitty knew the victories over the Confederates gave President Lincoln hope that the Union would transition from war to reconstruction to carefully reintegrate the southern states back into the fold. Smitty would be part of that transition.

Smitty knew that with reconciliation, a new country would be born—a country that would need reconstruction programs to provide financial opportunities for all, including dishonorable men like himself. Smitty knew that future was coming quickly or at least his southern friends would ensure of it. Timing was everything on the streets. He had to move quickly before the window shut. Otherwise, he would end up in the Union stockades or worse yet, back in South Carolina pulling cotton. He hated the notion of city folks looking down at him as a poor dirt farmer.

Living in the capitol city created an internal riff inside Smitty. Over time, he began to question his loyalty to the South and his desires for private gain. Why not question? He knew his usefulness would go away once the war was over, so he had to think ahead. He would have redefine himself and take steps to finagle fortunes of the future. To do so meant he would have to disassociate himself from his current profession without jeopardizing his life, but then they may not let him go. He would terminate that relationship in due time.

Since it was past noon on Independence Day, he thought he would go celebrate just a bit at the corner saloon appropriately called The Crow's Nest since the navy yard was not two or three blocks away. Smitty walked in and, as usual, went up to the bartender, laid down two bits for draft ale, then returned to his normal table with his back to the wall, facing the double doors. Smitty learned a long time ago to sit against the wall and never in the middle of a watering hole.

After taking a drink, he saw the double doors swing open and a young, dark-haired man shuffle in carrying his hat over his right hip. The man looked familiar, but Smitty could not place him. The young man walked toward the bartender and slid onto a stool behind the long oak bar with brass foot rails. The young man propped his boots up as he quietly drank a shot of whiskey.

Smitty thought he would join the young man armed with two pearl-handled Colt .45 revolvers and figure out his story. It was unusual to see a man wearing two Colts around the city with all the constables and military men walking around town.

Smitty sat down on the stool next to the right of the young man since he noticed the young man drank with the left hand. Smitty always positioned himself on the weak side of a man knowing how to disarm in case of an unplanned confrontation. Looking at the large wall mirror behind the bartender, Smitty could see the young man was uneasy, constantly wringing his hands and fiddling with his pocket watch.

Smitty turned to the man and said, "You all right, fella?"

Not looking at Smitty, the worried man continued looking into his glass and said, "I am fine. I don't think my business is any concern of yours, mister whoever-you-are."

Smitty gripped his glass a little stronger and replied, "Just trying to be friendly, young man. Whatever is on your mind, let me buy you another drink to take the edge off."

The young man put his hand in his pocket and realized he had only two bits. A smile cracking on his face, he said, "Thanks, mister meant-no-harm."

"Not a problem, young man, been worried myself. What is your name?"

"David…David Herold. What might be your name, mister?"

"My name is just Smitty." Smitty thought he looked mighty familiar.

Over the next couple of weeks, Smitty came up with a business idea that would move him closer to the prosperity and respect he so desired. Smitty knew that soldiers on both sides needed a full stomach to fight—well at least the Yanks. He knew his rebel brothers lived on little to fight and win. Here was the opportunity: find a way to sell food to the Union and skim back some for the south but add a tax—his tax.

Before summer's end, he knew he had to make a move to get into business with a large-scale farmer. Timing was critical. The growing season would be ending soon and all the crops would be harvested and shipped to the west. Smitty thought he would have to create a fictitious reputation to break into the stringent government contracts given to local farmers. His first step would be to travel the western counties in Virginia just outside the capitol. Remembering his conversation with David Herold, a long-time resident of Washington, D.C., his first stop would be Herndon, Virginia. There was old money in those parts.

The next morning, he packed up his clothes and moved out of Ms. Surratt's boarding house. While walking down the stairs, he ran into a familiar face—David Herold. Smitty just nodded and kept on moving, thinking something was up with that boy. Once outside, he tied a dirty bag to the old mare he had bought for fifty dollars from a drunkard two days before. The horse was old and looked like it had been ridden through hell and back with all the saber scars on her withers. What Smitty did not know was that that old mare was a cavalry horse that had fought in the First Battle of Manassas in '61. Even warhorses could not escape the memories haunting us until our last breath.

Smitty made his way through the back alleys until he found the bridge that crossed the Potomac River over into Fairfax where he rode west to Herndon, Virginia, a prized farming community recently named after Captain William Lewis Herndon, a native of Fredericksburg, Virginia. The bartender back at the Crowe's Nest said Captain Herndon was some famous sailor. He was not sure about his naval exploits.

Old Smitty crossed some fields where large oak trees lined the properties covered with tall green stalks of corn and in others, barley. Turning left onto Squirrel Hill Road, he rode two more miles to a general goods store owned by a local who did business with the federal army. The word back on the streets in Washington, D.C. was that several commissary support contracts were given to notable farmers around Herndon. There was old money there, and Old Smitty figured he would work, befriend, and betray his way into the mainstream of who was who in the area. Before getting to the store, he had one more job to do. Smitty stopped to place a sealed note under a large flat rock. The Ghost would pick up the note later that evening.

Back on the trail, a farmer told him that a general store where farmers traded was not more than two miles ahead northwest. The farmer said, "The store was called Moran's General Goods located off Squirrel Hill Road."

Smitty and his nagging mare of a horse rode down a country road that ran by a couple of cornfields owned by a local, Dr. John Moran. Smitty thought to himself, *If I can do some work for this fella, perhaps he can show me the ropes. Besides, I know how to make hay. Been doing it most of my life until in South Carolina before the war started.*

As Smitty approached the general goods store, he could see farmers and wagons coming and going along the main street. Wagons were loaded with vegetables of all kinds to be sold in the city outdoor markets. After tying his horse up to the hitching post, Smitty walked up on a set of old creaky planks to the storefront's door. The sign above it had been whitewashed, saying Moran's General Store in black letters. Walking in, he heard a bell ringing above his head announcing his entrance. A young plain-looking, redheaded girl behind the counter said, "Welcome, sir? How can we help you?"

Smitty was smitten with the lassie. After brushing off the dust from his dungarees, he took off his hat and said, "Miss, or is it Mrs.?" She replied with a bright red face, "My name is Miss Bella Moran. I mean, I am not married." Smitty's eyes lit up hoping he could smooth talk his way into a good situation.

He took off his hat, smiled, and said, "Miss Moran, I would appreciate your assistance in helping locate your father, Dr. Moran. I am interested in working a business proposition."

Smitty was very careful not to let his southern accent find its way back into his spoken word, not since the day he was almost shot in the back alley of a DC pub where a stranger had challenged his origin. That man drew his last breath after meeting Smitty.

"My father will be here soon for dinner. He is riding back from Falls Church where he is helping care for the injured soldiers returning from Gettysburg. Oh, how awful that was for our soldiers! You heard we won?"

After making that statement, she realized that Smitty should be serving. Quick to respond, Smitty replied, "I remember serving back in the First Battle of Manassas, I mean, Bull Run as a ninety-day enlistee. Glad my term expired before getting myself killed, which is why I want to serve the Union in a different way by bringing them fresh farm goods.

Grinning, Miss Moran replied, "Oh! That would be an honorable gesture on your part! We must all contribute to the war effort."

Smitty nodded his head forward and closed his eyes. *If she only knew.*

⌒

Colonel Butler was talking aloud as he did more frequently when he and I were alone on the trail. As we got closer to the Smith farm, he spoke, "Lucky, ole fella, do you remember the man and family south of Middleburg, the man who gave you this saddle blanket?" I shook my head up and down, but I don't think Colonel Butler caught it. In any case, he continued on. "Lucky, I think his farm is not three miles from here. We can take a shortcut over that field to get there quicker."

The hard grass beneath my hooves made a loud crunching noise. With no wind blowing in my ears, I could hear the horse and deer fly chasing my rear. I hated those bugs. As we moved closer to the farm, everything seemed so strange. My senses went into overload for some reason. Then a memory flashed like lightning before me, stopping me in my tracks; my Red was there. She was so close then; she still had to be there safe and sound.

I stretched out my neck and picked up the pace a bit. Colonel Butler said, "Wow, boy! We are in no hurry." I disregarded his command and moved into a trot. He had no idea how fast my heart was beating. The sweat poured down my back and the dryness in my mouth did not deter me. As we approached the crest of a rolling hill, the smell of battle alerted me that something bad happened. Looking down across the Smith Valley Farm, not all was well. Colonel Butler kicked me in the sides hard, "Come on, Lucky let us fly like the southern wind." I ran as fast as I had ever in my life toward the main house that seemed to be okay. Colonel Butler leaned forward and held on. As we got closer, I could see the red barn was no longer standing. It had burned down along with the rest of the property storage sheds. There were no crops in any direction; the Yanks had burned everything down. They reduced the summer golden wheat to black ashes. Did the Yanks take my Red, or did she die in the barn?

We stopped at the lane entranceway. Looking toward the main house, I could see wilted rose bushes lined up perfectly along the lane, looking nothing like I remembered last fall. Colonel Butler said, "Well, Lucky, at least their house was untouched. I suspect they are all inside." No sooner had he said that than Dr. Smith and his family emerged through the front door, waving at us. Once in front of the house, there was Dr. and Mrs. Smith standing on the front porch steps. With a wide smile on his face, Dr. Smith said, "Welcome back, Colonel!" Dr. Smith approached me to scratch my forehead and whisper, "Good to see you, ole boy."

Looking up at Colonel Butler, he said, "Please come in and sit with us for spell."

As Colonel Butler dismounted, he said, "Thank you Dr. and Mrs. Smith. We would be glad to." Colonel Butler looped the reins around the saddle horn and walked away. He knew I would not leave him.

I always kept an eye on my colonel. Looking through the window, I could see and hear them. Inside, Dr. Smith motioned Colonel Butler to sit on the green velvet-covered setae. Colonel Butler removed his hat but before he could take another step forward, Mrs. Smith stepped in between them and said, "Colonel, if you don't mind, please stomp your boots on the door mat. I just cleaned these old oak floors."

The colonel complied and proceeded to sit on the settee. Mrs. Smith brought in a hot cup of coffee and bread and butter. Looking up, Colonel Butler said, "Thank you kindly, Mrs. Smith. I do appreciate your hospitality. First, I must ask the obvious, what happened here? You barn is burned down along with all your crops."

Dr. Smith replied, "Colonel, the Federals came through here not a week ago. They slashed and burned the countryside. The Union Captain said he was part of a forward scouting patrol attached to General Philip Sheridan's cavalry division from the west."

Colonel Butler placed his delicate china cup on the table and scratched his head. He said, "I wonder what troopers attached to a Western theater are doing out this way."

"The officer was rather full of himself and a downright disrespectful young man. He was very much unbecoming of an officer. He told me in no certain terms that they were here to assess food supplies. That is all he said."

"I see. Perhaps the Union is thinking about living off the land maybe."

"I don't think so. Why would they burn my crops? The North has plenty of supplies for their soldiers. In any case, before they left he gave me a few hundred greenbacks for my four horses. He did not ask nor request but just handed me the money and left.

"Well, I am sorry to hear that. Honestly, we do the same but with permission."

Mrs. Smith said, "Colonel, can you get our horses back for us. We need them to grow our crops and get us to and from town."

"I will see what I can do. I am headed to Richmond. If I see any loose horses running around, I will have them sent your way. By the way, did they take that red mare?

Dr. Smith said sadly, "Yes, yes they did. In fact, the captain took the saddle, blanket, and halter off his horse and tacked up Red for his own."

Colonel Butler stood up and said, "Dr. Smith, Mrs. Smith, if you would excuse me, I need to get going. The information you shared needs to get back to Richmond soon as possible."

As the Colonel walked toward the door, Dr. Smith put his hand on his shoulder and said, "If you see that Yankee captain, please get our Red back. She was this farm's future and livelihood. I want to get away from farming and simply raise horses. We have no need for slaves to help me with that. Oh, excuse me! They call them 'contraband' in the North."

As Colonel Butler came down the steps, I walked up to save him a few steps. Grasping the reins, Colonel Butler mounted up on my back and said, while touching the front brim of his hat, "Dr. Smith, Mrs. Smith, thank you again for your hospitality. If I don't see ya'll again, I want you to know that God's speed is with you."

We turned around toward the main road. Dr. Smith yelled, "Lucky, I see you still have that saddle blanket!"

I shook my head up and down twice.

Dr. Smith turned to Mrs. Smith and said, "I think that horse understood me!"

As Colonel Butler and I departed, I overhead Mrs. Smith say, "Like I told you, Dr. Smith, a woman's intuition is always right."

⸺

Back on the turnpike, Colonel Butler and I continued at a gingerly pace toward Richmond so he could survey the area and make use of his time. We did not see many people about the countryside, and the road to Richmond was not busy. Occasionally we would pass by Confederate messengers going to and from headquarters to their divisions and not stop to talk. Those riders were on the move. However, on the seventh day since leaving Leesburg, a man on horseback came up behind us, almost spooking the Colonel and I as we did not hear him. The dapple-gray horse wore no shoes staying in the ditch. The rider's civilian clothes made Colonel Butler suspicious.

The man approached us on the left and said, "Colonel, request by your leave."

Colonel Butler replied, "Who is asking me?"

The man said, "Lieutenant Henry Thomas Harrison. My friends call me HT."

Colonel Butler grinned. "I will call you lieutenant."

"Colonel, looks like you are headed in the direction of Richmond. Might that be your destination?"

"Now it might be and might not be. Since you are not wearing the proper clothes of a uniformed Confederate officer, how can I trust you are who you say you are?"

The lieutenant scrunched up his shoulders and cracked a smile. "I have proof for you. I know a trooper who served for you just before the Battle of Gettysburg. His name was Sergeant Wilson."

Colonel and I both took a deep breath and wondered how he knew that. Colonel Butler replied, "Why do you use the words 'served for me' in the past tense?"

"Because I killed him," the lieutenant replied.

Before he could say one more word, the colonel pulled out a revolver and pointed it at Harrison's head. "Don't make one move or your days end on this earth."

The lieutenant held his hands up. "Wait, sir, hold on! I killed a traitor not a brother."

His pistol leveled at Harrison's head, Colonel Butler said, "I need more than your word."

"Sir, I am going to reach into my saddle bag and pull out signed written orders from General Longstreet." I could see sweat beading on the man's forehead. Colonel Butler nodded a yes. Harrison pulled out a rolled-up piece of parchment paper and handed it over to the Colonel.

Colonel Butler carefully balanced the pistol with his right hand while spreading the paper with his left hand. Glancing from Harrison to the paper, the colonel recognized the hand-written signature of Brig. Gen. J.E.B. Stuart and a signature he did not recognize at first. That signature was of the honorable CSA Secretary of War, Mr. James A. Seddon. Colonel Butler's eyes narrowed, showing suspicion. Passing the paper back to Harrison, Colonel Butler said, "Your credentials appear to be in order. Now tell me about Wilson while we move on down the road. Go ahead and put your arms down."

Harrison smiled. "I will after you lower your weapon."

Both men talked about the Battle of Gettysburg and the tragedy of so many dead and wounded. Harrison talked most of the way. He said he was from Tennessee.

"You have a different accent." Colonel Butler said. "What happened to your southern accent?"

HT replied, "Sir, I have been spending a bit of time keeping my eyes and ears open while living amongst the citizens of Washington, D.C. these months. I had to train myself not to speak in our southern tongue.

Colonel Butler glanced at him with a suspicious look, thinking, *He could still be a spy for the Union. How would I know the difference? The orders could have been forged.* He remained guarded as I did.

On September 6, we approached the outskirts of Richmond. I could see that not all was good. Grief and despair masked the homeless citizens' faces as they roamed a dark and dirty place. I did not understand how that could be. That was our capitol of the south. The smoke from the factories bellowed above the city skyline. War production was in full speed. Tredegar Iron Works, the paper and flourmills were working around the clock near the James River. Colonel Butler whispered, "Lucky, I don't remember Richmond looking so gray."

Broad Street along the railroad tracks was lined with women and children begging for food. One emaciated woman with a baby suckling at her small breast yelled, "Mister, can you spare some food. We are starving!"

Colonel Butler, the officer and gentlemen he was, reached back into his saddlebag, pulled out some hard tack, and carefully placed it into the woman's free hand. She said, "God bless you, mister! God bless you."

Colonel Butler turned to HT and using a firm tone said, "Feeling generous?"

HT then reluctantly felt obliged the same.

We continued toward Ninth and Capitol Street where President Jefferson and his cabinet worked on the Capitol grounds. Across the street was a horse stable behind St. John's Episcopal Church. Colonel said, "Lucky, let us get you and HT's horse settled in first. We will come back for you both once we are done meeting with our business." Mr. Harrison led his horse, Chance, to a stall next to me. While the Colonel and HT went to report to the secretary of war, old Chance and I chewed the fat.

Chance was an interesting gilded horse. He told me General Longstreet had requisitioned him from a farm outside Antietam. I found out that Chance had never seen a day in battle. While waiting for our food and water, Chance asked me, "So, Lucky, where are you from?"

"From the great state of South Carolina," I replied. "My service to our Confederate States of America began back in June of 1861 when I participated in the First Battle of Manassas."

Chance's brown eyes widened with disbelief. "That was our first victory and you were there! Tell me about it."

I wished he had not asked me that question. I hated the idea of talking about battles. I felt bad for those who asked and could not possibly understand what soldiers had gone through and what we had done and seen as the worst part of war. In any case, I replied, "Chance, everyone has a different perspective on war. Mine is no different and in that, time will tell. The only thing I can say is I witnessed the actions of a traitor. The wagon master, whom I hauled from South Carolina to Virginia, left the battlefield without permission. In other words, he became a traitor and left us for the other side."

Chance squinted his eyes in anger and shook his head. "What was his name?"

"Private Smith or as the men called him, Smitty. You could pick him out of any crowd. He smelled bad, looked skinny, and had a missing left thumb."

Chance searched his memory in a hard way. He replied, "Lucky, that fella sounds familiar. I think my master has met with him a few times back in the Yankee capitol. He was not skinny, but he did have a missing left thumb. But then lots of wounded soldiers could have a missing thumb. However, HT did refer to him as Mr. Smith."

"We will see. I intend on kicking him in the head next time I see him."

"Lucky, please tell me about the battles you have fought in. I have yet to fight."

"I can tell you only one thing: war is not for everyone. I have seen both men and horses die and been with those who lived to fight another day. Those who died have escaped lifelong nightmares reserved for those like me and Colonel Butler. We spend every waking moment wishing it would end. So my friend, you don't want to go to war. I wish this on no one." Chance shook his head, not understanding what Lucky had said. When he was about to ask another question, the stable's back door opened.

Secretary Seddon, an honest broker when it came to serving President Davis, always painted the truth, so Davis trusted him to plan and win the war. With that said, Secretary Seddon knew he had to work closely with military leaders that in his opinion were too narrow-minded. He shunned the idea that wars were only won on the battlefield. Seddon knew that advance knowledge of the Union's military and political decisions were key in crafting an offensive response to an unknown future. He needed intelligence to help make those decisions.

While contemplating military strategies in the White House of the Confederacy, Seddon's military aide knocked on the door three times. The First Lieutenant said, "Sir, Colonel Butler and Lieutenant Harrison have arrived. Do you want me to escort them in, sir?"

Before responding, Seddon paused and pondered on the thought that advance knowledge in question is gained from trusted individuals employed as intelligence collectors. One of his most productive spies was there. HT Harrison. *Colonel Butler will help me build a better view of the future.*

"Let them in, Lieutenant, you can be dismissed."

"Understood, sir." The lieutenant hurriedly grabbed his slouch hat and left the office.

Secretary Seddon motioned both Colonel Butler and Lt. Harrison to sit on the European-style, red velvet couch positioned directly across his desk where they remained quiet until spoken to. Colonel Butler looked at the well-dressed man sitting across him. The balding Secretary Seddon was dressed in light gray trousers and a matching vest over a white silk shirt accented with black braces. A gold pocket watch fob draped from his left vest pocket. On the oak coat rack behind the secretary, a black frock coat hung from a silver peg. He sported facial hair that was dark and gray. His remaining hair on the back of his head touched the collar. Seddon then began to speak. "What are you looking at, Colonel?"

HT interrupted him. "Good to see you again, sir."

Colonel Butler looked at HT, relieved to know he was who he said he was.

Seddon replied, "Yes, Lieutenant, it has been a few weeks since your last correspondence."

Before Harrison could reply, Seddon put his finger to his lips, indicating silence. "Gentlemen, let me show you the capitol grounds."

Back at the stable, I was finally enjoying eating fresh oats and water that were a rare treat outside Richmond. I felt like a king for the day. I neighed at Chance. "Chance, why is all this food and water so fresh?"

"Lucky, this is where President Davis keeps his horses."

To me, those horses looked as though that have not seen a day in battle.

Chance added with a noticeable look of disapproval, "All they have to do is look good and pull President Davis's carriage."

"Chance, you and the rest of us horses are serving our country. Getting shot at is not the only way to serve our country. In fact, I do not wish war on any living thing. It is the last resort our citizens should ever have to do to feel free."

"I suppose you are right, Lucky. I just want to be respected, like you. We have all heard about your actions at Antietam, Fredericksburg, and now Gettysburg."

Lucky, raising his head high, said, "I am only following the commands of my rider. I am driven by my unyielding need to find Red. I will stay alive to do just that."

Chance's eyes widened and with a loud hoof tap on the ground, he said, "I salute you, war horse!"

Meanwhile, Secretary Seddon, Colonel Butler, and Lieutenant Harrison were walking up Franklin Street when Seddon pointed down Thirteenth Street. "This way, men. We can continue our ᵉ

discussions at a secure office set up for me in the stable behind St John's."

Secretary Seddon asked both men, "Gentlemen, after we finish our discussions, would you be interested in joining me for dinner tonight? There is a wonderful place not two blocks from here at the Powhatan Hotel."

Both the Colonel and Lieutenant Harrison replied in unison, "Yes, sir."

I heard Secretary Seddon open the back door, letting a flood of light into the stable. Chance and I noticed all three men walk inside and turn right into a small entrance I had not noticed before. A lantern was lit and straight-back chairs were arranged around an old oak desk next to a long wooden table. Seddon pulled his watch chain that had two keys attached, one brass and the other silver. With the brass key, he unlocked the rolltop desk and pushed the slider upwards until it stopped. He then used the silver key to unlock desk panels that inconspicuously hid long drawers containing roles of paper.

Seddon pulled out one roll and stretched it across a table. Pointing to Vicksburg, Mississippi on a small hand drawn map, he said to both men, "Gentlemen, my sources indicate that General Ulysses S. Grant may be selected by Lincoln to become the Union's next general-in-chief. I need to know more about Grant. General Longstreet told me he was one of the best horsemen in their West Point class."

"Sir, they went to the military academy together," Colonel Butler asserted.

"Colonel, there are many officers who fought together during the Mexican War but who are now shooting at each other, brother against brother, which brings me to you, Colonel Butler. I understand you have survived many battles these past couple of years. How can that be true?" Seddon said in a concerned voice.

I could not help but overhear the discussions amongst those three. I caught the "best horsemen" comment by the secretary but did not understand the name of the man he was referring to: Grant. However, I kept my ears up and continued listening.

⌒

Colonel Butler replied, "Sir, as a senior officer, I am sworn to follow the orders of those appointed above me. My oath and love for our country are inscribed in my heart, weapon, and even my horse, Lucky."

Seddon interrupted him. "Colonel, I am not questioning your loyalty to the cause. I am simply trying to understand where you have been. I need to fill in some missing pieces of a puzzle we here at headquarters are trying to put together to give our soldiers in the field an advantage. General Grant will be problematic for us. His tactics and more importantly, his understanding of how his chosen generals make battlefield decisions will help us forge future battle plans for an assured victory for the Confederacy. One of Grant's trusted lieutenants is General William Tecumseh Sherman. I understand from our Joe Johnston that this Sherman is a dangerous man, meaning he does not play by the book."

HT, sitting quietly, asserted, "Sir, what do you mean Sherman does not play by the book?"

"Lieutenant, I mean Sherman seems to carry forth a bit of anger not born of this world."

"Sir, you mean he is devilish?"

Seddon replied, "Of course, he is not the devil, but from what my field reports indicate, he prefers fire over rain."

Colonel Butler added, "Sir, if I may, on my way here, I passed though Middleburg farmlands which had been torn up by the Yanks. What was unusual to me was that all the crop fields had been burned up. According to a farmer I had befriended, he said the Union trooper was working under the orders of another Union general called Sheridan. Evidently, the new tactic of the

Federal side is that they live off the land and then burn it after they take what they need. Those Yanks are borrowing a chapter out of our book—with the exception of burning their crops."

"Yes, that may be so," Seddon replied, frowning. "However, it is time for us to make changes to our war strategy. The battlefields have been chosen by the Union, and we don't know where they are. We need to get more intelligence from our loyal networks around the country. I need to know Grant's and Sherman's movements before they receive their orders. How can we do that, Lieutenant Harrison?"

HT replied, "Sir, I have established contacts in Washington, D.C. who are loyal to our cause. One man, whom I call Smitty, has been working closely with locals who are familiar with soldiers attached to the Union Army's newly created Bureau of Military Intelligence. The BMI helped the Union preposition their armies before Gettysburg. My source is reliable and committed to the cause.

Smiling, Seddon said, "Very good, Lieutenant Harrison." He continued. "Colonel Butler, you are here for a specific reason. After I hear from General Beauregard, I need you to travel to the Carolinas, Georgia, and Alabama to assess and recruit local men not technically attached to the CSA. We need to create a hit-and-run presence in those states."

Colonel Butler replied, "Sir, you mean recruit groups of guerillas like Mosby's Raiders in the north?"

"That is exactly what I want. Those hardened men will report only to you. You can think of them as militias if it makes you feel better. I noticed the disgusted look in your face when you mentioned Mosby. I agree. Major John Mosby is not the type of military officer one wants leading a professional army. However, his hit-and-run tactics get the job done. Colonel, I need a trusted capability in our southern and western states that not only provides me with reliable intelligence about enemy movements, but can also deliver a lethal response to the enemy. You will report only to me. Do you understand?"

Colonel Butler nodded. "Yes, sir, but why down south in protected areas?"

"The Yanks are coming. We need to be prepared for the worse."

Seddon looked at his watch and said, "Gentlemen, there are a couple of rooms waiting for you at the Exchange Hotel two blocks from here toward the river. I have made arrangements for clothes and provisions to be delivered and waiting for you. See my aide tomorrow for tender. He will disperse enough gold and greenbacks for you to execute my orders. Here are your written orders signed by my hand. Only present them to Confederate officers who introduce themselves as Richmond couriers. Colonel Butler, make sure you change into civilian clothes. For the next six months, you are working for me, and my soldiers do not wear uniforms."

Seddon turned toward Harrison. "Lieutenant Harrison, you are now promoted to the rank of major. Congratulations!"

HT raised his right hand to his forehead in a salute. "Thank you, sir!"

Seddon made one last comment. "Gentlemen, do not correspond with me directly. Do not send me wires or letters. All communications must be protected and go through my aide. He can be trusted. I will excuse myself now. Wait ten minutes before you emerge from this stable. Meet me at the Powhatan at six p.m. sharp. My carriage will pick you both up around five-thirty. Make sure you are properly dressed."

Both Colonel Butler and Major Harrison stood at attention as Secretary Seddon left the room.

HT looked at Colonel Butler. "Well, looks like you are in the spy business with me now. I will be glad to assist you in getting started. It is not so easy at first, but once you get the hang of making a lie sound like the truth—which is a perception—then you will discover that serving our great nation can be done not just on the battlefield, sir, but with the word. This business is dangerous though. I can't tell you how many times while meeting an asset that I thought a sheriff, constable, or Union soldier would be waiting around the corner to pick me up."

"Pick you up for what?"

Looking squarely into Colonel Butler's eyes, HT replied, "For treason!"

Colonel Butler looked down at his uniform. "Well, I guess we better get going. I need to change out of these dirty clothes."

HT replied, "Remember, clothes are waiting for us in the rooms. However, you will need to get a different saddle, one that does not have the letters *CSA* punched into the horn. Colonel, you will be surprised how well funded our operations will be even though many of our soldiers go without shoes or socks. I felt bad in the beginning about spending the gold for intelligence and secrecy, but then it did not take me long to see the results of how our intelligence saved lives on the battlefield. You will too."

Colonel Butler was a bit critical of the intelligence organization Richmond was trying to build, but then he thought maybe it worked. All he had known on the battlefield was looking into the eyes of the men he killed or who were trying to kill him or Lucky. Perhaps this profession would be better.

"Where are you going major?" Colonel Butler said. "I thought you were going to check in with me?"

"Colonel Butler, I have some personal business to attend to over at the Exchange Bank. I will meet you and Seddon for dinner at the Powhatan Hotel at around six o'clock."

Back at the stalls, Chance looked me over and said, "Well, Lucky, sounds like you have a new job. No more saber cuts, thrown shoes, tight cinches, short grass, and dirty water."

"What do you mean?"

"I mean you and Colonel Butler will not be fighting the Yanks on the battlefield for the next six months or so. You have new orders. Like my master, you will be serving Secretary Seddon's wishes until he says otherwise. The key to keeping this job will be keeping your Colonel Butler alive."

I did not know what that spy business meant. Colonel Butler would explain to me soon enough I suppose. From my stall to the right, I saw him walking toward me and opening the gate. "Come on, Lucky. We need to get out of here. We got a new mission and, well, a new life for six months. I will tell you more about it once we are cleared to leave Richmond. Until then, my temporary home is two blocks down the street from here. You will have to come back here for the nights. Let us go and scout this place out for the remainder of the day, but before doing so, I need to go check into my room."

Damn, I would rather be on the road going south, where I would be closer to home. Don't care for stables. Don't care for tight spaces and dark rooms like the blasted darkness of this stable.

Colonel Butler saddled me back up. I was kind of enjoying not having it on for a while because of a back sore that had not healed up yet. Colonel put my halter back on and said, "Lucky, need to make our way over to the tack shop. You need a different saddle."

I did not care for that idea either. My old saddle was just fine. Broken in like a glove. As if he had read my thoughts, the colonel said, "Don't worry, Lucky, I don't like new leather boots any more than you like hard, stiff leather saddles. We will find a good used one that fits you to the tee, but before we do that, I need to get to the Exchange boarding house and change." He laughed and added, "No pun intended."

He is turning into a real a comedian.

After making a couple of turns left and right down Capitol Street, we found the Exchange Boarding House right off Main. After fixing me to the hitching post, the colonel walked through the double-stained glass doors of the boarding house, looking like he did not belong there. After getting his key from the desk man, he went up two flights of stairs to get into his room. Once inside, he immediately noticed clean civilian clothes already laid out for him on the bed. He counted two pairs of brown, lightweight woolen trousers; two white cotton shirts; a black cotton vest with four small brass buttons; two pairs of gray, woolen socks; a pair of black cinches; tan leather riding gloves; a brown leather shoulder holster; one tanned half-flap holster attached to a brown leather belt; one pair of cotton long johns; one pair of preacher boots; one tan caped over coat, and one brown slouch felt hat. Also lying on the pillow was a .44 Colt Walker and one .36 Colt Navy. The .36 fit into the gun shoulder holster. The only thing missing were the bullets. Colonel said aloud, "Lucky, I guess I need to stop at the general store and get ammunition for these pistols and.56 cartridges for my Spencer. I will need about a sixty cartridges since it holds up to twenty."

Colonel Butler changed his clothes and wondered what to do with his uniform. He knew he could not take it with him. He went to the front desk and asked for some brown wrapping paper and twine to secure his uniform and saber. Colonel Butler thought, *Okay, now what do I do with them? Oh yes, I am sure Seddon's trusted aide would have no problem stowing these away for me until my return. And I will return! Seddon's aide can simply hold them for me. I should inscribe my name into this saber. Don't want that aide thinking he can take it on his own journey.*

When I first saw the colonel coming out of the boarding house, I thought my eyes had betrayed me again. He certainly did not look like Colonel Butler. Instead, he looked like some well-dressed highwayman who looked like a civilian in place. He had blended in with everyone else around there.

Colonel Butler approached me and held out his coat lapels. "What do you think?" he said to me. I did not think anything other than he must have quit the army. "Lucky, I am supposed to blend in according to the Major. Don't worry, ole boy. You are getting some new gear as well. We are heading over to the tack shop." Before mounting, he strapped a brown saddlebag on me that I had not seen before.

Our ride to the tack shop was short, as it was just around the corner. In front of the shop, the colonel tied me up again to the hitching post since we were in the city. I briefly wondered if he did not trust me anymore. Even though I would not go anywhere, he had to do so to keep me safe. While I just stood there looking at the street sidewalk, he walked into the store and came back out within minutes, holding a used western saddle in his hand. Without asking me, he plopped it onto my back and tightened the cinches and girth strap. I turned my neck toward him and shook back and forth, neighing a no. He understood.

So the colonel took off that saddle and went back in and came out with another brown saddle. He cinched that one to my back and said, 'Well, Lucky, what do you think about this one?" I turned away shaking my head back and forth. Colonel Butler's face reddened, but he relented, took the saddle off, and went back into the shop.

He took much longer that time, finally emerging with a black saddle with a silver quarter stitched into the horn. After carefully positioning my favorite horse blanket, he carefully positioned the black saddle on my back, attached the girth strap, and cinched me up. It was the one. He noticed my head bobbing up and down in approval. He said, "Figures! A gambler lost this one. Now we own it."

"Lucky, we have a couple of hours before dinner. I think a tour of the city is in order. What do you think?" What could I tell him, I don't speak! We had only gone three blocks before he stopped and smelled the air. He said, "I smell a baker's shop. They must be making ginger bread." Then out of nowhere, my rear legs kicked up. Colonel Butler held on to the saddle horn, wondering why I did it. That smell reminded me of a bad experience. It was the smell of ginger coming from the small house near the rock wall along Marye's Heights in Fredericksburg, December of '62.

Colonel Butler said in a low voice, "Lucky, it is okay, boy. I know the last time I smelled that gingerbread. You and I are going to be okay. It is hard to leave the battlefield knowing we may lose our edge, but we have a new mission." I did calm down after hearing his reassuring voice.

We rode over to a smelly place by the waterfront with all sorts of noise and smoke bellowing out of tall, red, cylinder-looking structures. I didn't know what the place was but the colonel did.

"Lucky, take a close look. This is where our artillery and iron is produced to support our soldiers in the field. It is called Tredegar Iron Works."

As we got closer, I noticed that the buildings were sitting right on the banks of the James River. The colonel and I stopped at the first building on the compound. I only saw a few soldiers walking on the compound between the buildings. Colonel Butler yelled over to the soldier, "Lieutenant, what building is the State Armory?

The young officer replied, "Sir, why do you ask?"

"Need to pick up some ammunition."

"Sir, that ammunition is issued only for our troops."

Looking down at his civilian jacket, Colonel Butler realized he was not in uniform.

"Thank you, Lieutenant. I forgot I was not in uniform. My name is Colonel Butler. Would you please point me in the right direction?"

"Sir, I need some identification."

He realized that he had only a piece of paper signed by Seddon, but he could not even share that unless the soldier was a Richmond courier.

"No worries, Lieutenant. I made a mistake. Do you know where I can pick up some ammunition in town?"

"Sir, there is a market on the corner of Marshall and Sixth Streets. A gun shop is right near there. I am pretty sure the sign says Gun Smith."

"Thank you, Lieutenant," the colonel replied with a crooked smile, knowing he was being a smarty pants.

After talking with Miss Moran, Smitty decided to ride back to the Surratt boarding house and pack up his belongings. He needed to relocate his operation nearer to the Morans's properties. He would go back and visit his downtown contacts once he had settled into Herndon. While riding back to the Union capitol, Smitty planned his next moves. Living in Herndon would get him access to Dr. Moran, and of course, his gullible daughter Bella. Smitty thought, *I will take advantage of a notional romantic relationship with Miss Moran. She seems attracted to me and will be my means to an end. Her father and his current dealings with the Federals is what I need. I will become his business partner all in the name of God and country. He is one of the key players I will need for my plan.* Smitty smiled. "And then I will have no more use of Mosby and his foolish ways for winning this war. The South can't win, but I will."

On the kitchen table were several unattended newspapers stacked in the center. With a fresh cup of coffee, Smitty tried his hand at reading the news printed by Yankee hands. The first paper was the *New York Herald*, and it had the headline "All Tennessee Redeemed." That caught his attention. He thought, *Redeemed by what?* The newspaper recounted the efforts of Union General Rosecrans to organize his scattered troops in Tennessee into a fighting force headed for Georgia. Smitty thought, *Where in Georgia and where was Confederate General Bragg?*

Two weeks later, on September 18-20, Union forces led by Major Generals William S. Rosecrans and George H. Thomas were defeated by Confederate General Braxton Bragg and

Lieutenant General James Longstreet at the horrific Battle of Chickamauga, Georgia. Though it was a Confederate victory, 34,624 were killed, wounded, and/or missing between the two sides; 18,454 were Confederate soldiers.[20]

Colonel Butler and I turned around and started along the river back toward town. Looking to our right, we saw a most unusual sight that looked like a warehouse floating on the water with large ropes and anchor chains securing it. Colonel Butler said aloud, "Lucky, what in the heck is in that building? There are armed guards standing on the dock leading to the warehouse on the water." I looked back at him and snorted, "You might not want to go over there since you are a civilian-looking fella."

Colonel Butler pulled my reins to the right, and of course, we went right over to the guard shack. The young private immediately challenged the colonel with a firm voice, "Halt, sir. You are not permitted in this area."

Colonel Butler raised both hands up to say who he really was, but then he remembered he was not wearing a uniform. Though his curiosity was burning, he could not play his Seddon card.

"My apologies, Private. I was just heading back to town and had never seen a floating bridge like this. I will be moving on."

What we had seen was the front end of what the newspapers in 1862 called the "Rebel Monster." Colonel Butler said, "I thought that odd-looking ship was sunk." Of course, I had no idea what a ship was. All I knew was that thing had four-inch cannons sticking out the front. Those cannons on the battlefield would be deadly. Colonel Butler and I moved on down the riverbanks until we came across the Tobacco Warehouse with a signpost reading Eighth Street. The colonel turned us onto the street, went one block, and then turned left onto Cary Street. "Boy, Lucky. We sure could have used these signs pointing the way for us back in Antietam." I did not know if I was supposed to laugh or stomp on the ground. I was not sure why he was behaving that way, trying to be humorous. I was thinking he was finally able to relax by then. I sensed there was much less anxiety as compared to what we had experienced since '62. Actually, I was feeling better myself. It was good not having to think if the day one woke up was a good day for living or dying.

Once we were on Sixth Street, we crossed over Marshall and saw the gun shop on the corner, facing Sixth Street. The place had no customers inside. After hitching my reins to the sidewalk rail, Colonel Butler went through the single door with a glass window stained with gray letters saying "God Bless Dixieland." I could hear the bell above the door ring.

"Good afternoon, sir, my name is Billy," said the silver-haired, pot-bellied old man behind the counter. "How can I help you? We have a fine selection of Yankee rifles, pistols, even a couple of blue-belly sabers if you are interested."

The colonel replied, "Sir, I appreciate the offer, however, I am only in need of .44 caliber and .36 caliber ammunition. And oh, yes, I need sixty .56 cartridges."

The old man said, "We can fix you right up! Yes, we can, sir." Mr. Billy went into his backroom and came back with two boxes of each caliber. "Mister, do you want the shells in a sack or do you want to put them in your saddlebag on that horse of yours outside?"

Colonel Butler looked back at Lucky, then at Billy. "No, sir. Just put them in a burlap sack with a drawstring." He walked out of the shop with a brown toad sack loaded with boxes of shells for each pistol and his rifle.

Colonel Butler sure loved that Sharps repeater he had taken from a Yankee Trooper back at Brandy Station. I remember at Brandy Station while I was galloping across the field, he held on to the saddle horn with his right hand, bit the reins in his teeth, and leaned way over to the left toward the ground to pick up that rifle off the dead trooper he had just killed. He then continued to shoot more troopers with it as they charged toward us. Sometimes I think my colonel had a death wish or something. All I knew was that it was my job to keep him alive to keep me alive.

After the colonel secured the sack to the saddle horn, we made our way back to the boarding house. He wanted to get back into his room to load up his weapons and freshen up a bit. After about thirty minutes, he came back outside. Standing on the porch, he looked at me and said, "Lucky, I better get you over to the stable for the night. I need to meet up with Seddon and Harrison for dinner." I looked at him and thought how okay I was with that as I was getting hungry myself.

Back in the stable, old Chance lounged in his stall, eating from a bucket of oats hanging off the stable door. He pulled his head out of the bucket to get a breath. After the colonel pulled all my tack off, he walked me over to the stall near Chance. Inside was a fresh bucket of water, clean hay, and of course, my own bucket of sweat oats. The only thing missing was a teaspoon of molasses, like what Sir Drayton gave to me back at the Magnolia Plantation. Before I could think more about home, the colonel came back and said, "Lucky, I got a surprise for you, old boy. I got some molasses back at the gun shop that Old Billy wanted you to have." As I watched him pour that sweet smelling, dark syrup onto my oats, my thoughts took me back to South Carolina.

Widow Drayton worked hard every day, trying to keep the plantation going since Sir Tom's death in June '60. She had relentless work ethic and, being Irish, would fight and die for what she believed and loved. She revered Magnolia Plantation and all the history it represented for the Drayton family. Mrs. Drayton thought she would never marry again until her daughter Allison became of age. Allison was just like her mother, protective of the family name and proud to work the land with her mother.

Mrs. Drayton continued with Sir Tom's approach for managing plantation workers. She refused to call Mr. Joe's family slaves. After she had read about Lincoln's Emancipation Proclamation, Mrs. Drayton told Mr. Joe that he and his family were free to leave because she could not afford to pay or feed them. Mr. Joe told Mrs. Drayton that he and his family never felt like slaves owned by her and Sir Drayton Jr. He just regretted having to live under Sir Drayton's father who wronged him and a hundred other African souls back in the late eighteenth century.

Sitting at the kitchen table, Miss Allison said to her mother, "When will you get married again mother?"

Mrs. Drayton smiled. "Daughter, I think you are enough for me to handle right now."

Allison laughed. "Oh, mother! You don't mean that. I am already ten years old."

"Darling daughter, you are still a little girl to me and always will be my little girl."

Allison shrugged her shoulders. "Yes ma'am. I figure you will be calling me that until I am thirty."

Mrs. Drayton hugged her. "Let us go. We need to go feed the chickens out in the horse barn."

"Mother, where do you think Lucky is now? Do think he is happy?"

Mrs. Drayton stood close to Allison and cupped her cheeks with her hands. "Sweetie, I am sure he is grazing on some tall alfalfa grass up there in the north somewhere."

Allison frowned. "Mother, I want him to come home soon. I don't want him staying up there where he has no family."

Mrs. Drayton said in a soft voice, "That is up to the Lord."

That night, I opened my eyes to noises I had never heard while out on patrol in the field. Day and night, there seemed to be people everywhere in Richmond. How did anyone sleep in that

town where both drunks and the homeless roam the streets? I did
not care for the city life. It was in that stall in Richmond when
I remembered that I had a family back in South Carolina. I felt
bad that I had almost forgotten about Ms. Allison, Mr. Joe and
his family, and of course, Mrs. Drayton. I wondered how she was
doing since the death of her husband, Sir Tom. I wish I could tell
her that I knew who shot him. I wish I could tell her that I would
make that wrong, right as soon as I saw old Private Smitty.

The sun rose, even as city shadows darkened the eastern horizon. The stable doors opened up, and there standing in the light
was Colonel Butler. He was right on time. He brought my breakfast, brushed my back, and tacked me up with that gambler's
saddle. Filling the food bucket, Colonel Butler looked over at
Chance. "Your master will be around shortly. He consumed quite
a bit of spirits last night at dinner. I am thinking he will be coming around to pick you up around midday." Chance glanced over,
neighed twice, which I interpreted as, "Better show up quick."
Colonel Butler put a handful of oats in front of Chance who
gratefully took them all in one gobble.

We left the stable without saying goodbye as Colonel Butler
said we were on our way south. "Lucky, we are going to follow
the Richmond–Danville Line out of here. In other words, we
are heading south to Atlanta then to Savanna, Georgia. You will
be happy about this patrol. From Savanna, we head back up to
Charleston, South Carolina to meet up with a couple of politicians. From there, we will make our way back to Richmond and
report our findings to Secretary Seddon." I was not familiar with
the town name of Savannah; however, I recognized Charleston.
My home was not too far northwest of there. I wasn't sure I knew
the way, but surely, locals would tell Colonel Butler how to get
back to old Magnolia Plantation.

After crossing over Mayo's Bridge, we found a trail going
toward the R&D depot. Outside the water tower, we got a clear
view of the boxcars loaded up with military supplies and many

wounded men destined for hospitals in Danville and Atlanta. I could see dozens of rail cars full of our wounded. The colonel went over to see if anyone he knew was in the hospital boxcar. A man in a long white coat helping with gurneys looked up at us. "I am Doctor Wilson. Care to give a hand, mister?"

Colonel Butler nodded and dismounted to help the soldier who was missing his right leg from the knee down. I noticed the bandage on the soldier's leg was dirty and bloodied. The colonel and the doctor spent the next hour loading up forty half-alive men.

Colonel Butler remained silent the whole time, but his face spoke a thousand words. Once the boxcar was loaded up with all that it could take, he and the doctor stood to the side and talked. The doctor said the men in this car received their wounds from Gettysburg. Colonel Butler lowered his head and stood there with his eyes closed. I understood the sadness that overcame one's heart when he witnessed a fellow soldier maimed and beaten down. At that moment, I flashed back to my friend Old Virginia back at Gettysburg. May he rest in peace.

Colonel Butler mounted and turned us away from the sight. Looking down at the last car, he noticed men in leg shackles, dragging themselves to the boxcar, two by two. Colonel said to the doctor, "Where are they taking those prisoners?"

Doctor Wilson looked up at Colonel Butler and sighed. "They are taking them to Camp Sumter, Georgia."

Colonel Butler understood why he sighed. As we turned away from the train, the doctor yelled out at Colonel Butler, "I did not catch your name."

Colonel Butler replied, "Just passing through…just passing through."

We followed the banks of the James River for about two miles southeast of town. The colonel said we would reconnect with the R&D about five miles from there. I didn't know why we could not have just hitched a ride on a rail car, but then the rail cars were all full and the colonel seemed to be in no hurry. The trip to Danville would cover about 160 miles. Traveling about thirty to forty miles a day, we should get there in four or five days. Once we were out of the city, the countryside quickly changed to rolling hills, creeks, and rivers. Since it had not been raining, there would be no problem negotiating those waters. We followed the R&D rail, staying smartly just inside the tree lines when we could.

Colonel Butler said, "Lucky, no need to draw attention to ourselves. You never know when a wayward Union patrol may come up on us. I remember what Doctor Smith back in Middleburg said about the forward Union Cavalry Patrol. They were part of General Sheridan's Division, coming in from the west, though not sure how far south they are going.

On October 26, 1863, we finally made it to Danville, Virginia. What should have taken a week took us three weeks to accomplish since Colonel Butler and I were chased and in some cases shot at by farmers, confederate deserters escaping to their homes, and of course an occasional deer hunter. The journey from Richmond to Danville certainly should have been safer. While we were crossing the railroad bridge spanning the Appomattox River, a locomotive came up on us and gave us little time to get over the trestle without being pushed off into the river. We had only seconds to spare. Colonel Butler said trains could not stop on a dime, so even though the conductor saw us, he had no way of avoiding us. How could we have known?

Once we were in Danville, Colonel Butler wanted to visit the Danville General Hospital where wounded soldiers lay in anguish. I knew he felt a sense of responsibility for his men who were wounded or killed. The Battle of Antietam, Battle of Fredericksburg, Battle of Brandy Station, and of course, The Battle of Gettysburg showed no mercy. We road down Main Street which took us to a tobacco warehouse converted to accommodate wounded soldiers who needed long-term medical care they could not receive on battlefields. If a soldier was lucky enough to survive the trip from wagon to rail, they stood a good chance of getting well enough to go back home, or in some cases, return to their units. Visiting these hospitals probably gave Colonel Butler a sense of closure or something to help him understand why he struggled with his own feelings about the war. No doubt, war is hell. The problem with men killing one another ends on the battlefield but continues forever in the minds of those who fought them.

The first hospital we visited was Confederate Hospital #1 off Market Street between the R&D railroad depot and Piedmont Railroad (P&R) railroad depot. Colonel Butler saw a wagon teamster unloading supplies by the hospital. He took me over to the wagon and asked the man, "Muleskinner, where does that rail line go?"

The old man replied, "Mister, that line goes south for about fifty miles toward Greensboro, North Carolina."

"Thank you kindly," Colonel Butler replied.

We continued down Market Street for a ways looking at the tall, red brick buildings that stood like giants to me. Colonel Butler said, "Lucky, these buildings used to store vast amounts of tobacco before being shipped out across the world. Now they are only holding prisoners or the sick."

We stopped in front of a tall brick building Colonel Butler called Hospital #1. He secured the reins to a hitching post while he went in to find someone Secretary Seddon had told him to meet. If memory served me correctly, Colonel Butler had said the man's name was Major William T. Sutherlin who was in charge of the Danville Depot. The Confederate Subsistence Department had established the depot to control the receiving, storage, and distribution of goods soldiers needed in the field. Evidently, Major Sutherlin was unable to serve because of poor health and perhaps because he was one of the richest men in the county.[21]

The tall double doors of the warehouse were open. I could smell tobacco in the cool air drifting out of the building. I could also smell the odorous stench of rotting flesh. That smell just never left Gettysburg. Colonel Butler stared through the shadows inside, hoping someone would walk out. My ears went back, sensing danger, but then it was only a hunch that played out far too often over the past two years. The colonel glanced back at me. 'Lucky, what do you think?" About the time he said that, a short, older man wearing a worn and wrinkled Confederate officer's uniform came out and pointed a cocked rifle at Colonel Butler.

Colonel Butler raised his hands, quickly saying, "Sir, I am looking for a Major Sutherlin. Do you know where I can find him?"

"Why do you want to see him?"

"Just need to discuss some tobacco business."

The old man glared into Colonel Butler's eyes. "Looking for a Richmond courier to pick up my tobacco. Do you have a bill of lading?"

The colonel reached into his inside vest pocket and pulled out a small rolled-up piece of paper and handed it to the old man.

Opening it, the man said, "I have been waiting for you, young fella, or should I call you Colonel?"

Colonel Butler stepped up onto the loading dock and walked with the man just inside the double doors. I could hear both of the whispering as my hearing was better than a human's. The old man said, "Colonel Butler, I am sorry for bearing arms against you, but one has to be careful around here in Danville. Though our security is tight, one never knows what yank-love'n spy walks these parts. I have a package for you to take to Savanna. It is pretty heavy, but it looks like that big stallion you have there can handle it."

Colonel Butler said, "I do not want to know what is in the package, but I have been instructed to protect it from all hazards."

The old man then replied, "Our country depends upon it."

Colonel Butler followed the old man into the depths of the warehouse. After about one hour, Colonel Butler emerged out of the double doors, carrying a pair of leather saddlebags over his shoulders. Based on how lopsided he looked while walking, I suspected the weight was more than he could handle. He came up to me, breathing heavily.

"Lucky, our stay here in Danville has just ended. I was hoping to see some of my men, but we need to get on out of here toward Savanna, Georgia. I remembered Sir Tom taking me down there back during the winter of '61 to sell his cotton. From there, the cotton made its way all the way to England on board a tall ship."

We left Danville on the same day we got there. I am thinking that was the plan all along. That evening, we stopped at an abandoned farmhouse with a partially burned horse barn. It was around eleven o'clock at night when Colonel Butler said, 'Too tired to ride anymore, Lucky. Let us go inside that barn and rest a spell. We are about 350 miles from our destination. I figure that if we go about twenty to twenty-five miles a day, we will get there just before Thanksgiving. I can't remember the last time I had a baked Turkey. By the way, we will have to go through the Carolinas. Maybe we can stop and see family and friends."

My ears perked up. There was hope.

Original artwork by Ryan Goodwin and Rebecca Calderon.

HOME HAS CHANGED

After about two weeks on the trail, Colonel Butler and I stopped in the South Carolina town of Florence. About halfway between Danville and Savanna, I was hoping we would stop and rest a bit. A warm stall with fresh water and hay sounded good to me. However, like many Confederate soldiers, we lived off the land and southern generosity. I do not know why the Colonel avoided most of the towns since leaving Danville, but he did. On the trail, the colonel talked frequently to himself. He said he needed to pay a visit to a Major Frederick Warley, who worked at an important railroad supply center located in Florence. I wasn't sure what the connection was between the Major and Colonel Butler. Like many of the new faces the colonel had been talking to, I figured it had something to do with Richmond and Secretary Seddon.

It was November 13, a Friday, when we arrived outside of Florence. The colonel thought Friday the 13th was an unlucky day. I thought not, for I was born on April 13, a Friday, back in the spring of '59. Things weren't so bad. I was still alive. My mother had told me before she died that God had a purpose for me, otherwise I'd be lying dead on a battlefield somewhere in the North. With Colonel Butler on my back, there was hope that we would survive the war. However, losing was not an option to Southerners. We would press on no matter what the odds.

Getting to Florence was not easy. Since entering the Carolinas, we had crossed swamps with more gators and poisonous snakes than I cared to meet. Five miles north of Florence was a wide stretch of low wetland; a river ran across it which the locals called Pee Dee Swamp, through which the Pee Dee River flowed. The area around Florence was awfully wet. The colonel said the Carolinians grew lots of rice that grew best in wet, humid weather. Unlike the cotton we grew on Magnolia, rice was pretty much a year-round harvest in those parts.

We traveled through the Pee Dee Swamp on a corduroy road that had been elevated with cut logs covered with sand and small stone. It made it easier to get wagons over the mud. However, I still did not care for those types of roads, as running over them was not an option. Colonel Butler kept me on a slow walk to ensure my hooves did not catch a stone, which would cause me to go lame. Looking across the swamp about halfway over, we saw a railroad trestle, which would have been easier to use for crossing. However, we did not want to repeat the Richmond–Danville railroad narrow escape that we had experienced back in Virginia. The colonel decided getting muddy and wet was a safer option.

We passed by an old plantation that reminded me of home. There was a large, white two-story house with four front pillars supporting a walk-around porch. An old man was sitting in a white rocking chair, smoking a corncob pipe. To the right of the house around back was a huge red barn, standing two stories high and tucked back beneath a stand of tall lodgepole pines about a hundred yards from the main house.

The plantation was beautiful. Getting to the house required passing through a closed black wrought iron gate. Hanging above the gates was a white wooden sign shaped liked an eagle with its wings spread out. It said, "God Bless the Confederacy— Cannon Plantation."

Looking at the sign, Colonel Butler said, "Yes, need all the help we can get." It was a sunny afternoon, and the rice fields glistened like a mirror reflecting the sun. I stuck my nose toward the sky to smell what was in the air and found it thick with moisture. That told me rain would be coming soon. The colonel nudged me forward toward the town.

The dirt road into town widened into two lanes where wagons and carriages passed by each other without colliding. I noticed there were signs of Thanksgiving celebrations on the store windows. Why humans use soap to draw turkeys on the storefront windows is beyond my understanding. At least the tack shop should have had horse figures on their windows. We stopped in front of the closest hotel we could find.

Colonel said, "Lucky, I need to get a room. Why don't you wait here while I go clean up a bit. I will return to get you settled in that blacksmith shop with some stalls for rent." I was thinking maybe he could just take me over to that wide-open field full of hay and let me run for a while. I think the last time I had a full gallop was back at Gettysburg.

Colonel Butler dusted off his pants and coat to look somewhat civilized before he entered the fancy-looking Harllee Hotel. As he walked toward the swinging double-oak doors, I heard him say, "Be darn glad to get these saddlebags off my hands." I wish I knew what was in those bags, but it didn't matter, as Colonel Butler's orders were my orders. The mission always came first. He checked his pistols before swinging those bags over his left shoulder. Since he was right-handed, he always made sure he could pull his weapon.

Thirty minutes had gone by and I was starting to worry about the colonel. I was tired, hungry, and just a little bit chilly since my winter coat had not grown in yet. An hour had gone by. Finally, the colonel walked out of the hotel, but he had no saddlebags. That was a curious thing as he had never let those saddlebags out of his sight since we left Danville. The colonel came up and said, "We need to get you to a better place tonight. The hotel bartender said rats infested the blacksmith's stables. I do not need to be paying for sideboards you kick out in trying to kill them. Lucky, remember that plantation we passed coming into town? The bartender said they had a horse barn you could stay in while we are in town for a couple of weeks." Wow! I could finally get to relax myself.

Back to the Pee Dee Swamp we went. We turned right off the main road into a winding lane that led to the Cannon Plantation mansion. The black gates were open. Walking under the white arch above the lane entrance, I remembered the redbrick arch Sir Tom had built at the entrance for Magnolia Plantation. Looking left and right, I saw rose bushes lined up along the graveled path leading to the main house. The place reminded me so much of home. I hoped that we would continue farther south after the colonel completed his business in Florence. I hoped to see my home again, just one more time.

We stopped in front of the white mansion where a manicured lawn lined with lilac bushes formed a half circle in the front. A redbrick walkway led to the mansion's front porch, which was also made of red brick. The black hitching posts ran parallel to the sidewalk, and on top of each post was a bronze horse head with half-loop rings attached to each side. As Colonel Butler dismounted, an older-looking man, wearing a short-vested brown coat over tan stripped trousers, walked out and said, "How can I help you young fella?"

Colonel Butler answered, "Sir, my name is Matt Butler. Major W.T. Sutherlin sent me to deliver a package to you sir."

The man replied, "My name is Colonel William Cannon, but I was expecting a Richmond courier. Do you have anything to prove who you are, young man?"

I saw the old man's right hand slip just inside his vest, a movement that did not escape Colonel Butler's eyes either.

Colonel Butler said, "Sir, I am going to lay these reins over the middle post. I will then reach into my left pocket to produce a letter for you. I will keep my left hand up."

The old man nodded a go ahead. Colonel Butler handed Colonel Cannon the letter. After a close examination, all hands relaxed.

Colonel Cannon smiled. "As I said, welcome to my home."

"The secretary sends his regards as well."

Handing him back the letter, Colonel Cannon replied, "Leave your horse there, and I will have one of the servants take care of him while you and I go to town and take care of business. But first, we can drink a cup of tea and eat an English tart or two."

"Sounds good to me, sir."

Colonel Cannon smiled and waved his hand "Please. Please, do come in. We have much to talk about."

Colonel Butler removed his hat. "Thank you kindly and thank you for offering to stable my horse, Lucky."

As both men walked through the doorway, the old man said, "Lucky? How did he get that name?"

I overheard Colonel Cannon's comment and wished I could somehow tell him that that was my birth name, but we horses don't talk. However, we do understand.

While the colonels were inside, I got a little restless, stomped the mud off my feet, and swatted a few horse flies with my tail. The horse bit in my mouth was bothering me. The bridle needed to come off for a few days. I waited outside for a farmhand to get me over to that barn. I sure looked forward to a good brushing down, a fresh water bucket, and maybe, just maybe, some oats and molasses. Until then, since the sitting room windows were open, I could hear both men talking. What I did not hear was a woman's voice. I suppose the old man was a widower, or maybe he never married. On the way over here, Colonel Butler said Mr. Cannon owned the largest rice plantation in the county. Everyone in town just called him Colonel. I wondered what war he served in to earn that title.

Finally, I did hear a woman's voice, but she had a different accent than the ones I had heard from other parts of the south and north. Her voice was soft, but she had a curious dialect in which words beginning with a "t" sound were pronounced with a "d" sound. She sounded almost like Mr. Joe back at my Magnolia Plantation, but she spoke a little bit faster. I could barely see her through the window as her dark skin blended in with the shadows. Carrying a silver tray of cups and tarts, she moved closer to the men, so I got a clearer view of her face in the sunlight. She was beautiful in human terms. Her black hair was pulled up into what I remember was a bun. Mrs. Drayton had once told Miss Allison, "Put your hair up in a bun so your hair won't get caught in the door, little girl."

The dark-skinned woman also covered her head with a white-laced bonnet tied under her chin. She wore a dark blue skirt with a white apron wrapped around her waist. I also happened to notice that Colonel Butler's eyes were fixed upon her as well. I was not sure how to interpret his gazes. She laid the tray on the table and departed. Colonel Cannon did not even thank her. I thought that was rude of him.

Both men picked up their cups of tea and sat back in their individual opposing settees. Colonel Cannon was the first to speak. "So, how was your trip from Danville?"

Colonel Butler took a sip of his tea and winced. "Different tea. Where did you get this?

The old man replied, "Make it myself using that rice I grow. Pretty good stuff, I think."

Colonel Butler replied, "Well back to your questions. We pretty much stayed away from the towns. I did not want to bring much attention to ourselves, considering what I was carrying. Poor Lucky. He had too much unwanted gator attention while we were moving through those swamps."

Colonel Cannon smiled then said as the smile faded, "Speaking of the package, did you deliver it to Major Warley?"

"Yes, sir. Major Warley accepted custody of the package back at the Harllee Hotel after verifying the contents were accounted for."

Colonel Cannon looked Colonel Butler directly in the eyes. "Very good, Mr. Butler. I will wire Secretary Seddon this afternoon and tell him the mission is complete. I will also tell him that you continue to serve our great nation with honor and loyalty. Thank you for your service, Colonel Butler."

Colonel Butler remained silent and humble as he always did when someone complimented him. I knew he never cared for recognition or medals. He would always tell me, "Lucky, we are just doing our jobs. Rewards are measured in the heart and by good deeds, not on the chest."

As they continued talking, a large black man came up to me and said, "Come on, boy. Going to take uze over to dae barn and fick you up." As he walked me over to the barn, the man talked. He said, "You are a mighty handsome stallion, fella. What does your master call you, Blacky? I get called Blacky all the time by them white folk. I wish they would just call me by my real name, Bo. You can call me Bo, okay?"

When Bo said "my master," that seemed wrong to me. When I was young, I knew Sir Tom was my master, but then I did not know any better. Now that I have fought in war and have done what I have done for the war effort, I only consider God above my "master."

Bo walked me over to that big red barn I saw from the main road earlier that day. It was even bigger when we got to it. I was amazed. The double doors were each at least twenty feet tall and ten feet wide. When Bo opened them up, the smell of other horses clung to the wind that swept in from the other open end of the barn. The horse stalls were large; they were the largest stalls I had ever seen. I was thinking Colonel Cannon must have built these stalls to hold two horses at a time. As we walked down the breezeway, a very large head hovered over the stall gate. Its nose was almost twice the size of mine. Bo said, "Boy, know giz a stallion and all, you may want to stay clear of this one. She is what d' Colonel call a Belgian Horse. She will mess you up, boy." "Don't worry," I neighed. I had no intention of messing around with her. She looked like she could break my back. However, there was something cute about her. Her blonde forelock was rather attractive to me. I have been on the patrol too long."

As Bo walked us by her stall, she said, "Who are you, good looking?"

"Just passing through ma'am," I replied. "Not looking for any trouble here."

"My name is Greta. However, you can call me Gertie. What is your name?"

"My name is Lucky."

"Lucky, see you out in the pasture."

I rolled my eyes. I snorted, "That's an old line. Where did you get that line from…a sack of flour?"

Bo put me into the last stall on the left nearest to the rear barn door. I learned a long time ago that when you walk into a bar, you should always sit with your back to the wall nearest to the door. Okay, horses do not go into bars, but we do go into barns and I thought the same rules applied.

Bo took off my saddle, slid it off my back, and then swung it over the stall door. He then replaced my bridle with a halter. Boy, it felt good to get that halter off! I was secured with crossties between two sturdy posts to keep me in place, like I was going anywhere! When Bo brought over a grooming box packed with brushes and picks, I was so happy I almost kicked him.

Bo said to me, "Now you'd need to calm down boy. We gots lots of work to do here now." As he brushed off the mud from my left flank, he said, "Lucky, looks like you and I have somethin' in common, yes sir-ee." At the time, I thought the only thing we had in common was that both of us were stuck in the war. "Lucky, youz from Magnolia Plantation. That was where I was born after my mama came from Africa. That place was owned by Sir Tom Hayden. He was my first masta. How did you get here from there? Well guzz it don't matta. I go home once in a while to see my wife Harriet. Uz split up a few years back when my mastah's son took over the Magnolia Plantation. Not sure why, but he just did."

I knew what it felt like to be involuntarily separated from a family. I was sold to the CSA. I reckon the black humans were sold the same way horses were. Thinking about it hard, I decided that made me and Bo brothers. After getting me brushed and my hooves picked, Bo led me into my stall. He put fresh water in one bucket and four cups of oats in the other.

Bo said, "Lucky, knowing yuz grew up on old Magnolia, I bet you would like a teaspoon of molasses. I usually save it for myself, but since you are like family to me, you can have some." I really liked Bo. He was a kind man who had suffered and continued to suffer from the absence of his family.

Bo said, "Gots to get back to my work, Lucky. I will see you tomorrow morn'n. I let out all the horses in the morn'n for exercise. You gets some rest. Looks like those scars on your neck tells another story." As he turned away, I noticed he had several long scars on his shoulders. I wondered if he fought in the war as well.

On the next day, Colonel Butler came out to the barn just before sunrise. He walked up to my stall and said, "Lucky, you look like you need a brand new set of shoes." Looking down at my front legs I neighed, "No, still looking like a horse."

"Lucky," the Colonel said in a low voice, "I am going back up to Danville with Colonel Cannon for a few weeks to spend Thanksgiving up there with his friends. He has invited me along. We are taking the iron horse, so you don't need to make the trip. I am sure you are happy about not going back over those swamps." He was sure right about that. I just didn't care for them gators. Colonel Butler said as he left, "Remember, I will be back for you. I never leave a man behind or in your case, a horse." He saluted me, then turned and walked out of the barn door. As I watch him leave, I felt sad. He had never left me alone before.

After Colonel Butler left, Bo emerged from the front stall where he slept. He made sure the front barn door was latched, and then turned around and started walking toward the end of the barn unhitching the stall doors. I saw several big Belgians walk out and trot toward my direction while Bo yelled, "Get on out of here, you big lugs." I swear the barn dirt floor moved as those big Belgians went by my stall. Gertie stopped at my stall before heading out into the back pasture. "Lucky, come join me over by the pond. Good water there." I just nodded without a reply.

Bo got to my stall and said, "Lucky, you better stay clear of those Belgian stallions. They can be mean. The good news is dey are slow runna's. You have the edge on them that way boy." I was not looking for a fight, so that would not be a problem. As I emerged from the barn, the sun was just rising over the horizon behind those tall lodgepole pines. The sky was in an orange hue. The wispy-looking clouds high in the sky above the sunrise looked like silver stripes overlaid with red and orange colors. Colonel Butler always said, "Red sky in the morning, soldier take warning. Red sky at night, soldier's delight." I reckoned a storm was coming.

The rest of the week was pretty much the same. I guess you might say I got bored. It was hard not to think about the battles Colonel Butler and I had fought in. The memories of horses dropping and men screaming with agony woke me up at night. Sometimes I would kick the back stall boards for no reason. The sound of a board cracking made my spine tingle. I always had mixed feelings about being on temporary duty. There were many times I wished I was back up North fighting alongside my friends. I shook my head and realized that I was not far from home. How I wished to see Magnolia just one more time.

Bo came to my stall in the middle of the night, whispering, "Lucky. Lucky, stay calm boy. You and me going on a short trip.

Yuz like this idea. We gonna go see my wife Harriett at Magnolia for Thanksgiving. Maybe you see your brother." My eyes lit up. What did he mean?

Bo said, "Harriett told me all about the troubles Widow Drayton had after Sir Tom died. She sold most them horses except your brother. Don't recollect his name, but you and him looks alike. Now letz get a bridle on you. Needs no saddle since we be taking the swamp back trails. Been sneak'n to see my wife and brother Joe, when Master Cannon gone. She be glad to see me. I reckon Widow Drayton be glad to see you."

We traveled all night through the swamps. Bo took me down trails that looked like deer used to skirt their way around hunters and the like. I was used to riding in the darkness. Colonel Butler and I patrolled many times when the only light you could see was the stars and moon. Bo said, "Lucky, whenever you get lost in da woods, always remember to find and follow a deer trail. Theyz aldwayz lead yuz to water and food."

The first early morning in the swamp was familiar. We settled down by a small creek on top of piece of high ground that was a good ten yards wide and about thirty feet long running along the creek. It looked like someone had staked a pile of leaves all over. The ground must have been used for bedding. Bo said it would be safe to stay there for the day. He built a small fire to cook some bacon with a couple of pieces of cornbread the woman serving Colonel Cannon had cooked up. He even brought me a couple handfuls of oats. We both ate our food slowly. Bo said we had about eighty miles to go before we reached the Magnolia Plantation, meaning we needed to forage off the land for about three more days.

After moving all night, I was very tired as was Bo. He slept on a pile of dried moss he pulled down from the palmetto trees. *The swamp was very thick with trees and covered with tall, sharp saw grass.* I slept standing up near a large palmetto covered with Spanish moss that drooped down from the limbs touching my back. I tried a bit of that moss but was not very impressed. My stomach gave me a little trouble for the rest of the day. With stomachaches, I would go in and out of sleep. I also could not stay near Bo as the burning campfire had wet wood in it. Wet wood always caused white smoke. Bo said it kept the mosquitoes away. The smoke burned my eyes, so I decided to stand away from the camp.

Now the smoke and stomachache happened for a reason. Sometimes God makes things happen as a part of his plan. As it was, since Bo was sleeping soundly and snoring like a saw, I pretty much kept watch over the camp in between naps. Standing by the tree, I listened intently to every sound out there. I could tell the difference between a morning dove hoo, hoo, hooing and a squirrel making a high-pitched, raspy bark. The swamp could be loud with noises of other small animals like raccoons giggling at night and crickets chirping loudly.

Then for no apparent reason, the swamp got silent. You see, the silence was what woke me up that first day in the swamp. Since I am a horse, the smallest noise did not escape me, at least in my right ear. It was around noontime when I woke up and heard leaves and small sticks break from over near Bo. Something low to the ground was moving toward Bo from the tree line along the creek. Since the palmettos blocked the sunlight out, it was hard to see through the shadows. My internal alert system kicked in but not soon enough. By the time I looked toward Bo lying on the ground, a big, dark green alligator was slowly creeping toward his blind side. The thing was big. The rows of flesh spikes running on top of its tail were at least six inches high. The gator's outer skin looked like the armor plating on the ship we saw back in Richmond.

The gator must have been at least twelve feet in length and wide as an oak tree. Then things started happening quickly.

Bo woke up just in time to hear the alligator's growl. He turned toward the side and saw a wide-open mouth. From twenty feet, I could see the whites of that gator's teeth. Bo was a big, strong man, but he wasn't big enough to keep that gator from coming at him. With his two hands, Bo put one on the lower jaw and the other on the upper jaw of that monster. Both began to twist and turn wildly. With the smoke stirring, I briefly lost sight of Bo. I would not let death come to him. I ran over to get behind the gator. Bo looked up at me and his eyes told me everything. He was losing his strength. I reared up and planted both hooves into the back of that gator's midsection. He stopped moving. His massive head just dropped on Bo's chest. Bo pushed himself out from under the gator's head. He quickly stood up and said, "Lucky, yuz saved my life. Da Lord's hand guided yuz to save me from a pain I could not takes. Thanks you boy."

I stepped away and stuck my nose down at the gator. He smelled like the rest of the swamp—foul. Bo took out a knife from his bag and began cutting away at the gator's front teeth. Those teeth must have been five inches long. Bo said while cutting. "Lucky, I am gonna make my Harriett a good-luck necklace out of these. Shez know da meaning of this. Thank yuz again. Much appreciated."

Since we had a few hours before sunset, we decided to stay up until it got dark. We had another eighty miles or so to go. The remaining three days were not much different other than we did not sleep near a creek on top of an alligators home. There were no more big gators to contend with, just little ones. The occasional cottonmouth snake would cross our path. A big black one came after Bo who quickly dispatched it with his knife. He skinned it and saved the meat to cook for dinner. He said to me, "Lucky, do you want some? Taste like chicken." I just turned my head up and walked toward his bag sniffing for oats.

We had to stay in the swamps for a couple of days. Bo said traveling during the day was not safe. I got to know him a little more while he fished, and I ate swamp grass. He was a proud man. He said life without his wife Harriett was painful and lonely. I thought about Red as my strong feelings for her kept me going with the hope we would reunite someday.

The final leg into Magnolia was easy, considering all that was on my mind was getting home. As we got close to the plantation, my memories flooded back with visions of little Allison bringing me oats, Mr. Joe putting shoes on my hooves, and of course, Sir Tom riding down that dusty road where he was shot and killed back in '61. Everything had changed at Magnolia from that day on.

It was early Thanksgiving morning when we made it to the Magnolia Plantation. I could not see how it had changed, but I knew that once the morning came, the sunlight would give me a full view of what I had been missing for so long. The smells triggered memories that were long forgotten. My heat beat faster at each step taken closer to home. I was nervous and did not know why.

Magnolia Plantation looked as grand as it was during my younger years. The morning air was fresh. No one was up yet, so we quietly made our way to the barn I was born in. Bo slowly cracked open the barn doors and tried hard to keep quiet. Inside, he found an oil lamp hanging next to the door and a box of matches sitting on the support frame. Once we got light, I could see that nothing had changed. The only thing different was the smell. There was nothing inside except for chickens roosting in the stalls. I did a hard stop to look at the stall where I was born, and sadly, where my mother died. Bo was tugging at me to go, but I refused. I had to stand there to remember. Bo saw that there was something special about that stall. He knew just to leave me be for a few minutes. I sighed then started walking forward to the rear left stall. Bo let go of the lead and followed. As I turned to the stall I wanted to be in, Bo quickly unlocked the latch and let me walk myself in. I just wanted to take in the moment. Bo said, "Lucky, I see you need to be left alone. Ize go'in to sleep in the stall next to you. We can go see Mrs. Drayton and Harriett later this morn'n." Bo turned out the lamp before setting it on the ground. I lay down on the cool dirt stall floor and fell asleep. I had no nightmares for the first time since Antietam.

Around midafternoon, Bo got up and came to my stall with some water and hay. He said, "Lucky, need to get you brushed down before we take you over to the main house. I knoze Mizza Drayton gonna be mighty glad to see you 'gain." I blinked the sleep out of my eyes and snorted to get my head clear. I stepped out of the stall so Bo could get me brushed down. He found the old groom box. The brush and hoof pick looked recently used. Funny, I did not hear or smell any horses around. About the time Bo started brushing me down, a dark frame of a woman walked through the front barn doors. She then started running toward Bo who dropped the brush and ran toward her. They collided and fell into each other's arms.

Bo picked up the woman with one arm. "My darl'n Hariett. I have missed you soz much. Da you been alzright?" Harriett whimpered. "I have missed you so, husband. I have missed you so. You take big chanzes whenz you come'n da see me you know. Someday that Colonel Cannon not go'in to be so firgiv'n to yuz. The last time he gave you twenty lashes." Bo replied, "Now don'tz yus worry about that. The pain is worth all the luv you bring me'z Hariett."

I stood there thinking how much I missed my Red. It was on this place where I met her and her master, Mr. Goodwin. She was not there anymore. Was she up north somewhere? I knew I would find her someday. For the time being, I will just live in the moment here and enjoy being here at Magnolia while I can. But I will have to go back. I know it. It was my duty.

Mrs. Drayton was outside trimming her rose bushes when she heard all the commotion in the barn. She yelled at Allison who was helping her. "Come on, daughter, sounds like Mr. Bo is paying us another visit."

Allison smiled. "I will run over to the field and get Mr. Joe. I just know he will be glad to see his younger brother again."

Allison left her mother to get Mr. Joe. Mrs. Drayton walked, looked at Bo then at me, and said, "Where did you get that black stallion, Bo?"

"He'd be stay'n at the Cannon Plantation for a few weeks while his master is gone with the Colonelz to Danville for a bit. I thought you might like to see him. Mizza Drayton, that horse gotsa the Magnolia brand on his left flank."

Mrs. Drayton ran by Bo and Harriett and stopped just in front of me. She put both of her hands on my nose and said, "Is it you, Lucky? Is it you?" I shook my head up and down. I carefully placed my nose on her shoulder thinking, "It is me. It is me." Tears ran down Mrs. Drayton's face as she embraced my neck. I was home. As she ran her fingers along my neck, she felt the rough scars, which had left gaps in my mane. I could see her expression quickly change from cheerful to sad. I could not tell her how hard the war had been on me, yet she silently understood the truth.

~

Old Smitty convinced Dr. Moran that his wartime business would grow beyond his imagination. Dr. Moran was impressed with Smitty's vision and the fact that Smitty had won the heart of Dr. Moran's daughter Bella. Smitty played his cards carefully. After courting Bella for two months, he asked for her hand in marriage. She fell for him—and his tricks—and said yes. The wedding would be a grand affair since Dr. Moran did not think his daughter would ever get married. Recognizing this, Smitty skillfully pretended to be a gentleman, only to later on sadly dupe another innocent victim whose heart would become the casualty.

Now that Smitty was part of the Moran family business in a true sense, he could expand his dealings to the South once the war was over. Smitty was smart that way. He knew that all wars ended and with that came a period called post-war reconstruction. Smitty knew the South, and he knew how to take advantage of people. Someday, that would get him killed. Somehow, he had to back out of his agreements with Harrison. Smitty did not want to spy for the Confederacy as that interfered with his business. He would have to end his business relationship with Harrison before war's end.

Mrs. Drayton invited Bo and Harriett back to the house for dinner. If other white people knew what she was doing, they would surely shun her from the community. However, she had her own mind and her own way of living. Coming from a country where the Irish were suppressed by Great Britain royals, she would not treat people the way southern people treated their so called property. If Mr. Joe and his family had not stayed with Mrs. Drayton to work the land, the Magnolia Plantation would have fallen to shambles. Mrs. Drayton considered her "help" as family members.

Harriett and Mrs. Drayton fixed up a light supper that consisted of baked yams, fresh bread, and some fried chicken that Mr. Joe fixed up. With everyone at the table, Mrs. Drayton said, "Now we must bow our heads. Father, thank you for these many blessings you have laid upon this table and for our family. We thank you for our love, joy, and most of all, our health. Thank you for these many blessings. In Jesus Christ's name, we pray. Amen."

Mrs. Drayton continued on. Now we are going to have a light super tonight, for Thanksgiving is coming and we will be baking fresh peach pies, mashed potatoes and gravy, and of course, a big ole turkey, depending upon Mr. Joe's shooting skill this year."

Allison let me out into the pasture to graze. It felt good to run, buck, and snort to my heart's content. Though I was by myself, I did not feel alone. Looking across the pastures I could not see my brothers. Bo had said my brother was there. I did not know which brother, but one was here. Maybe he was mistaken. I stuck my nose down to the ground and picked up fresh scents, but there was no other horse in this field but me and those mules that I considered half breeds. I suppose I shouldn't be judgmental about their heritage, as it seemed the war had only escalated because of someone's differences in heritage. I felt bad for thinking that.

I walked over and stood in front of the largest gray mule that looked like he was in charge of the team. He looked worn and had dried red mud attached to his tail and mane. The mule raised his head. "What do you want, horse? Can't you see I am minding my own business?"

I replied, "Just trying to be friendly, mule. I just came back home from the war up north where I learned some hard lessons. Listen, I know us horses have not treated your kind very well over the years on this place. I want to change that. Would you give me a chance?"

The mule raised his head, looked me in the eyes, and said with a skeptical tone, "You mean that horse?"

"Of course, I do. I have seen enough hate between humans to last a lifetime. Our kind can learn from their mistakes."

The mule snorted. "Oh, I suppose you are right. What is your name?"

"My name is Lucky. I was born here back in '59."

"Oh, I remember you and your father, mother, and three brothers. Sorry about your mother. She was kind to us mules."

"Well, thanks for the sentiments. I did not know her very well as you already know, but I did hear good things about her from my father."

"Well, sorry about that. I know the Confederate army came and forcefully bought them and you from this place. I was glad we were with Mr. Joe down in Savannah that day. I am sure the

CSA would have taken us as well. By the way, how did you make your way back here?"

"That is a long story. We can talk about that some other time." I really did not like talking about the war when asked. I then remembered I did not know the old mule's name.

"Sir," I said, "What is your name?"

The old mule replied in a gruff voice. "Son, I don't have a name. Also, don't be call'n me sir."

"Sorry about that. However, you are older than me and I will show you that respect. I will call you by whatever name you want."

"Oh, okay. Well then, just call me Mister."

Mister and I talked until sunset. Allison came out to the field before dusk and put a halter on me. She said, "Come on Lucky. I need to get you back into the barn. It looks like it is going to rain." She did not know that all she had to do was ask and I would have followed her. While stepping forward, I glanced back at the mules. I stopped and shook my head side to side for Allison. There are plenty of open stalls back in that barn. My mule friends must come back with me. Allison kept tugging at me to go, but I could only look back at the mules to get her attention. She said, "Lucky, why won't you come?" I snorted in a way that told her what she suspected. Allison sighed. "Okay, Lucky. Tell your friends to follow us back."

It took time for everyone to reacquaint themselves. Once she got me and my friends back into the barn stalls, I tried shaking my head sideways and up and down to get her to tell me about my brother. Bo said one of my brothers was supposed to be here, but I did not know which one. Allison looked up at me and smiled. "Lucky, it is good to have you home again. Is that what you are saying?" She could not understand me, so I would have to wait for another time to get her attention. Maybe then she would understand.

After they finished their Thanksgiving meal, Mrs. Drayton, Miss Allison, Mr. Joe, Mr. Bo, and his wife Harriett came out to the barn. They were walking down the center of the barn wondering why the mules were in the stalls. Miss Allison said, "Lucky would not come out of the pasture unless they followed."

Bo said, "Sounds like Lucky is learn'n how da treat others who don't look thu same az him."

Mrs. Drayton said, "Allison, that way of treating others is what you must always remember to do. The Lord teaches us that in the Bible."

"Yes Mama. I will.

They all came down to my stall and stood outside talking. Mrs. Drayton said, "Bo, tell me more about Lucky. Who brought him to your plantation?"

"Mizza Drayton, it was a colonel, uhm, what was his last name? Yeza ma'am, I rememberz now. His name was Colonel Butler. That was the name my Masta Cannon called him. He sure could have fooled me all dressed up as a civilian and all."

I was wondering why they all came out together.

"Well, perhaps Colonel Butler was on leave or something. In any case, I sure would like to talk with him about how he came to owning Lucky."

"Well ma'am, I can't ask when I get back. Then Masta Cannon would knowz I wuz down here seeing my wife again. He sure gave me a beat'n the last time."

Mrs. Drayton looked at Bo in the eyes. "Now don't you worry. Me and little Allison need to make a trip to Florence for some Christmas shopping. I will just happen to be in the neighborhood."

Bo bowed his head. "Thank yuz, Mrs. Drayton. Thank you for your kindness."

The next day, Bo came out to feed me my oats and hay. Standing at my stall gate, he said, "Lucky, better get a nap in this afternoon. Me and yuz go'n back to the Cannon Plantation. I want to get back before Masta Cannon returns from Danville."

The couple of days here had been good for me to see all were healthy, but it was not the same without my Red who was back north. I swore to myself that I would survive the war to see her again—someday.

⌐

We needed to leave just before sunset. Standing outside the barn, Bo said goodbye to his wife while little Allison hugged me and didn't let go for some time. Mr. Joe said, "Bo, you and Lucky be careful now. That swamp has more than just wild animals."

Bo smiled. "Nowz brother, you know da Lordz with us."

Mr. Joe looked at me and said, "Well, you also got Lucky."

Bo and I made it back to the Cannon Plantation on Tuesday, December 1 before the sun showed its glory peering in from the backside of the plantation along the stand of pines near the barn. We did not see Cannon's carriage parked near the barn, so the smile on Bo's face was not hard to see in the dark. He put me in my stall where we both simply lay down and slept until about noon, when the barn door opened and two men walked inside. I could tell one of them was irritated and the other was trying to calm the older man down. Once the men were halfway in the barn, I could see it was old man Cannon and Colonel Butler.

Old man Cannon said in a loud voice, "Lucky, have you seen that slave of mine?"

Out of anger I pulled my ears back. We are not slaves.

Colonel Butler said, "Now Colonel Cannon, your boy probably took Lucky for a long workout which he enjoys. I know Bo is your property and business, but remember, no harm no foul since Lucky is my property."

Colonel Butler's comment concerned me. I never considered myself his property. Remember, I choose not to buck him off. There is always a first time.

Colonel Cannon looked into my stall, saw Bo lying down behind me, came into the stall, and raised his riding crop against

Bo. I carefully pressed my broadside against the old man. He was now trapped against the stall wall.

Colonel Cannon gasped. "Butler, get your horse out of here. He is crushing me!"

"Cannon, I think Lucky will do worse if you don't lower that crop, slowly." The old man realized he was in a disagreeable situation, so he lowered the crop. "Okay boy, you can let me go. I will not punish Bob. Just let me go."

I was waiting for that submissive cue. I pulled back but put myself between the old man and Bo who by then was standing in the stall corner behind me. Colonel Butler said, "Come on, Cannon. We need to go get some lunch. Let them be for now."

Reluctantly, Colonel Cannon replied and walked out of the barn with Colonel Butler. I think his pride was hurt more than his ribs. Bo ran his hands over my nose and said, "Thank you againz, Lucky. Yuz saved me again. I wish da I could do somth'n for you. How about some oats and molasses?" My ears perked and with a snort and shake of my head, he left to get my reward.

Colonel Butler came out to my stall about an hour before sunset to take me for a ride in the pasture, but he did not put a bridle or saddle on me, just a halter and blanket. We rode out along the property line near the main road. As we walked, Colonel Butler said, "Lucky, figure you have been on an interesting trip, but I don't want to know the details. I am just glad you are back. We need to talk about our future." I was thinking in the same vein.

He said, "Our trip to Danville went well. Secretary Seddon met us down there to talk about the future as well. He said he needed me to come back to Richmond after I had taken a few months to think through some things. I have had enough of war and wanted to resign my commission, but he convinced me otherwise. Secretary Seddon gave us until spring to actually rest and recuperate. He said General Stuart did not need me back until May in any case. I was thinking maybe you and I could go to

Savannah and try to find your home." I laughed and thought no worries there. I knew exactly how to get there.

Colonel Butler and I stayed on the Cannon Plantation through the winter months of '64. I was glad for it never got colder than thirty or forty degrees. I was okay with staying put for a little while, but the need to fight again grew stronger every day. I became restless. During the cold nights, I lay in my stall thinking about our troopers and their horses fighting the battles. For some strange reason, I wanted to be there with them.

Colonel Butler and I did not wander too far from the plantation during the winter months except for a long trip we took to a place called Camp Sumter, Georgia. Most of the locals there called the prison Andersonville. Little did I know the trip to Andersonville would be our way back up to Richmond, Virginia. I would never see Bo or the Cannon Plantation again. I worried about Bo and the Magnolia Plantation. It warmed my heart, yet it made me sad to see home again for it had changed.

Getting to Camp Sumter did not take long even though the camp was about 360 miles from Florence. It would have taken me two weeks to get there carrying Colonel Butler. However, he took us south toward the Monroe Railroad. At a train's water stop, Colonel Butler convinced the train conductor to let us ride in an empty boxcar. Since the Monroe Railroad ran west to Macon from Savannah, we only needed a couple of days to reach Macon.

The train stopped in Macon on April 30. While we were disembarking from the boxcar, I looked around and felt thankful that we had not retraced our steps through those swamps. I had had enough of those gators for a lifetime! Them gators liked to eat just about anything and I didn't plan on being on their menu anytime soon.

During our train trip, Colonel Butler told me that Macon was a very important CSA war production location. He said the CSA produced a large number of Confederate firearms, uniforms, and saddles in Macon. No doubt the Yanks would like to destroy this place.

Colonel Butler said, "Lucky, this town may not survive the war. As we did to the Yanks' Harper's Ferry arsenal, I suspect the Yanks will take this place and Atlanta as well."

The colonel mounted me back up and said, "Lucky, welcome to Macon, Georgia." I looked to my left and right and saw wagons of all types coming and going from the many factories Colonel Butler had told me about. The place was full of people busily walking, riding, or hauling wagons to and from large warehouses that produced lots of smoke and noise. Colonel Butler said that from Macon, the trains transported the war goods up to Atlanta. From Atlanta, the CSA shipped the uniforms, firearms, and saddles to where General Lee needed them. Colonel Butler said the Atlanta hub was a major Confederate production and distribution center for the South. I would not be surprised if the Yanks were making plans to destroy Atlanta and Macon; we just did not know when.

The colonel said, "Lucky, we don't have much time, so we'll just get a bit to eat here then get back on the railcar. The next train to Andersonville comes by at around three o'clock this afternoon. We will cross over the Ocmulgee River to get to a place the train conductor said cooked up a tasty plate of shrimp and grits. I also need a bottle or two of joy juice before we get to Camp Sumter. I am not sure how that will go for us."

Once we had crossed the river, we rode down Main Street looking for a place called Perry's Saloon and Eats. Colonel Butler said, "Lucky, let me know when you see the Perry's Saloon and Eats sign." As we made our way toward the center of town, I realized that what made that journey exiting for me was that it was a reunion of sorts. On the way to Perry's, we passed by several horses I had served with back in the First Battle of Manassas in '61. They were not in the best of shape, but at least they were alive and hauling wagons loaded with uniforms, not heavy caissons full of cannon balls and grapeshot. I was glad to see my friends had survived and come home.

Once we saw the Perry's sign, Colonel Butler stopped, dismounted, and walked up through Perry's double-oak doors. I became irritated since he had forgotten about my oats, molasses, and water. Bo had spoiled me back at the Cannon Plantation. He had given me some of his molasses ration every day. Well, I guessed I would have to wait until Colonel Butler was finished eating lunch and drinking.

While the colonel was inside, I stood outside pawing the ground next to an old horse that called himself Buck. He remained silent until I said something. From my perspective, he was an unusual-looking horse, all tan with a black mane and tail and white socks over his hooves. The humans called his type "buckskin." I reckoned that was why his name was Buck. He was smaller than me, but he looked every bit as fast. I looked over at his saddle and noticed the letters *CSA* on the horn.

"What unit are you with?" I said.

He replied, "I am with the Eleventh Texas Cavalry. Colonel George R. Reeves is my trooper."

That cavalry unit was familiar to me, but for some reason I could not place it. Buck looked at me and proudly held his nose high. "Lucky, my rider and I fought in the Battle of Chickamauga, Georgia back in September '63. General Braxton Bragg was our commander. It was one heck of a battle."

"Yes. I heard from my colonel that it was the second bloodiest battle fought in this war thus far. My colonel told there were about thirty-four thousand casualties and countless horses were killed."

"I'm glad I was not one of them."

"I understand just how you feel."

For a moment, Buck looked a little irritated. "What do you mean you understand how I feel?!"

I calmly replied, "Buck. I am a veteran of the First Battle of Manassas in '61, the Battles of Antietam and Fredericksburg in

'62, the Battle of Brandy Station in '63, and the last big one, the Battle of Gettysburg. As I said, I understand how you feel."

Buck lowered his head toward and said, "You're the legend our kind is talking about. Please accept my humble apologies."

At about the time Buck apologized to me, Colonel Butler and another uniformed colonel joyfully emerged from the saloon. Judging from their burping and hiccups, they were a bit intoxicated. Colonel Butler looked at the man and said, "Glad to have tipped a few with you, Colonel Reeves."

The colonel, stumbling somewhat, said, "You bet. I need to get back to my Regiment. They will think I am meeting with the president Jeff Davis, or Abe Lincoln."

Colonel Butler laughed. "You take care, Colonel. Here now." Colonel Reeves untied the reins to Buck's halter and said, "Let us go Buck. We have a date with manifest destiny."

Colonel Butler untied and mounted me, and we proceeded down the street to the train station. He said, "Lucky, we need to get to Andersonville soonest. I am expecting visitors from the North." I looked back at Buck and his Colonel Reeves who looked like he was having a tough time staying in the saddle. From the feel of Colonel Butler's legs, I could tell he was having trouble as well. I considered that a signal for me to express that I wanted my oats, water, and molasses, so I started drifting back and forth to create the effect of a moving ship on water.

Colonel Butler burped. "Lucky, you feel like a ship in rough seas. Stop. I am going to get sick." Seeing there was a feed store on the way back to the train terminal, I thought, "Uhm, I will stop there and then let him off. Maybe he will get the picture." My oats and molasses topped off with a bucket of cool water tasted good. Colonel Butler promised he would never again forget.

Once we arrived at the train station, I could see several rail lines connected from all directions. We were waiting for the inbound train from Atlanta. The colonel said we would catch a car from Macon to Andersonville. He gave the ticket man a gold coin and all was well. I did not mind riding those iron horses one bit! Knowing that I was getting to a destination in less time was truly a marvel to me.

At about five o'clock in the afternoon, the train from Atlanta arrived. I counted about ten boxcars, and as the train pulled by us, I could see Yankee prisoners tightly crammed into each car. They smelled of stench, which literally made my eyes water. The prisoners' faces were so dirty that they looked black. Their clothes looked like rags hanging off them. I also noticed none of them had any boots. Colonel Butler said, "Looks like them Yanks have had a rough going. I am sure General Lee will pardon and exchange them for our men held prisoner by the North. That has been our custom during this war."

We hopped on the last car where the guards and their horses were riding. Colonel Butler stayed with me during the whole trip from Macon to Andersonville. During the trip, I noticed a young prisoner staring at us. The boxcar's wooden slats partially covered his face. The periodic shadows from the trees we passed flickered on his face, making it harder to discern. One thing was for sure: his deep blue eyes looked very familiar to me. Colonel Butler noticed me looking straight into the boxcar in front of us. "Lucky, what are you doing? See some Yank who tried to shoot you?" No, I think I see someone who saved our lives.

The ride to Andersonville did not last long, for we were on that train for little over an hour. The train tracks came into Andersonville from the northeast. After we got out of that boxcar, Colonel Butler double-checked the saddle girth strap and mounted up. He evidently knew where he was going, so off we went to Camp Sumpter located east of town.

The CSA had built Camp Sumpter to house a reasonable number of Union prisoners. Like he said, the prisoners were paroled soon as practical. However, that gentleman's custom changed in '64. The Union's General Ulysses S. Grant stopped paroling Confederate prisoners, which meant the Confederacy would not parole Union prisoners. This created an unintended problem, and it led the CSA to make a choice: feed Union prisoners or feed Confederate soldiers.

Obviously, the latter was chosen. However, that choice created dire consequences for the many souls who ended up in what the Northern newspapers called Andersonville, House of Horrors. Colonel Butler told me that Camp Sumter was built in February '64. Since then, the CSA would transport over four hundred Union prisoners to Camp Sumter on a daily basis without the possibility of parole.[22]

We rode up to the camp's command officer's house occupied by a Colonel Alexander W. Persons. The little white sign outside his bunker door said so. I stood by the hitching post while Colonel Butler met with the prison commander and a Mr. Henry Wirz. While the men talked, I took advantage of the time to look over the new prison yard. It was an unusual prison. The prisoners wondered about the "pen" which had no walls. The prison builders positioned the sentry houses every thirty yards along the stockade walls, which were fifteen feet in height. I heard a prisoner yell at a newcomer, "Don't cross the Dead Line. They will shoot and kill you."

It appeared that the Dead Line was an invisible nineteen-foot line extending from the walls. All prisoners knew not to cross at any time, or they would be shot. Flowing in the middle of the yard was a small creek called Stockade Branch which the prisoner drank from.[23]

After thirty minutes had gone by, Colonel Butler came back outside with Colonel Persons onto the porch. Colonel Butler looked at Colonel Persons. "Thank you for the discussions. Will you please have one of your guards bring the young Gettysburg prisoner, Otto Poffenburger, to me?"

Colonel Persons yelled at a soldier, "Private, come here." The young private came over and saluted.

"Yes sir."

"I need you to canvass the yard for a Private Otto Smith from Sharpsburg, Maryland. Once you find him, bring him back here."

"Yes, sir." The private saluted and ran back toward the stockade.

Mr. Wirz said, "Colonel, why do you need this boy?"

"He has information that will help us in the cause. I am not at liberty to share that with you."

"Well, good. You then have responsibility of his actions. That German boy had been a problem. We were getting ready to just shoot him."

"I can handle him. Just make sure he brings all his things."

"The only 'things' the Yanks have is the shirts on their backs, if they were lucky."

Private Otto Smith, not really himself, approached the colonels and Mr. Wirz. He looked at Colonel Butler but showed no reaction. His eyes were empty.

Colonel Persons said, "Private Smith, your stay here in Camp Sumter has been terminated. It appears that Richmond wants you up North. What do you do so good, cook sauerkraut?"

Private Otto did not respond.

Colonel Persons handed Colonel Butler some shackles. "Here, you will need to put these on him. Don't want him running on ya."

Colonel Butler said, "He can't run faster than a bullet." He tied a rope around Private Otto's hands and waist, then mounted up and tipped his hat. "Colonel, Mr. Wirz, thank you for your cooperation." He then turned me around and steered us back to the train station.

Once we were out of sight from Camp Sumter, Colonel Butler halted, dismounted, pulled out a pocketknife, and walked toward Private Otto. I knew Colonel Butler did not like the Yanks and had killed many. However, killing in the battlefield was part of the job. What I thought he was about to do would be murder. The colonel walked up and looked intently into Otto's young face that was covered with dirt and mud. Otto cringed at the sight of the knife blade.

Colonel Butler showed him the knife. "Turn around." Otto reluctantly turned around, saying something in what sounded like a French to me but with a German accent. Colonel Butler took his knife, and with one movement, cut the ropes free from Otto's waist. Grabbing Otto by the shoulder and turning him around, Colonel Butler looked at him closely. "Present your hands, Private." Colonel Butler then cut those bindings with one movement of the hand and knife.

Otto looked at Colonel Butler. "You look much different now in civilian clothes, not like how you were back at Antietam, sir."

"When I saw you on the train coming here, I knew it was you. Who could miss that German blonde hair and squinty blue eyes of yours? Plus, you were giving other prisoners—Irishmen, I believe—a hard time. You have an attitude, son, and that has obviously kept you alive. Of course, your disregard for your own life helped save ours at Antietam. Lucky and I thank you. Otto, I will get you back to Richmond, but from there, you will have to get yourself back to Maryland. Our debt will be paid."

"You mean that is the same horse you carried me on?"

Colonel Butler quickly brushed aside the remark. "You will have no problems getting back home. The Yanks are thick in Northern Virginia now. I am sure you will find safe passage through there."

Colonel Butler reached into the saddlebag and threw Otto a pair of britches and shirt. "Go change. We will get you some boots once we are back in Macon. You will have to be my prisoner until then. These ropes go back on after you change."

"Thank you. My mother will thank you."

Colonel Persons gave Colonel Butler written orders stating that Union prisoner Otto Smith was going back to Richmond for more interrogation. That note was used to ease our passage back to Macon through Atlanta, and finally to Richmond. Between stops, the Colonel made sure Otto and I were watered and fed. In fact, the Colonel gave Otto some coins to go get a bath and new shoes in Atlanta. Otto looked like a new young man when he walked out of that bathhouse. Colonel Butler then took me over to the blacksmith to get some new horseshoes, water, feed, and a brush down. I was not sure what got into the Colonel with wanting everything cleaned and in order.

We left Andersonville on May 8. The trip would take us only two days. On the way, Otto sat with the colonel and I in the last boxcar with boxes of uniforms stacked high. The obvious military supplies needed were missing. Where were the shoes? Our men had suffered through winters without shoes. They often had to tear up their blankets and wrap them around their feet to march in the snow.

Since the boxcar was actually a cattle car, we could see outside through the wooden slats spaced out about three inches. The light of day made it easier to see outside. Pressing my nose against the slats, I could get glimpses of southern crops of corn and tobacco growing and springtime flowers sprouting up on the hills. For a moment, it was hard to believe all of that would change, and change it would.

Colonel Butler asked Otto how he had ended up with the Federals. Otto replied, "Captain, I mean, Colonel, after the Battle of Antietam, I turned seventeen and was drafted into service like most of my friends. My mother cried for days knowing I was leaving. My father, well, he just looked at me and said, 'Go serve our great nation then come home. It is honorable to die for what we believe.' He gave me neither a smile nor a hug when I left. If you know Germans, they typically show no emotion when the times get tough. It is our way."

"I can understand that as my father was also from the old country. Back to where you have been with the Federals. Tell me more."

Otto looked up. "I mustered into service on Saturday, April 4, 1863. My mother was none too happy about it. She insisted that I stay and go to church one more time, but the Union lieutenant would not respond to her pleas. I grabbed what little personal effects I could take with me and stood in formation outside. Then we all marched over South Mountain toward the east. The rest were our community volunteers who were eager to fight you rebs. Not me! I remembered what the Battle of Antietam did to you, Lucky, and tens of thousands of others who fought in that battle. I was one of only a few, including my mother, who looked into the eyes of death."

With a serious voice, Colonel Butler asked, "Yet you still mustered in. Why?"

"Because I wanted to show my father that I was a man like him." Colonel Butler put his hand on Otto's shoulder. "You became a man the day you saw what men did to one another on the battlefield. I wish you could have stayed a boy as long as you could. That was what my father always told me. Because once you step forward with being a man and all, there is no going back to a simpler time in life."

"Well, I suppose you are right, but it is too late for me. You see, I fought in the Battle of Gettysburg. It does get worse."

We arrived at Richmond on Thursday morning, May 12, 1964. After getting off the train, the colonel opened the boxcar door and led me onto a ramp. From there, the colonel, Otto, and I made our way over to the Exchange Hotel where I remembered the colonel had left his uniform and saber.

On the way there, Colonel Butler said, "Otto, I have some gold coins to help get you back to Maryland. I would suggest speaking German to avoid questioning by our patrols. Go to that bathhouse across the street and get yourself cleaned up before you leave town."

Colonel Butler smiled and handed Otto a burlap bag. "Otto, there is a sidearm in there for you along with a pair of clean britches, a shirt, shoes, and a jacket. Oh yes, here is my hat. I won't need these extra civilian clothes anymore."

"Thank you, sir. I am still not sure why you feel you owe me this."

"I owe you nothing now. The next time we meet on the battlefield and you're wearing Yankee blue, I will have to kill you, so we part ways on good terms now, showing respect." I looked at Otto and then at Colonel Butler. Both saluted at the same time then turned never to see one another again.

I watched Otto walk across the street, occasionally looking back to make sure we were going somewhere he wasn't. I wasn't sure if he was unsure of his newfound freedom, or if he was nervous about the colonel's remark. That would be the last time we would see young Otto. I often wondered if he ever made it back to his farm and into his mother's arms. I knew what it felt like to not have a mother's love.

The colonel said, "Lucky, we need to head over to the church stable and get you situated for the night." Colonel Butler mounted up and clicked his tongue, knowing I would move forward. Once we were at the stable, Colonel Butler took me inside where he saw the old caretaker. He said to him, "Sir, you may remember me from back in October of last year. I left my horse's saddle and bridle with you.

The old man replied, "Yes, suh. I do remember you and that other young man. What was his name?"

"His name was H.T. Harrison."

The old man scratched his chin. 'Yep, I do remember now. He moved out of here in a hurry a few months ago. I overheard him and Mista Seddon arguing about someone not doing their job on the Yankee side. No matter to me you know. So, Mr. Colonel, I recon you would like your tack back."

"Yes, sir. How much do I owe you?"

"No charge, son, we both see to the needs of Mista Seddon, yes we do. No charge, no suh. You needs me to take care of your horse? What is his name again?"

"Lucky."

"Awe, yes," the old man said with a smile. "I will brush him down and feed him before night. No suh. Don't you worry about that."

Colonel Butler looked at me. "Lucky, I got some business to take care of with Secretary Seddon. His carriage will get me back to the hotel tonight. You just enjoy your stay. We will be heading back out on patrol before long. By the way, it looks like your old friend is gone."

The old man interrupted. "Oh no! That old horse is not gone. Chance is just down the ways pulling a water truck. He will be back soon."

I was happy to know he was still kicking. Before long, Chance was back in his stall next to mine. We had a lot of fat to chew.

May 13 came quickly. With the morning sun hiding behind the clouds, it looked like the day was going to be dark and gloomy. I didn't know what it was, but that day felt like it would not start well. I had my breakfast and water. I was anxious to get back out on the trail. Being trapped inside a horse stall never sat well with me. I always imagined the possibility of the stable hay catching fire with no way out for me.

Colonel Butler picked me up just a little after nine o'clock. Something was very wrong. He looked very angry and overwhelmed. We made it back to his hotel where he tied me to the hitching post and ran into the hotel. After about thirty minutes, he came back outside looking like Colonel Butler. He was wearing his uniform that had been cleaned and pressed by the hotel servants. I looked down and saw him carrying his saber in one hand and a burlap bag in the other.

He said, "It feels good to be back in uniform." Since I had my CSA tack on, Colonel Butler sensed my thinking and said,

"Lucky. We are going back on patrol." I felt a strong sense of pride as we rode back toward the hotel and bathhouse. The people on the streets looked at us, smiled, and said, "Remember, General J.E.B. Stuart's spirit is in you." Enlisted soldiers saluted the colonel as we rode by. Colonel Butler had always said, "The uniform does not make the man, but the man makes the uniform." I understood what he meant.

Colonel Butler and I rode back up to the capitol grounds to pay a visit to Secretary Seddon. Colonel Butler mumbled something like, "Need to submit my final report and request immediate assignment to the north." I knew he felt like I did, lost and lonely for the fight, a strange sense of commitment that only combat veterans understand. Some soldiers avoided loneliness through drinking, while others embraced it by fighting. Colonel Butler and I wanted to keep the battle in front of us though the loss of life would mount.

When the colonel came back from his meeting with Secretary Seddon, he had a serious look on his face. I could not tell if he was happy or mad. Mounting up, he said, "Lucky, we are headed for the Army of Northern Virginia headquarters encamped south of Fredericksburg. I am to report back to General Stuart on May 12 for further orders."

Holding our heads high, we stepped out of Richmond. We wanted no more of civilian life, which was too soft for us. We were going back to fight with our comrades-in-arms. It was our job.

SHERMAN'S RIDE TO THE SEA

In 1864, Union generals Ulysses S. Grant and General William Tecumseh Sherman would literally change the landscape of our Southern homesteads. Secretary Seddon said he would come, and come he did. After burning Atlanta to the ground, General Sherman marched his soldiers, all three corps to the Atlantic Ocean. After all, he had the blessings of the Union President Abraham Lincoln and that of his superior officer, General Grant. However, Colonel Butler and Lucky were bent on stopping them.

In General Robert E. Lee's mind, the Civil War must have turned against the South on May 12, 1864. On that day, a dismounted Federal shot Cavalry Commander Major General J.E.B. Stuart during the Battle of Yellow Tavern. General Stuart's death caused great concern for General Robert E. Lee. The loss also brought memories of his trusted officer and friend, General Stonewall Jackson who died in May 1863.

General Lee lost key generals he needed to defeat the North. However, there were still superb officers capable of filling the leadership gap in his mounted service. To fill the gap, General Lee recalled all senior cavalry officers on temporary duty back to Richmond, meaning Colonel Butler and I would be heading back to battle.

The news of General Stuart's death spread quickly on the streets of Richmond, but his death took on a different meaning for Colonel Butler. Back at the Exchange Hotel front desk, the clerk handed Colonel Butler an urgent telegram from Secretary Seddon's aid. It said: "Start. Colonel Mathew Butler report to Commander, Army of Northern Virginia Headquarters. Stop. Start. You are to report to Lt. General Wade Hampton, Cavalry Commander, Hampton's Legion, no later than May 20, 1864. Stop."

As I stood outside near the hitching post, Colonel Butler emerged from the hotel double-doors holding his head high. Taking a deep breath, he said the words, "God be with us," then mounted up as he did a thousand times before. This time, he tilted his old gray slouch hat forward to cover his face. I believe he wanted time alone to think as we rode toward the train station. After a long ten minutes, Colonel said to me, "Lucky, General Wade Hampton is a good officer and one heck of a horseman from Charleston, South Carolina. We will follow him to any battle he chooses. I reckon your owners back at Magnolia Plantation probably knew him. You also may not remember, but General Hampton fought with us at Brandy Station last June. General Hampton also fought with us at Gettysburg."

He continued. "With General Stuart gone, General Lee will certainly put Hampton in charge of the Northern Virginia's Cavalry Corps.[24]

General Robert E. Lee knew he needed a strong defense in front of Richmond to interdict General U.S. Grant's Overland Campaign. Lee had always defeated the past Union generals like McDowell, McClellan, Hooker, and Burnside because they would not stay engaged. General Grant would be different. Grant would be the first Union Commander with the wherewithal to stay on course, a serious concern for Richmond. General Grant had made it clear to President Lincoln that the Federals would invade the South and capture the Richmond leadership to end the war. We paid no attention to their rhetoric. Our fighting would stop with our last breath.

On May 19, Colonel Butler and I arrived at General Hampton's headquarters located southwest of Fredericksburg, Virginia. It was early morning. The campfires were burning with soldiers tending to breakfast. Low-hanging smoke over the fields carried the smell of fried bacon and boiling coffee through the air. There were tens of thousands of tents and campfires in rows upon rows in the open fields. On the highest hill behind the fields was a lone white tent.

We rode by an officer as Colonel Butler asked, "Where can I find General Hampton's tent?" The baby-faced captain saluted and then pointed toward the tent on the hill.

"Suh, there yonder is where you will find General Hampton and his staff, suh."

"Where are you from, young man? And how old are you?"

The captain bowed his head. "Suh, my name is Captain Charles Irving Harvie, from Amelia County, Virginie, suh."

Colonel looked at him with intense eyes. "Who are you attached to, young man?"

Standing with his chest out, the soldier said, "Suh, I am with the First Virginie Cavalry, suh!"

"Very well then, carry on." The colonel smiled.

We turned toward the hill, moving in and out among the men and tents. At the base of the hill, a young captain walked toward us. Judging from his fresh uniform, he was evidently General Hampton's aide-de-camp.

Colonel Butler dismounted and returned the captain's salute. He then pulled out his orders and handed them to the captain who read the orders out loud.

"Sir, we have been expecting you. I will escort you to General Hampton's quarters, sir."

As we walked up the hill, the captain said, "With our armies battling it out over in Spotsylvania, General Hampton has been very busy planning an offensive response should Grant move around General Lee within the next couple of days."

"Very well," Colonel Butler replied. "Please take my horse to get him watered and fed."

"Sir, you may want to keep a close eye on this one. General Hampton has been complaining to Richmond that our horses are in need of replacement. In fact, General Hampton just returned from South Carolina last month with fresh horses. Those horses have already put some miles on them. Good horses are getting harder and harder to find."

Naturally, my ears perked up. I refuse to carry another trooper other than Colonel Butler. Otherwise the rider will be on his back.

While Colonel Butler met with the officers, I stood behind the tent with the other officer's horses, which seemed to be rather stuffy. I heard the captain call one of them—of all names—*Butler*. I walked over to Butler and asked him how the battles were going.

He said, "Why do you ask? Who are you? Do you know who I am? I carry General Wade Hampton into battle."

I felt the urge to kick ole Butler. "My name is Lucky, and I don't appreciate your tone. I am tired and not inclined to put up with your disrespect." I raised my head high above his and turned my flank closer to his nose, within kicking distance, and he knew it.

Butler then saw the Magnolia Plantation brand on my flank and said, "My apologies. I thought you were just another arrogant black stallion who had not seen battle yet."

I turned toward him and said, "Brother should not fight brother, don't you think?"

Butler turned to me. "I heard about your exploits at Brandy Station when General Wade and I fought there last year. Another horse veteran at Brandy Station told me that you ran a zigzag maneuver where the Yank sharpshooters could not hit you. It is understandable why the enemy always shoots us first, not the rider."

"Not sure where I learned that move. I think it was back in Antietam. In any case, it kept me and my rider alive."

General Hampton and Colonel Butler came around the tent. The general was a big man whose full beard extended to the top of his chest. I could not help but notice he had a piece of egg on his beard. I suspected no junior officers would say anything to him. I snorted to get his attention but to no avail. Colonel Butler looked at me wondering why I was trying to get his attention. I snorted one more time at the general. Colonel Butler saw the egg and simply shook his head at me. I wonder where the expression "get egg on your face" came from.

General Hampton introduced Colonel Butler to Butler. General Wade said, "Colonel, I named him after your brother. I know his recovery will be a long and painful one. He was and still is one heck of a horseman. I am sure you gained the same skill as he did growing up in North Carolina."

Colonel Butler replied, "Our father taught us every aspect of getting a horse to do what they don't like and in the end like it."

General Wade grinned. "Much like leading soldiers into battle."

The general looked at me and said to Colonel Butler, 'Where did you get that horse? I have seen him before."

"Sir, he went lame and was almost put down after the Seven Days Battle in spring of '62. At that time, I think General Stuart rode him. The quartermaster said this horse had a mild limp. Instead of putting down the horse, the old quartermaster fixed him up. I was in need of a new horse and took him from the quartermaster. I call him Lucky for many reasons."

General Hampton replied, "Son, looks like you are going to need his luck. My orders are for you to penetrate the Union lines northwest of here and collect intelligence as a scout. Secretary Seddon said you became very proficient acting as the civilian doing his business down in Danville and Andersonville. I need you to do the same but under specific orders to collect intelligence on Union movements. No interrogations involved. General

Lee thinks Grant is trying to get into our rear by skirting the Rappahannock, and maybe move down south around Petersburg. However, Grant may change course and come straight at us along the James River. We need to know when and where. I have assigned half a dozen riders to shadow your movements and work as messengers.

"Sir, I kept a set of civilian clothes, but the saddlebag was left back in Richmond."

"See my quartermaster. He has horse tack without the CSA markings. Have one of your messengers report back to me every evening or soon as you see the Federals turning toward Richmond."

"Yes, sir."

General Wade nodded his head and saluted Colonel Butler. "Godspeed, mister. Remember, I need to know the movements of General Sheridan's cavalry divisions. I am most concerned about their ability to disrupt our supply routes to the west of Richmond. Keep your eyes on Gordonsville and Charlottesville. We have to keep the Central Virginia railroad tracks open. General Fitzhugh Lee and I will be moving to the west once we are sure where Grant ends up to the east of us. "

Colonel Butler changed back into civilian clothes as I sported a different saddle. I was not very happy about losing my old saddle again. At least the leather on that one was broken in. Colonel Butler looked different. The clothes he wore were not as fashionable. He looked like a poor scavenger. I suppose that was the intent in case the Yanks captured us. Colonel Butler mounted up, "Move out, Lucky. We need to meet with some fellas over there by that stand of trees. They will be riding with us." I was excited to be back on the front lines again. Even though I did not have my lucky saddle, I did have my lucky blanket Dr. Smith had given me back in Middleburg. That luck was still good.

When evening came, Colonel Butler and I traveled with the other six troopers westward toward the Virginia Central Rail Line. This railroad provided a critical link between Richmond and Northern Virginia outposts. Before the Union could tear up the tracks, we had to interdict the Union movements. It would take a corps of infantry and a division of mounted troopers to do so.

Since the weather was starting to get warm, water became more and more important to us horses. While we rode across the fields and hills of Luisa County, it occurred to me that that summer would be my fourth in those parts. I did not mind June, but I sure did not care for the heat in July and August. The June grass was still green and water ran plentiful. For us horses, life was not as challenging. However, for our soldiers, the lack of food, ammunition, and clothing made it more difficult to fight.

While we rode during the day, the colonel said the plan was to stay just inside enemy lines. That meant watching for Sheridan's reconnaissance patrols performing the same mission of intelligence gathering. Once we had crossed the North Anna River, we patrolled between the North and South Anna Rivers about twenty miles east of Gordonsville.

The men made no fire that night and slept on bedrolls and saddles. The men tied us horses to a rope line strung between two oaks trees. I could overhear Colonel Butler plot out how the seven would patrol the area over the next few weeks. Compared to a field battle, moving at or within enemy lines that moved was dangerous business. That type of warfare was nothing like brigade fighting brigade in an open battlefield during the day. It was the war of wits and silent reconnaissance against the unsuspecting enemy.

During the first week of June, we saw more movement northeast of the Virginia Central Rail. The Union scouts were operating fifteen miles northeast of Gordonsville or about twenty miles north of Luisa. On June 6, Colonel Butler and I stood on a hill overlooking a place called Clayton's Store, where at least two cavalry divisions were encamped in the valley, so we quietly turned and quickly moved back toward Luisa at a predetermined meeting place with the other riders. Colonel Butler handed a small piece of paper to one of the men who said, "Sir, I will ride like the wind to get this to Generals Lee and Hampton."

Colonel Butler replied, "Make it so. The Federals looked like they were making preparations for moving out."

As General Hampton suspected, the Federals were targeting Gordonville along with the Virginia Central. Since the Gordonsville was a critical railroad junction city for moving confederate supplies, we were not surprised. Colonel Butler was pleased. "Lucky, we now have verified Sheridan's intent and assessed his cavalry strength. We must use this information to our advantage."

On June 8, Generals Hampton and Lee moved two divisions of our own cavalry to the west to intercept the Federals. General Hampton's plan was an offensive plan. We would attack. Colonel Butler and I maintained our positions just outside Sheridan's divisions to make sure we had eyes on their movements in case they turned east toward Richmond. Colonel Butler and I did not engage the enemy. "Lucky, we need to get back to headquarters soonest. The Federal Troopers are moving in mass—at least two divisions, dozens of guns, and most likely hundreds of wagons in the rear."

June 10 was spent patrolling south along the Virginia Central rail to a place called Trevilian Station just about six to seven miles west of Luisa. Colonel Butler and I stayed put at that rail station. In the afternoon, the other six scouts made their way back to our position. One of them, not sure of his name, galloped toward us, stopped, and, breathing hard, said, "Colonel, just got back from headquarters. Our men are already on their way. The plan is to stop Sheridan here. General Wade said his regiments would be here tomorrow morning."

Colonel Butler said, "Men, we will not be in this battle. Once General Hampton gets here, we will have to move toward Charlottesville to get eyes on Charlottesville. I saw a small Union

patrol headed that way. I think they were going there for a purpose which needs to be determined."

Generals Lee and Hampton arrived at Trevilian Station just
before sunrise on June 11. It had rained the night before so the
trails were muddy. However, the sun rose from behind clouds
blowing north. That day would be a good day for fighting. Colonel
Butler and I rode over to the great General Hampton who was
riding Butler.

General Hampton said, "Colonel Butler, you and your men
did an outstanding job. You information was sent to Richmond.
General Robert E. Lee was most appreciative in knowing
Sheridan's movements from the north. What we do not know
is where General Hunter is located. Is he still operating in the
Shenandoah Valley, or is he coming up from the Appalachia in the
west? Hunt was last reported moving east from the Shenandoah
Valley through the Blue Ridge Mountains. Unreliable reporting
has him going toward Charlottesville. I need to know where he
is at."

Colonel Butler saluted and replied, "Yes sir. We are on our way."

Little did we know that day that the Battle of Trevilian
Station would be the largest cavalry engagement since Brandy
Station. We had heard one of our messengers say the Yanks were
surprised, whipped by tough Rebel hearts. Sheridan had brought
about nine thousand troopers and horse batteries to the battle,
and we had mustered up five thousand brave troopers and horse
batteries. The Battle of Trevilian Station raged on for two days. In
the end, General Sheridan's forces had enough and pulled back to
Clayton's Store. For the moment, Richmond avoided Sheridan's
strike. Sheridan would not connect with Grants Forces moving
toward Petersburg while Colonel Butler and I were in the field.

Between July and October 1864, we continued scouting for
General Hampton. Our mission was to detect and report any
Federal movements west of Richmond. During the first week of
November, while patrolling in the southernmost parts of Blue

Ridge Mountains, we saw signs of the enemy moving their armies in the direction of Atlanta, but then it could have been a military feint. Army commanders oftentimes faked a movement to draw the opposing force away from their real objective. Sometimes, the only way we could validate the truth was through interrogations of captured Union officers. Colonel Butler rarely detained enlisted Yanks. He did so because they were removed many levels from the Union's decision-thinking. We did not want to waste our limited food and water, so Colonel Butler would keep their weapons and horses, then send them on their way, much the same way we treated the highest-ranking Union General we took captive during the war, Cavalry General George Stoneman.

During the summer of '64, the notion of mounted Union patrols penetrating deep into the south was just that—a notion. However, during the month of July, General George Stoneman had it in his mind to lead a raid into Georgia and bust up the South's war-making capability in Macon. He would then set free the prisoners in Andersonville. That did not work out for him so well. We captured Stoneman and his aide-de-camp, Major Myles Keogh, on July 31, holding them both as prisoners for three months until Union General William T. Sherman negotiated their release in exchange for Confederate General Daniel C. Govan. Those were the rules of war that most everyone followed—except for General Sherman.

General William T. Sherman was our cross to bear. Grant kept us busy defending Richmond while Sherman scooted around to our south toward Atlanta, the Atlantic Ocean, and all points in between. Sherman literally burned Atlanta to the ground on October 26. From there, General Sherman and his three Corps made their way to the Atlantic Ocean. The newspapers would call his plan the March to the Sea.

Sherman began his invasion on November 14, 1864. His army consisted of three corps, all marching in the same direction but spread out over a sixty-mile swath, making it difficult for our commanders to anticipate where to concentrate our defensive positions. The Union pillaged in most cases, destroying both military targets and civilian properties. Attacks on civilian property flipped the rules of war upside down, making it difficult for us to identify and protect our citizens.

Many in Richmond speculated that Sherman would hit Macon, Georgia, first since Macon was a key war production facility, and thought Charleston, South Carolina, would be his number one target since that city fired the shots that started the Civil War. Sherman also held my home close to his heart in that he wanted to destroy South Carolina. My South Carolina was the first state to secede from the Union. Because of this, I worried for Mrs. Drayton and the Magnolia Plantation.

While Sherman's march went unabated, all Colonel Butler and I could do was to remain focused on Richmond. It was our job to provide defensive reconnaissance support to ensure the Union did not penetrate any further north from Petersburg south of Richmond. This task became even more difficult as the winter of '65 settled in, making this long war harder on all of us. We seemed trapped by the Yanks. Colonel Butler said General Grant had positioned well over one hundred thousand soldiers in front of our Petersburg breastworks. The situation was becoming more difficult for our side. It would only be a matter of time.

After Sherman's successful March to the Sea, he made his way back up north from Savannah. The Union's General Rosecrans was making his way toward Richmond from the west. Uncontrolled events were moving quickly, and I feared that hope was beginning to waver. The Union had three things better than the CSA. They had food, warm clothes, and ammunition. Our men were fighting on empty stomachs. Our men's ammunition was in short supply since Sherman had destroyed our munitions manufacturing capabilities in Georgia and North Carolina. Northern civilian were coming down hawking their goods for unbelievable prices on the black market. I called them thieves taking advantage of the starving South. I could only hope something big would happen for the better. The South needed it!

———

While the South was crumbling, back in Washington, D.C., Private Smitty was already making plans to invade his own homeland with his pen instead of bullets. Shrewd he was. Smitty and his father-in-law made lots of money selling food to the Union. Smitty convinced his wife that they could make much more money once the war ended. They would become carpetbaggers, a term used for Northern civilians who would travel south to buy up burned-out plantations for practically nothing. Smitty knew the first place he wanted to buy—the Magnolia Plantation. He despised the Draytons. The killing of Sir Drayton was not enough.

Smitty woke up his wife Bella. "Darl'n, how would you like to live on a big ole plantation where the crops are as green as money?"

Bella tried to sit up in bed to speak, but her stomach was too big with a baby. Using her elbows, she pushed herself up to sit. Smitty put a couple of pillows behind her back. She smiled at Smitty. "Husband, now why would we want to own a plantation? Daddy said he would give us a hundred acres here in Virginia."

"Bella, we are going to have lots of kids. We will need more money to raise them properly and I want to earn it with my own two hands, not with your father's money."

"You are always your own man. I will follow you wherever you go honey, but right now, I need to have this baby first."

Smitty got out of the bed and put his pants on. "I think I am going to go south to scout out some places. I heard Sherman burned up quite a few plantations on his way to the sea. I want to make an offer those owners cannot refuse."

Bella slipped back down under the patchwork quilt. "Well, just make sure you get back in time to see your first baby being born. Mama says I got about two weeks."

"No worries, honey. I will only be gone a week. I figured I would take a ship down to Savannah since our Federals occupy it. They must need to be resupplied by now."

Bella pulled the covers up over her chin. "See if Daddy wants to go with you. He has never been beyond the James River."

Smitty squinted his eyes. "Naw, honey. He is busy, and well, it is still a little bit dangerous down there. I will do this on my own. I will be okay. I will send you a telegram once I arrive in Savannah."

Smitty grabbed a small bag made out of a carpet with a purplish background and black-and-brown paisley patterns. He stuffed in three pairs of britches, shirts, and socks.

Bella, peeking out from under the covers, said, "You only gonna be gone a week or two. Why take so many clothes?"

Smitty hesitated and said, "It rains down there in the winter. I will need warm clothes to change in."

Bella seemed satisfied with that answer. Little did she know her husband would not return for a long, long time.

LEE'S SURRENDER AND GRANT'S VICTORY

In March 1864, President Lincoln promoted Union General Ulysses S. Grant to Commanding General of the United States Army. His orders were basically to end the civil war. It took a year and some months, but eventually, General Grant would do as he promised, but not without causing more suffering and death on the battlefield. Lucky's final battle would be the longest he experienced: the Battle of Petersburg. The battle was actually a siege that the Union held over the Confederates for nine long months. Both sides had soldiers hunkered down in the dreary mud trenches of Petersburg, Virginia just thirty miles south of Richmond. The siege would consist of a prolonged series of fighting between the Union and Confederate armies between June 9, 1864 and March 25, 1865. General Lee desperately needed to protect his primary supply line to Richmond. To do so would require more men. This is how Lucky tells it.

⚊

Colonel Butler and I understood that General Grant's primary objective was to take Petersburg to force General Lee to surrender. Since General Lee was short on troops, he requested from the Confederate Congress to pass pending legislation to arm and enlist black slaves in exchange for their freedom. On March 13, the Confederate Congress passed legislation to raise and enlist companies of black soldiers. The Confederate legislators and President Jefferson Davis promulgated into military policy General Order No. 14 on March 23, 1865.[25] This policy forced many plantation owners to give up their property. As such, the Petersburg Campaign would force human beings like my friends Mr. Joe and Bo into service. People who looked like them would participate in six major engagements and earn fifteen of the sixteen Medals of Honor awarded to African American soldiers in the Civil War. I wondered how Mrs. Drayton would get by without Mr. Joe.

Mrs. Drayton woke up to another lonely day on Magnolia Plantation. It was early March and she knew getting the fields ready for planting was going to be tough without the many hands she needed to get the job done. They were barely making enough money from selling the few crops they had harvested last summer. Thank God Mr. Joe and his family did not run away. They showed mercy and stayed on to help out. Mr. Joe had said shortly after Sir Tom's death, "Mrs. Drayton, ma' am, Magnolia Plantation is our home and you treat us something good. Sir Tom would have wanted noth'en less from us."

Like most Saturdays since the war had started, Mrs. Drayton got Allison up to help bake bread for the church's efforts to send food to the front lines. Their men were starving and needed food and clothes. The 1865 winter had been hard on the soldiers encamped throughout the north. To help, Miss Allison had learned to sew company flags, but at thirteen, she could do more to help the cause.

Later that day, old Sadie started barking her head off outside. Curious, Mrs. Drayton looked out the front window and saw a Confederate soldier riding up the road toward the house. Within a few minutes, he had stopped and tied his bay horse to the hitching post in front of the main house. By the time he dismounted, Mrs. Drayton was on the front porch. A plank creaked as she stepped forward. *Funny*, she thought, *the noise it made started after Tom had passed on. I need to fix it, or maybe not.*

Stopping at the edge of the porch, she said, "How can I help you, soldier?"

Removing his hat, the young man replied, "Ma'am, my name is Corporal John Brown. I have written orders from General Robert E. Lee to inform all plantations in this region that the Confederate States of America's leadership will soon pass legislation that will draft all able-bodied Negro men between the ages of sixteen and forty-two to serve as soldiers in the Confederate States of America Army. We need all the men we can get to the front."

With concerned eyes, she said, "Well, Corporal. I wish I could oblige the cause, but we only have one male here who is of fighting age, and he is all we have to keep this plantation going."

"I am sorry ma'am, but you really have no choice, otherwise their owners will be arrested. Ma'am, I will be back this afternoon to take charge of your servant. What is his name?"

Turning away toward the front door, Mrs. Drayton replied in a shaking voice, "We have always called him Joe. I do not rightly know what his real last name is. However, I suspect that from this point on, he would not mind being called Joe Drayton."

The beginning and ending of the Civil War had many twists of fate. Colonel Butler said to me while we were on patrol, "Lucky, you know, the first Confederate General Officer at the beginning of the Civil War in Fort Sumpter will also participate in writing what may be the final chapter of this war."

I knew who he was talking about—the general who took me from my home, General Pierre Gustave Toutant Beauregard, who commanded the defenses of Charleston, South Carolina, at the start of the Civil War at Fort Sumter on April 12, 1861. Three months later, he and I were the victors at the First Battle of Bull Run near Manassas, Virginia. During the Siege of Petersburg, General Beauregard had ten thousand men protecting the Confederate capitol of Richmond, Virginia. One of his cavalry officers would make his way down to Petersburg. His name was Colonel R.W. Goodwin, the first trooper I carried in the war.

Colonel Butler would not make it through the end with me. During a skirmish with Union Brigadier, General George Armstrong Custer's scouts shot Colonel Butler off my back. I tried to get him up with my nose, but he only waved me away with his pistol. I knew he was down but still alive when I zig-zagged back to the tree line. I stood just inside the line, watching to see if the scouts would simply ride away. They did not. Instead, they rode over to Colonel Butler who tried to lift his pistol but dropped it. He refused to be taken alive as he felt a soldier who surrenders will surrender again. Since Colonel Butler was an officer, he stood a good chance of getting medical help, if not taken for questioning. At that time, I thought I would never again see this man who proudly wore his Confederate uniform and protected me from unreasonable odds. I could only turn and quietly move south toward Petersburg.

It was during the Siege of Petersburg when I almost gave up on life. The Confederates survived on little food; we horses fared no better. There were days when all went without clean water. The soldiers would improvise and catch rainwater. I was in no better shape. The trooper from the Sixth South Carolina Cavalry who shared his canteen water with me was shot off my back during the Battle of Fort Stedman on March 25, 1865.

During the confusion of battle, I tried to find a safe place to rest and figure out where to go. It was hard for me to see through the smoke and understand any sounds suppressed by gun and cannon explosions bellowing in all directions. Since it was still dark in the early morning, I remembered what Sir Tom had said about getting lost: "Find the Orion stars." The top of the kite pointed to the North Pole. I used the Orion as my compass. I slowly made my way through a stand of trees to get clear of the smoke. Once I was in the thickets, I saw the stars and then finally the Orion, lying just to the east. Tracing my nose from top of the kite to the tail, I found south.

Eventually, I made it to a muddy trench full of Confederate soldiers and cannons. One soldier yelled, "Look yonder fellas. Food has arrived." Before the soldier could take the shot, a big black man pushed down the soldier's rifle, "Stop! We need that horse to move our cannons."

There was something familiar about the black man in the gray uniform. I stood perfectly still as the familiar deep voice walked slowly toward me. "There now, boy, everything will be fine. I will take care of you. We will soldier on together."

Those words came back like a floodgate pouring water from a damn. I then remembered who he was. It was Mr. Joe who had made me my first saddle, fed me, and trained me!

Private Joe Drayton approached me and saw the Magnolia Plantation brand on my left rump. "My, my, sweet Lord. This cannot be. This is little Lucky! How did you make it here boy? You have grown so tall—seventeen hands it looks like."

Mr. Joe looked into my eyes. "I see you are confused about my name. I took the last name of my master. This was a common practice for us slaves who came from Africa." I glanced to the left and right and noticed some of the soldiers were wondering why Mr. Joe was talking to a horse.

Private Drayton quickly took me over to the earthwork used to protect the soldiers and artillery. Once we were in front of the cannon limber, Private Drayton removed the cavalry saddle, blanket, and bridle. He then put the old leather harness that connected the cannon limber jack to my harness. Needing five other horses, the soldiers would have to pitch in.

Drayton called over to the men. "Come here, men, the great state of South Carolina needs you all's help. We need to move that cannon over to the north side. Grant's men will be coming that way soon." With all their might, the men and I repositioned the cannon to where it could best protect our position—pointing over the ridge where the Union soldiers were expected to charge. It has been awhile since I had to move one of these darn things. The smoothbore Napoleon weighed over 1200 pounds. It was going to be some trick.

Mr. Joe and I heard some commotion behind us. We looked behind and a young cavalry officer galloping over yelled out, "General Lee has ordered retreat, retreat!" Without wasting any time, Private Drayton unhitched me from the limber. After removing the heavy leather harness off my back, he said, "Godspeed with you, Lucky. Get out of here!" I stood there not knowing what to do. Then all of a sudden, a Union shell came screeching in, exploding not ten feet in front of the earthen works. Mud, shrapnel, and wooden splinters showered everyone. I felt several stings burn in my left front leg and chest. Disregarding the pain, I looked down and saw Joe Drayton covered with blood and mud. His legs were motionless, and his arms were pointed south. With a drawn breath, he said, "Go home, Lucky." I never saw Private Drayton again.

My wounds did not keep me from running. Though the red, thick mud stuck to my hooves, I pulled them out and jumped over that caisson, landing safely down the hill onto an open tobacco field. Keeping my balance and head down, I raced for a stand of woods maybe five hundred yards away. The pain in my front leg was throbbing. It seemed like time had stood still from the time of the explosion until I reached the far tree line. Like how it was back in Manassas, my ears were ringing again. Things were in slow motion for some reason. Finally, while standing under a large oak tree, I took a deep breath hoping the enemy would not come after me. Looking back at the ridge, I saw fire, smoke, and hundreds of men in dark blue uniforms swarm over Private Drayton's position. I hoped the Union would show mercy on my brothers.

Wandering through the trees and small meadows, I came to a small stream the soldiers called Harrison's Creek, which was running slower since the rain had stopped. I was terribly thirsty, so I stopped to lap up much needed water. With my nose close to the water surface, I could see my reflection. How old I looked. My face was so dirty and worn. My eyes looked dark and empty. The whites of my eyes were bloodshot and red. Was that what war did to God's children?

Refreshed, I continued trotting southwest. The trees and brush were thick with new leaves. I felt so lost. None of the scents in the area were familiar to me. Early in the morning, the forest was dark and silent. I could hear my hooves breaking the small tree limbs that cluttered the forest floor. I would stop periodically to listen for anything that might be a threat to my life, though my ears were still ringing a bit. Suddenly, there was a crack of a limb to my right. I stopped, frozen, carefully controlling my breath. Was it the enemy? Did they come for me after all? My eyes did not betray me. With my head down, my eyes focused on the direction from which the sound came, I saw it. A couple of deer were making their way along a trail that divided into two trails, one leading to the left where the does went, the other breaking off to the right.

Before I could take a step, I heard a deep snorting sound behind some thickets to my right. It was a big whitetail buck standing behind a large growth of blackberry vines. I could see his neck and massive set of horns. Gauging by the fourteen antler points, he was a large, old buck. When his eyes met mine, he took a few steps from behind the vines revealing a massive chest with V-shaped white hair traveling from his neck to the bottom of his chest. His front legs were muscled with large dewclaws coming out just above the backside of his hooves. At that point, I did not know if I should run or stand my ground. Mother Nature gave him a lethal weapon to defend himself. Those sharp antlers could easily penetrate my hide.

The big buck continued walking to my left until he came into full view. I then saw it: blood stains on his rear left leg near a bullet wound. He looked at my front leg and saw the blood from my wounds. We both snorted and understood one another. He motioned his head toward the trail breaking to the right, a trail going somewhere. I had to trust him. Cautiously, we both moved along the path for what seemed to be three to four miles. Finally, we stopped. I looked up and saw that the horizon was becoming more visible. With hope filling my heart, I could see the edge of the forest. When I looked back down, the big buck was gone. Thank God for small miracles and a big buck.

By following the big buck, I was able to make it out of the stand of trees. Stepping out of the woods, I came to an embankment that looked like a railroad track. I climbed up the small hill to see that it was in fact a railroad. Remembering the days during the Battle of Fredericksburg, I was sure the track would lead to the Confederates. The only problem was deciding to go left or right. The stars were not visible during the day. I had to choose. Seeing the smoke rise from the right, I knew my Confederate brothers were fighting. That was where I wanted to be. As Little Sorrel had said to me back at the Battle of Manassas in 1862, "It was our duty."

꒰ꜛ

It was our duty. Much had been the case when Mr. Joe encouraged the men to stand tall and get ready to fight. Lying in the trench full of mud and dead bodies, Private Drayton used all his strength to pull himself up to his knees. Looking down at his hands, he felt no pain though his left thumb was missing. He was in shock. Corporal Drayton did not realize what was going on around him. Dazed and confused, he shook his head, thinking it was only a matter of time before the smoke cleared and the Yanks would be on top of him. Reaching for his rifle, a big hand stopped him. It was a black hand which he had never shook. Private Emor Washington, a Union soldier from the Second Regiment of the Maryland Infantry, reached down, sweat dripping off his head. "No worries, my brother. You are free now. No need for uza to fight anymore. Let us get yuza back to the field hospital. Doctors won't cut that leg off too soon." He smiled. Corporal Drayton struggled to his feet and said, "Much obliged. I am free! Praise the Lord, sweet Jesus!"

While walking along the train track, I was able to find some young spring grass to graze on. It felt good to get food into my stomach. The grass was moist with dew. It tasted so fresh. "Live off the land" was what General Jackson had said before he died from wounds sustained during the Battle of Chancellorsville in May 1862. Stonewall Jackson was one of our favorite generals in the CSA, a true leader of men and horses. I was sad for his Little Sorrel. I wondered if he had survived the war.

I kept a watchful eye while moving along the railroad. After about an hour of walking, I suddenly heard men's voices ahead, so I quickly moved over to the tree lines to hide until I could see what was coming around the corner. Then there was the sound source—hundreds of Confederate Troopers patrolling the railroad moving toward my position. My horse brothers were snorting. They looked tired and hot, judging by the white froth foaming from the sides of their mouths. The men looked worn out. Their eyes told the story of how much fighting, killing, and suffering they had been through.

The officer leading the cavalry regiment was hard to recognize since dried mud and chewing tobacco covered his face. I saw him look back to call up another trooper who had a hemp rope in his free hand. I did not know what the rope was for until it was too late. Before I could run, the rope's noose was around my neck. Not knowing what they wanted, transportation or food, I did what I do best—I resisted.

Several of the troopers encircled me, and one trooper tried to tame my spirit, but he could not do it alone. The officer leading the patrol stepped down from his horse and said, "I got this. Back in Union County, I was known to tame both woman and horse at the same time." The men laughed as the dejected trooper walked away.

While I reared and stomped, the officer continued to say, "It is okay, boy, we only want to ride you, not eat you." When he spoke, my memories flashed back to Magnolia Plantation. My senses triggered what I thought was the smell of Red, but she was not there. Then it all made sense. It was the voice of Red's owner, Mr. Goodwin. Now, he was Colonel R.W. Goodwin, assigned to the Confederate States of America 7th Regiment, South Carolina Cavalry.[26] I was so relieved to see my master's old friend again.

Calming down, I felt more at ease at the hand of Colonel Goodwin. He seemed so much older than he was when I first met him and Red on that old, red dirt road in April 1861. Who could forget? He and Sir Tom were whooping it up, celebrating the Confederate victory at Fort Sumpter. Both men were yelling the rebel yell then.

Colonel Goodwin took off his tan leather gloves and approached me head on, keeping his eyes on mine as I kept my rear legs, ready for kicking. I wasn't sure of his intentions as I had seen many men change during the war, so I kept my guard up just in case. He placed his left hand in front of my nose, barely touching my whiskers. He then carefully took the rope from around my neck while keeping his hand on my nose. With a double look, Colonel Goodwin looked over to my left flank and saw a portion of the brand Mr. Joe had given me years back. I had dried mud covering most of it. Using his hand, Colonel Goodwin brushed away the dried mud and saw clearly the crescent moon and palmetto mark on my skin. He smiled and said, "Well, boy, it looks like me and you are both a ways from home. Perhaps we can go home together. However, we still have more fight'n to do. I have two riders on one horse back there. If you would be so kind, we would appreciate your help." I think he meant to feed and water me in exchange for carrying that young officer riding double on that poor brown mare in the rear. Why not? This is better than hauling 1200-pound canons in the mud.

After saddling me up, a young officer by the name of Lieutenant Silas Walker gently pulled my mouth bit to the right, saying, "Move out." With a clicking sound and a dig with his spurs, we moved out quicker than he had hoped. I felt at home again. It would not be long before I would be racing toward the enemy while my rider shot his rifle. This was the battlefield I knew and felt most comfortable working in. Lt. Walker eventually got control of me and turned us around toward the rest of the regiment. Once there, we both observed a young Confederate trooper riding fast toward Colonel Goodwin. He said with a broken breath, "Colonel, General Lee is planning a counterattack at Appomattox, Virginia. You must report to General John Brown Gordon at once. General Lee wants to break through the Union lines south of Appomattox. We need to help turn the Union flank."

Colonel Goodwin and the 7th Regiment South Carolina Cavalry reported to General Gordon on April 8, 1865. General Gordon and his staff were camped by Appomattox River two miles southwest outside Petersburg. It was General Lee's intent to break through the Union lines to reposition the Confederate leadership in North Carolina. On the morning of April 9, General Lee marched his troops south. General Gordon's troops charged through the Union lines and took the ridge, but as they reached the crest, they saw the entire Union XXIV Corps in the line of battle with the Union V Corps to their right. Lee's cavalry saw the Union forces and immediately withdrew and rode off toward Lynchburg.[27]

The 7th Regiment South Carolina Cavalry stood and fought briefly with the Union Cavalry. It was difficult, for the Union troopers carried carbine rifles capable of repeating shots without stopping to reload. Many Confederate troopers were wounded or killed by those weapons. As such, my Lt. Walker was quickly shot down from my back. A few rounds skirted by my front hooves. Not to become another target, I galloped to the left of the shooting and smoke to my right. Again caught up in the fog of war, I was confused about what to do.

Coming up from behind, several horses and their riders wearing dark blue uniforms passed me by. I felt relieved that the enemy troopers did not shoot at me for once. I thought I had escaped capture by the enemy, but my self-assurance was short lived. Suddenly, I could hardly breathe. A wire rope thrown around my neck tightened up quickly. A trooper sitting on a much larger black horse had tied the rope's bitter end to his saddle horn. His horse looked like a monster to me with its hooves twice as big as mine. Not sure what breed he was, but surely that horse came from across the oceans. I calmed myself down to not cause any more trouble. The Union trooper was very pleased with his catch of me. I suppose it was then that I realized I had become the soldier's captive or war trophy.

The morning passed and by the afternoon, all shooting had stopped. The battlefield had gone quiet. General Robert E. Lee had no choice but to surrender the Confederate Army of Northern Virginia. It was on April 9, 1865 that General Lee and Union General Ulysses S. Grant would sign the surrender documents. The signing took place in a house owned by a Mr. Wilmer McLean.

I did not know where I was going. The war was pretty much over. Part of me was glad, knowing that no more humans and horses would have to die. Another part of me wished I could go home. I simply wanted my Red and to go back to Magnolia Plantation where I was born and raised. Surely Mrs. Drayton and little Miss Allison would be there waiting for me. However, that would not be the case. Instead, I spent the next three days riding back to the Union capitol in Washington, D.C.

⌒

Smitty had been riding in that back of a settler's wagon, when out of the side of his eyes, he notice a Union patrol quickly coming up on left side of the wagon. He knew his troubled past would come back to haunt him now that the war was almost over. Many thoughts were screaming through his head at that moment. Lincoln has been assassinated by a young man who lived at the same boarding house where Smitty rented a room a few years back. Smitty knew he had nothing to do with it but then the boy's mother may have named him as a conspirator in Lincoln's assassination. Smitty was not going to stick around to find out.

Smitty tipped his hat over his nose as the patrol rode by. He was counting his blessings since the day he told his wife he would be right back. Instead, he hitched a ride with one of his store's immigrant customers. Smitty was lucky to have ran into an Irish couple at the general store. They had recently immigrated to America, coming through Ellis Island. Smitty knew they would take any help they could get in a strange new land. The husband, Mr. O'Malley said he and his wife and brother were on their way west to find gold. The papers reported that gold was pouring out of the mountains in Colorado, the Dakota Territory, and the Alaska Territory. Headlines read, "Come One, Come all to Stake a Claim."

Smitty figured the O'Malley's thirst for gold could be bargained with. Smitty offered to build a gold sleuth guaranteed to sift gold from water and rock. He would only do so in exchange for free passage. The O'Malley elder was a little suspicious of Smitty's grandiose claim. But the husband relented when his red-headed wife insisted that an American-born man would be better equipped with the right accent to negotiate with locals. Smitty sat in back of that wagon with the younger O'Malley bother, looking at the dust kicked up by the mules in tow. He was certain of prosperous future, even if it meant killing again. This time the enemy would not be wearing blue. The enemy would be far more lethal.

The black mule and creaky buckboard kept its distance behind the Irish settler's wagon. Since being freed by Lincoln, Mr. Joe vowed to track down the man who killed his master back in South Carolina. Mr. Joe said aloud, "Mr. Smith, you and I will come to terms with the law as my witness. What you did to the Drayton family would be forgiven by a better Christian than me. However, that war made me'za an unforgive'n man."

WITHOUT THE HORSE, THE CIVIL WAR WAS NOT

On April 13, 1865, I celebrated my sixth birthday in a horse stable owned by the United States Army in Alexandria, Virginia. It was Thursday, so I and the rest of the horses would enjoy the grooming in preparation for the weekend celebrations planned for the reelected President of the United States, Mr. Abraham Lincoln. The Washington, D.C. residents would be celebrating General Robert E. Lee's surrender at the Appomattox, Virginia courthouse on April 9, 1865. I and several other horses were selected to pull the presidential carriage. We needed to look our very best for the President. How ironic it was that a Confederate horse like me, who had fought the Union for four long years, would end up charged with transporting the most important human being in the free world: the President of the United States.

I often wondered if the soldier horse trainer knew it was my birthday that day. Using my hind legs, I tried to sidekick the soldier to get his attention. Hey, don't you know my birthday is today? I am thinking that extra oats and molasses are in order.

Sergeant Suozzi, my handler, said in his New York accent, "Hold on to your horses, boy. I know its Thursday and you are excited about the parades this weekend." No kidding, but it is my birthday Yank. Count my teeth.

While Sergeant Suozzi held my halter, I pulled him over to the feed bucket, shaking my head up and down. Suozzi realized that I was hungry even though I had had my hay earlier. "Okay, boy, why not? I will give you a cup of oats, just don't tell anyone." I was still not happy. I wanted a spoon of molasses mixed with those oats. Suozzi said, "It's a bit chilly today. Why don't I put some molasses in with those oats?" I could not have been happier since the day I had arrived in Washington, D.C.

While brushing the dust and dried mud off my coat, Suozzi noticed my unique brand showing a crescent moon over a palmetto tree. "Nice tattoo Blackie," Sergeant Suozzi said while brushing the knots out of my tail. I snorted, "Don't call me Blackie; my name is Lucky, Yank!"

Sergeant Suozzi continued grooming me to the point I felt alive again. "You know, Blackie, I have seen that tattoo before. On a black horse that looked exactly like you, not one year ago I think."

My ears perked up, thinking what other horse could have had my brand. No, wait! There was one other horse on Magnolia Planation with my brand. That horse was my father! Could it be he was still alive? I had to figure out where he went. What happened to my family? Where were my brothers?

I looked closely around, thinking the Yanks would have me hauling those damn cannon limbers again. Funny, I could not see any cannon limbers or caissons full of ammunition in sight. I looked for a way to escape. The fences were very high. I could not possibly jump clear of them. I would wait for the right time. Until then, I would need patience. I had to get back home and find my Red. I missed her.

After Suozzi finished the grooming, he hooked up a long lunge line to my halter and made me go around in circles. What did he think I was, a circus horse? I was a warhorse, a seasoned warrior. Looking at his brand-new black boots, the boy had lots to learn. He was probably one of those ninety-day wonders the

Union recruited by assuring families their sons and husbands would only be gone ninety days, hence a ninety-day enlistment. It was funny how we horses were not given a ninety-day enlistment or any choice on that score. We either lived or died.

While running in circles in the fenced yard, I noticed that my front leg's limp was not as noticeable as it had been right after the Battle of Fort Stedman. Several of the thousands of wooden splinters flying around that morning had stuck deeply in my front leg muscle. Fortunately, good old Mother Nature and time had healed them. The wounds had become infected, which helped push the huge splinters out over time. Only the big saber scars were left as unwanted reminders of the war. I thought I was darn lucky. Suozzi noticed the scars on my front leg and withers. He said, "Blackie, looks like you have been through hell and back. I change my mind now. Your name is now Lucky." Looking up, I thought Providence had a way of looking out for me.

I slept pretty well in my stall that Thursday night. Reflecting on the day, I had a pretty good birthday considering where I was. Friday, April 14 would come with another day of tender loving care courtesy of Sergeant Suozzi. He said the army had scheduled many parades for notable Union generals, like General Grant, General Sherman, and several others returning from the battlefront. The plan was for me and five of my finest Yankee horse friends to pull decorated carriages, seating six generals and their wives. Well, so be it. At least no one was shooting at me, or I wasn't being hunted by starving Confederate soldiers. As Sir Tom would say, I would soldier on and make the best of the situation by choosing my battlefield.

Later that evening, at about ten o'clock, I was standing in my stall half-asleep, when all hell broke out in Washington, D.C. People were yelling, and horses were hastily pulling carriages everywhere. Police were blowing whistles. I was alarmed, thinking the Confederates were marching into the Union Capitol. General Lee changed his mind, but that was just a fleeting thought.

Suozzi came into the barn to check on us horses, and he had a rifle in his hand. I was not sure why he was carrying a weapon; we were spooked. Suozzi yelled out, "Now calm down ladies and gentlemen, there has been a terrible shooting. Our orders are to keep a lookout for two or three men running fast to get out of town. One has a broken leg. My job is to ensure they don't come here and take you boys." What was he talking about?

Evidently, a man named John Wilkes Booth had shot their president, Abraham Lincoln, in the head. The act had been committed at the Ford's Theater in Washington, D.C. Not knowing what that shooting meant for our country, I could only guess that based on the look on Suozzi's face, it was bad for the Union. It could be bad for the South.

There would be no parades that weekend. I remained locked in the stable wondering when I would get a chance to run again. It was okay getting fed and watered on a regular basis but I needed to run. Suozzi came to our stalls at around six o'clock every morning. His face was not smiling nor was he in good cheer. He looked like he had slept in his uniform. I reckoned he was mourning the loss of President Lincoln. Suozzi made some comment about how we Confederates were responsible for assassinating President Lincoln. I hoped not. There would be little chance of peace during our country's reconstruction time ahead.

The rumors of who was behind President Lincoln's assassination would run rampant over the next few months. Eventually, the authorities did catch the men who had plotted and killed President Lincoln. Suozzi said they were Confederate spies, but I wondered if that was true. The killers had used several horses to get away. I had no doubt they were Yankee horses.

April 19, 1865, was a Sunday. In fact, it was Easter Sunday, one of the human's most cherished religious days to celebrate the life of Lord Jesus Christ. I already believed in him. Back home, I would pull the Drayton family carriage every Sunday to St. Michael's church in Charleston. While the Draytons worshiped and sang many songs, I would stand outside at the hitching post, listening to the sweet music intended for the Lord. One of my favorite songs was taken from a poem written for a dying child. The lyrics went something like "Jesus loves me! This I know, for the Bible tells me so. Little ones to him belong; they are weak, but he is strong."

I stuck my head out of the stall to see Suozzi bringing a bucket of oats for every horse in our stable. Maybe it was a special day. Outside our barn, a black-lacquered caisson was decorated with red, white, and blue ribbons. The center of the caisson was empty. Funny, I remembered hauling those caissons loaded with cannon balls, powder, and fuses for the Confederates.

Sergeant Suozzi led six of us out of our stalls to the front of the stable where we all stood wondering if we would be in a parade and what the parade was for. Suozzi said, "It is a very sad day for our nation, ladies and gentlemen. Our fort commander has ordered you six to pull the caisson carrying President Lincoln's body and casket down the streets of our capitol. There will be thousands of people watching, crying, and grieving. You warhorses must keep your pace deliberate and respectful.

Another soldier came up, quickly saying, "Sergeant Suozzi, the Whitehouse wishes to have six white horses pull the president's caisson."

Since this was an order from the White House, Suozzi led us back into the stable stalls. I guessed the army horses penned up on the good side of the fort were to be used. That was fine with me. I would rather be in a parade where the folks were cheering and laughing. Mine eyes had seen enough sorrow. Mine eyes had again seen the coming of the Lord.

⁓

It was now 1867. Many months had passed and countless parades were marked on my harness. I longed more and more to go back home. I missed the old Magnolia Plantation. How wonderful it would be to see home again. I wondered how Mrs. Drayton and Miss Allison were doing. I wondered if Colonel Goodwin had ever made it back to Union County. Then of course, where was my Red? Did she survive the war? I truly hope she did not have to go into battle.

＝

Fate had written Red's story. During the Battle of Gettysburg in July 1863, her trooper was shot off her back. Not long after the rider fell, cannon shot had exploded and knocked her down below a hill called Little Round Top. It had been the third day of the Gettysburg battle, and most of the dead were still lying in the fields of sorrow. Fortunately for Red, she was just knocked out by the shell shock. Rising to her feet, she could not believe her eyes. There was so much death. Tens of thousands of soldiers from both sides were killed in action. Countless were wounded. Hundreds of horses lay dead on the battlefield. Red was so confused as to who she was and where she came from.

Before long, a Union soldier walked over to Red. "Looks like you got spared. God must be looking after you. I will take charge of you now and give you a good home. My little Annie back in Maine will love you. My name is Private Emulous S. Fuller from Freeman, Maine where my wife Maria and I work a farm. Maria sure would love to have you."

Red was still feeling a bit groggy, but she understood the word *farm*. She was ready to go home. Red obliged the soldier's command and willingly went with him, sore, hungry, and thirsty. The kind soldier took out his canteen and poured water in his hand from which Red could drink. Private Fuller said, "Slow down girl, there is more of that back at camp."

The soldier took Red around Little Round Top and back to the rear where tens of thousands of Union soldiers were encamped. Red was amazed at the sheer numbers of soldiers, horses, and cannons. She could overhear men calling out, "We need to go after

Lee, not stay here and wait. Meade is acting like McClellan." Red remembered Dr. Smith talking about how General McClellan could have ended the Civil War if he had gone after Lee after the Battle of Antietam.

While they were walking to a makeshift horse pen made of rope and poles, a Union Cavalry officer rode up to Private Fuller and asked him, "Private, where are you taking that horse?"

"Sir, just taking the horse over to the horse master to check her out. She had been knocked out."

"What cavalry are you with?"

"Sir, I am not. I am attached to the Twentieth Maine Infantry, sir."

The officer issued a stern order. "Soldier, you have no business with that horse. Give me those reins and get back to your unit." Red was confused as to what would happen to her now.

The Union officer took Red over to the quartermaster who would record Red as a property of the United States Army. The trooper asked the quartermaster for a USA saddle, blanket, and bridle to replace the old Confederate-issued tack barely holding together on Red. Before long, Red was back in the roped horse pen Private Fuller had wanted her to stay in. While there, the horse pen attendant fed Red fresh hay, oats, and water. She thought, *No wonder the Yanks won, they are not fighting on empty stomachs and bare feet.*

~~

I spent all of 1867 at Fort Whipple pulling caissons along the streets of Washington, D.C., or tugging funeral caissons to the cemetery located down the hill from the horse stables. The white crosses, which marked graves in the field, grew in number every day. I was mentally tormented by pulling living, happy people during parades on Saturdays, and then turning around to pull dead soldiers to their final resting place at the national cemetery.

Suozzi said General Robert E. Lee's wife, Mary Anna (Custis) Lee, had inherited the Arlington Cemetery property. She was the great-granddaughter of Martha Washington. It was funny how history and fate worked in our lives. The land that had sustained General Lee's family would become the final resting place of the Union men who fell by the Confederacy's swift sword.

In January of 1868, the army promoted Sergeant Suozzi, which meant new orders requiring him to transfer. He was fortunate to have been asked to stay in the military. Most all of the volunteer army had processed out to return to their homes and families. To celebrate the event, Suozzi invited several of his Washington, D.C. friends to attend a private party he was having in our stables. About twenty of his close civilian and military friends showed up with liquor bottles in one hand and cigars in the other. I made note that his civilian friends were all females. I wondered if the army would approve of that.

As the evening went on, the party seemed to get more and more out of hand. The more they drank, the more they smoked. That was the problem. One of the soldiers was too drunk to know he had set his cigar on top of a stall door. Whitie next to me said, "Those dumb drunks. Don't they know that hay catches fire pretty quickly?"

Suozzi saw that it was getting late, and he suggested to the female company that they move their party over to the barn loft. Picking up their bottles, the crowd left the stables for the barn loft across the way. The one thing they forgot was the lit cigar. We all watched the still smoking cigar burn down, falter on the top of the door, and eventually fall to the ground. The lit cigar caused the hay to smolder at first. We all watched the smoke rise into the air. The horses that had never been in battle were the first to raise commotion in the stable; they started kicking and bellowing out for help. Whitie and I remained calm. We had survived many battles where smoke and the cries of the dying were the unwanted memories that never went away.

As the smoke increased in volume, we could barely see where the doors were. Whitie and I knew before long that the hay would turn into fire. With all our might, we kicked at our door stalls to the point where the hinges broke free. We then quickly moved out toward the stable door to once again breathe fresh air.

I turned to Whitie. "We leave no horse behind down South. That is the honor code we live by."

Whitie turned to Lucky. "We leave no horse behind either, which is the American way." Together we went back into the stable and convinced each horse to calm down and kick at the door hinges. We kicked the opposite side of the doors. The amount of force applied to both sides of the stall doors was incredible. Every horse got out alive. While standing together, we all watched the smoke turn into fire, as we were grateful to be alive.

Our friends came up to us and said, "We would all have died if it was not for you and Whitie. Thank you both so much." Whitie and I shrugged it off for we both knew life comes and goes. The war had changed Whitie and me. We did the changing, not our families and friends. We did not call it bravery; we called it our duty.

The army demoted Sergeant Suozzi down to private. In fact, he was discharged from the United States Army the very next day. The stable commander moved us over to the "special" stable located on the other side of the yard. As we walked along the groomed road and white picket fences, we could not help noticing. "Look," we said, "look at that stable. It must have room for two dozen horses." Greeting us at the door was our new barn manager, Sergeant Henry Jones of the First Regiment of the District of Columbia Cavalry. He led us all into the stable, putting each of us into a stall much bigger than the one we had been living in. Sergeant Jones was a big black man who seemed to take his job very seriously. I did not think Whitie or I would be giving him any grief like we did Suozzi.

Two hours later, a man in a white coat came around looking at each of us closely. I wasn't sure what he was looking for, but he touched and prodded every leg and hoof on all of us. When he came to me, he pulled my rear leg up and balanced it on one knee as he knelt down. I heard the man say, "This looks bad. There is significant swelling on the ankle. You must have hurt it kicking down those stall doors when you were saving your friends. It might be broken."

When I heard the word *broken,* I snorted. The memory of the Seven Days Battle came back to me. Anything broken meant certain death for a horse in those days. I pulled my leg back from his hands. "Now, now there boy. I am not going to put you down. I know how to treat wounded horses. You will heal up just fine."

Months had passed, and it seemed life was getting somewhat better. We still lived over here at the "special" stable while the army rebuilt our old stable. It was June 1868, an election year. The people from both north and south would decide together to elect the next president of the United States. We horses did not care until one day, a gentlemen and his small entourage of aides came to our post, requesting transportation down to the cemetery. Colonel Blake, the post commander, greeted them (Sergeant Jones called them our "distinguished visitors") and took them to our stables. The man in the center of attention had a familiar face. It did not take long but then it came to me—he was the Union general our General Lee had met with at the McLean home in Appomattox, Virginia: General Ulysses S. Grant.

One could not be surprised that the victor of the Civil War would want to be the president of the United States. Sergeant Jones said, "Lucky, the general wants you to take him down to the cemetery, alone. I will put the best saddle and blanket we have on you. Do a good job and don't throw him. I will give you some oats with a dab of molasses." Jones sure drove a hard bargain.

With the general on my back, we rode on down the hill toward General Lee's old home. Surrounding the house were thousands of gravesites where war heroes were buried. The general remained silent until we stood facing the hundreds of white crosses that were planted in perfect rows and were facing the Potomac River. We moved slowly between the graves showing respect and honor. I tried not to disturb a leaf with my hooves, but the silence was broken when General Grant started talking to himself. Or me, I wasn't sure.

General Grant said, "I can't and will not make any decision different than the ones I made to help free our country from the chains of misery and injustice that divided the hearts of great men charged with keeping the people of America free and safe. I am forever grateful to each and every one of you here that made the ultimate sacrifice for our nation. Our nation will forever be grateful to you. I pledge that I will commit my heart and soul to making our nation, one nation, under God, with liberty and justice for all."

General Grant pulled on my left rein. "Let us go back, boy. I feel a tear coming on." I did not waver from the command of this unique man. I had never sensed the same from a human like him before, well except perhaps when I met General Robert E. Lee. Both men truly loved their country.

Back at the stable, General Grant was most appreciative of the post commander's time and service. As parting words, General Grant said, "Commander, I would be interested in having that stallion should the United States Army agree at the right time and price."

The post commander saluted General Grant. "Sir, it was our honor and pleasure. We will put the paperwork through for transferring Lucky to your ownership. As you know, that may take several months."

"Understood. I would appreciate the consideration."

After the Grant delegation departed, Sergeant Jones came over to me. "Lucky, looks like you are going to muster out of the United States Army."

My ears perked up. I was thinking it could be a good sign. Jones was smiling ear to ear. I returned to my stall an indeed, there was a bucket of oats with a dab of molasses mixed in. Life was slowly getting better.

Six months later, the people elected Ulysses S. Grant as the Eighteenth President of the United States, the first US President elected after the nation had outlawed slavery and gave citizenship to former African American slaves by US constitutional amendments. President Grant would take his oath of office on March 4, 1869. I remember it well, for I stayed with his ceremonial carriage parked on the side of the street since he had refused to ride in a carriage. He actually walked to the East Portico where he said, "So help me, God."

After the ceremony, my driver took us back to the stable where I was unhitched and led back into my stall. That was a waste of time. I sure was getting tired of Virginia. All that pomp and circumstance just made me want to go home even more. I missed the southern ways of Magnolia Plantation. Somehow, I had to get back. I went to sleep that night dreaming of Red and what we could have been.

Later that week, a messenger from President Grant's office came to the post with an order to bring me over to the White House stable. Sergeant Jones came to my stall. "Lucky, you are one step closer to going home. If anyone can get you home, I am sure President Grant will. I recognized the crescent moon and palmetto brand on your rump. I was a slave down there in Charleston. When I came to this country, the word on the street was, 'our people at Drayton plantation don't get whipped nor chained.' They may have been nice people but I still did not feel that making a man work against his will was right. So, I made my way up north where us blacks were not treated so badly. When the war came, the United States Army felt our blood was just as red as the white men."

Stabled behind the Whitehouse, I was not alone. There was a small pig in the outside pen snorting up a storm, and a mule lived in the stall across from me. What the heck was a mule doing at the White House? The barn manager said the mule was a democrat; it was hardheaded and tough to deal with. I was not really impressed with my new home, as I had no other horses to talk to. Now what should I do? The president of the United States was my new owner and I felt more miserable than before. But I supposed I should be grateful for the mercy shown since I was a Confederate. I would figure something out.

⚊⚊

Red had made her journey from the battlefields of Gettysburg and Fredericksburg to the open fields of Northern Virginia where she grazed lazily on the spring grass covered with morning dew. With her head down, she wondered where Lucky was. Was he still at Magnolia Plantation, or was he drafted into the war? She had seen enough battles to know her fellow horses were shot first by enemy snipers and troopers. Oh, how she longed to see Lucky again!

Red wandered on the fields owned by a medical doctor practicing in Fauquier County, Virginia. His name was Dr. Thomas W. Smith who had moved from Middle Tennessee to Middleburg, Virginia, to practice medicine and breed horses for sale.[28] However, Red was not a good horse for breeding as she never let the stallions near her. She was what the other studs called "a mare with an attitude." She did not care. She would rather live and die alone if her Lucky could not be the father.

On the morning of Friday, April 5, Dr. Smith saddled up Red and decided that he needed a new carriage. He heard there was a superb carriage maker in Loudoun County who made one of the finest black-oak carriages in the area. His name was Mr. Opie Norris.[29] Mr. Norris was a thirty-six-year-old man born with one arm, but he could swing a hammer as if he had two hands. Due to his physical challenge, he was not able to serve in the Civil War, though he vigorously protested that he could shoot with one hand as well as anybody with two. Now, with the war over, Mr. John Norris was grateful he had a family and an ability to make a living.

Red and Dr. Smith made their way over to Leesburg, Virginia, where Dr. Smith had some important business to take care of while in Loudoun County. The daylong journey would be uneventful as the weather was holding up and the roads were dry. Without enough daylight to return to Middleburg, an overnight stay would be necessary. Once in Leesburg, Dr. Smith found lodging for both Red and himself. Riding down Loudoun Street running east to west in Leesburg, he saw a blacksmith's sign on the left and a hotel on the right. He stopped in front of the blacksmith's shop where Mr. Henry Steer charged eight bits for putting up Red in the town stable.[30] Dr. Smith checked into the Red Fox Inn owned by the same fella who owned the Red Fox Inn located in downtown Middleburg. The night would be uneventful for Dr. Smith and Red, but the next day would change their lives.

President Grant's daughter, Nellie, was one who loved horses. She would go out to the stables and care for Lucky when her dad was not in town. Nellie was only fifteen, but she acted older than her age. She said to her mother, "I want to go riding out in the country. I hear that there are many horse farms out in Northern Virginia. Can we please go? Dad's security soldiers can go with us."

Mrs. Grant was always trying to teach their kids discipline and frugalness, but then being a child of a United States president made it difficult to say no.

It was a warm Saturday morning on August 6, 1870. Four armed soldiers escorted Miss Nellie Grant and her mother to the Northern Virginia countryside. They crossed the Potomac River over to the Virginia side called Alexandria. Lucky pulled a carriage where Mrs. Grant and Miss Nellie sat. The carriage was flanked by two soldiers riding up front and two soldiers in back. The Grants' intent was to spend the day traveling the countryside toward Leesburg, Virginia, to see how reconstruction efforts were coming along. As a bonus, Mrs. Grant would surprise Nellie with a stop at a farm to purchase a new horse. Since Lucky was getting older, and Nellie wanted a horse of a different color and sex. Lucky always seemed to have an attitude according to Nellie.

Dr. Smith arose from a deep sleep at around six o'clock in the morning. The sun came up early during the summer, so sleeping in was not an option. He took a bath using the small pot of water heated by a small gas lantern. After getting dressed, he headed downstairs to where breakfast was being served. The smell of eggs, bacon, biscuits, and hot coffee permeated the air.

Dr. Smith smiled all the way down to the table. Pulling up a chair, he sat by himself until a young man came over and asked to join him. His name was Agent Wallace.

"Good morning, sir. My name is Brian Wallace. Would you mind if I joined you?"

Dr. Smith gladly said, "Do sit down. Your company would be appreciated. What brings you into town, Agent Wallace?"

"I work for Senator George S. Boutwell. He asked me to ride in advance of a family visit to Leesburg. I have been here for a few days, making sure all threats to the family were identified and of course, removed."

Dr. Smith said in a low voice, "Sounds like an interesting and dangerous job, Mr. Wallace."

"Yes, indeed," Agent Wallace said with enthusiasm. "If you don't mind me asking, Dr. Smith, what is your business in Leesburg, Virginia?"

After taking a sip of coffee, Dr. Smith replied, "I am in need of a new carriage for my wife. I heard that there was an expert craftsman by the name of Opie Norris who lives not four miles from here toward the Potomac River."

"Sounds like someone's birthday is coming," Agent Wallace said with a snicker.

"Your instincts are correct, my good fellow."

After finishing up breakfast, both Dr. Smith and Agent Wallace parted ways. Dr. Smith walked across the street to get Red. Mr. Steer had Red all saddled up and ready to go. Dr. Smith, once he was mounted on Red, said to Mr. Steer, "Do you know the carriage maker Mr. Opie Norris?"

"I sure do, sir. His farm is not four miles north from here toward the Potomac River. Follow the dirt road that goes right off Loudoun Street. You cannot miss his place. He hung up an old carriage in an oak tree to advertise his wares."

⌇

Mrs. Grant and Nellie traveled about fifteen miles and thought they would stop for a picnic at a creek outside Leesburg not too far off Loudoun Turnpike. The soldiers were motioned to clear the turn before Mrs. Grant and Nellie traveled through the intersection. Turning toward the creek, Nellie spotted a cleared green spot right by the creek. With Lucky tied to the tree, the soldiers positioned themselves by the main road to ensure Mrs. Grant and Nellie were protected from inquiring visitors.

Holding a sandwich in hand, Nellie asked Mrs. Grant, "Mother, why did Dad want to keep that old black horse, Lucky? He has so many scars on his legs and he does not look pretty."

Mrs. Grant touched her cheek. "Nellie that horse was like your father. He had survived many horrible battles during the Civil War."

"Is that where those scars came from, Mother, the battles?"

"Yes," Mrs. Grant said with a small tear in her eye. "No living thing escaped the suffering and sorrow our country experienced between 1861 and 1865. Your father and Lucky were blessed to have been spared death. Unfortunately, many like them did not live to see the rebirth of our nation, the newness your father has been charged with protecting."

"But still, Mother, Lucky rarely lets me get on his back. I am afraid of him," Nellie pleaded.

"Eat your sandwiches, Nellie. We only have a few miles to go before we are in Leesburg."

Dr. Smith and Red made it to the carriage maker's house at about ten o'clock in the morning. Mr. Norris was outside working on a carriage he had built out of black oak, one of the hardest woods in the area.

"Good morning, sir," Dr. Smith said. "I am interested in purchasing that carriage you have masterfully created. Many passersby have reported such a work of art being built by you. I am from Middleburg, Virginia and wish to purchase this carriage. How much do you want for it?"

"Not sure I want to sell it, sir. It has taken me six months to get her in shape. Mr. Steer in Leesburg finally brought out the wheels axles I ordered four months ago."

"Name your price, Mr. Norris. My wife would love this fine piece of art. Please consider the enormous amount of joy your artwork would bring for a woman's heart."

"Purchas'n a gift for the little missus, eh?"

"Okay, how about $250 in gold?"

Mr. Norris raised his head, took a breath and in a low voice, said, "It's a deal."

While walking toward Red, Dr. Smith hurriedly spoke. "Let me get my saddle bag."

The exchange of gold for the carriage was quick. Dr. Smith soon realized he did not have the right leathers to hook up Red.

"Oh, Mr. Norris!" Dr. Smith yelled. "Do you have a set of leathers I could buy from you? I completely forgot to bring the old carriage leathers."

"I do have a set, but I reckon I can part with them for twenty dollars."

Dr. Smith smiled. "Thank you. Thank you so much!"

Red did not like the new carriage. As she pulled it, the wheels seemed to drag her down and there was a squeaking noise coming from the real axle.

Dr. Smith said, "I hear it, Red. Let us go back to Leesburg and have the blacksmith look at it before we go back to Middleburg. We may have to stay another night in Leesburg."

Once we were in town, Dr. Smith took his new carriage over to Mr. Steer's place. Mr. Steer was outside hammering on a hot piece of steel when he saw Red and Doctor Smith.

"Good afternoon, Dr. Smith. How can I help you?"

"Well, it seems the rear axle is making quite a ruckus. Can you fix it?"

"No problem," Mr. Steer replied with a worried face. "However, the repairs will require you to leave it with me overnight. You can leave Red with me, and I will take care of her."

Dr. Smith turned to him. "You're a scholar and a gentleman."

Mrs. Grant and Nellie finally made it to Leesburg at around two o'clock in the afternoon. The sun was blazing hot during that time of day, so it was time to find some shade for Lucky and a cold sassafras drink for Mrs. Grant and Nellie. Once in Leesburg, the soldiers motioned the carriage driver over to the US Post Office on the right side of the street, just one block over from the Red Fox Inn. Standing in front of the post office was Agent Wallace, whom the soldiers knew but did not acknowledge. With his four fingers tucked in his right pocket, Agent Wallace lifted his right thumb up for the senior soldier who was glancing at him while tying his horse to the hitching post.

The soldiers assisted Mrs. Grant and Nellie down from the carriage. Once they were on the boarded sidewalk, they quickly walked toward the General Store that served cold drinks. Once inside, the two sipped on cold sassafras drinks while snacking on fresh popcorn. The soldiers remained vigil by the store's entrance.

Outside, the wind picked up, and as usual, a flurry of dust was kicked up on the road. I was uncomfortable with all the trash bouncing around outside the blacksmith's stable. The hot wind seared my eyes and nose. Suddenly, the wind quit blowing. I stuck my nose up and picked up on a familiar scent lingering in the air. Yes, that was the smell from long ago. However, it can't be. She was surely shot down during the war. The wind picked up and changed directions. I could definitely smell her. With all I could muster, I let out my version of a rebel yell. In response, Red knew I was there.

Inside the store, Mrs. Grant said, "What is that racket going on out there?"

"No worries, ma'am," the senior soldier said, "just the wind making Lucky unhappy."

"I see it is blustery out there. Please go unhitch him, and see if that blacksmith over there can give Lucky a stall and some fresh hay."

"Yes, ma'am," the soldier replied, who did an about face and went out to unhitch Lucky from the carriage. Lucky was not so cooperative at first, but then he settled down when he felt the soldier lead him over to where his Red might be.

Standing in front of Mr. Steer, the soldier said, "Mister, what is your name?"

"Mr. Steer."

"Well, Mr. Steer, would you mind putting this horse up in a stall for an hour or two? The owner would like him fed and watered, if you don't mind."

"That will cost you two bits," Mr. Steer said with a smile.

The soldier handed over the silver piece and returned to his post inside the post office.

The blacksmith grabbed the reins of my halter and said, "Come on, boy, I have what you are looking for." Once inside the dark stable, my eyes were out of focus for a minute. I could barely make out what was in there. However, my nose did not fail me. As I was led deeper into the stable, I could see small lights coming through the stall window slits. I saw movement of shadows breaking the light rays coming from the stall next to the stall the blacksmith led me into. With the door closed, I waited for the blacksmith to leave. Taking a chance, with bated breath, I let a low hello break the stable silence. After nine long years, I heard her voice again; it was Red.

"Is that you, Red?"

"Yes, yes it is me! How did you find me?"

"Fate found you; I was just tagging along for the ride. Mine eyes have truly seen the glory of the coming of the Lord."

⌐⌐

Mine eyes have seen the glory of the coming of the Lord;
He is trampling out the vintage where the grapes of wrath
   are stored;
He hath loosed the fateful lightning of His terrible swift
   sword;
His truth is marching on.

EPILOGUE

Lucky was one of thousands of horses that survived many battles during the Civil War. Though he received only superficial wounds throughout the campaigns, his spirit was wounded by sorrow and tempered by the unyielding desire to live. For many years after the war, my great-great-great-great-grandfather would not talk with his family about the horror he had witnessed and experienced. Lucky thought those memories had best stay in the back of his mind. Instead, he passed on to his children the stories of determination, loyalty, duty, and honor for his sons and daughters to learn from and live by.

Authentic sketch of "Lucky" by Russell Clint Goodwin

ABOUT THE AUTHOR

CDR Goodwin serving in Iraq 2007.

Clint Goodwin spent his childhood working on a small cattle ranch in Mineral Wells, Texas. Raised by Great Depression–era parents, Clint's life would become a story in itself. As a WWII veteran, his father, Russell, shaped Clint's disciplined thinking. Clint's mother, Jolene, raised him and his three siblings while Russell was away working much of the time. Jolene defined Clint's love for people and life. Together, both parents forged Clint's confident views on life and balanced it with reality. In the '60s, Clint thought, his future would be reins in one hand and a rope in the other. During the mid-1970s, he traded them in for a pen and weapon. He would travel the world supporting combat operations as a sailor and naval officer. For over thirty-four years, Clint has served the United States as a military officer and federal employee.

Towards the end of his military career in late 2006, the United States Navy mobilized CDR Goodwin to Iraq. He served there as Chief, Target Development Cell. During this tour, CDR Goodwin led a combined joint-team of agency, military service, and contractor personnel who developed intelligence packages to plan and support intelligence-driven operations throughout the Iraq Theater of Operations. According to his unclassified end-of-tour award write-up, his teams saved lives during combat actions. Clint is a father, husband, and grandfather. He and his wife Karen raised five children: three girls and two boys. Clint and Karen are also proud grandparents of seven grandchildren: four boys and three girls.

Mine Eyes Have Seen the Glory is the first of a series of exciting historical fiction books that bring to life the saga of Lucky and his offspring that fight for the United States of America on the deserts and high plains of the West to the muddy rice paddies and hills of Vietnam. It is a creative approach to learning American History while being entertained.

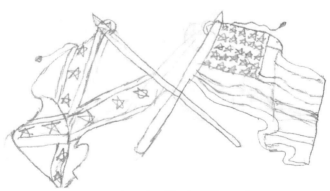

Original art by Gavin Womack.

NOTES

PROLOGUE

1. "Cavalry in the American Civil War," *Wikipedia*, last modified September 20, 2013, http://en.wikipedia.org/wiki/Cavalry_in_the_American_Civil_War.

LUCKY'S NEW OWNER

2. "P.G.T. Beauregard, General, May 28, 1818 – February 20, 1893, " *Civil War Trust*, last accessed December 6, 2013, http://www.civilwar.org/education/history/biographies/p-g-t-beauregard.html.

3. "Naming of the battles and armies," *Wikipedia*, last modified November 6, 2013, http://en.wikipedia.org/wiki/Naming_the_American_Civil_War.

4. "The Stone House, Manassas National Battlefield Park," *Wikipedia*, last modified July 6, 2013, http://en.wikipedia.org/wiki/The_Stone_House,_Manassas_National_Battlefield_Park. The Stone House, Manassas National Battlefield Park is a two-story, stone structure in Prince William County, Virginia. It was built as a stop on the Fauquier and Alexandria Turnpike in 1848, but it achieved its main significance during

the American Civil War, when it served as a hospital during the First and Second Battles of Manassas. Today it is owned by the National Park Service as a contributing property to the Manassas National Battlefield Park, which is listed on the National Register of Historic Places. To better understand what the soldiers and horses viewed as the ground truth, the author and his wife walked this battlefield on July 21, 2011.

5. "J.E.B. Stuart," *Wikipedia*, last modified November 14, 2013, http://en.wikipedia.org/wiki/J.E.B._Stuart. James Ewell Brown Stuart (February 6, 1833—May 12, 1864) was a U.S. Army officer from Virginia and a Confederate States Army general during the American Civil War. He was known to his friends as "Jeb", from the initials of his given names. Stuart was a cavalry commander known for his mastery of reconnaissance and the use of cavalry in support of offensive operations. While he cultivated a cavalier image (red-lined gray cape, yellow sash, hat cocked to the side with a ostrich plume, red flower in his lapel, often sporting cologne), his serious work made him the trusted eyes and ears of Robert E. Lee's army and inspired Southern morale.

6. "Williamsburg," *National Park Service American Battlefield Protection Program*, last modified December 3, 2013, http://www.cr.nps.gov/hps/ABPP/battles/va010.htm. Also known as the Battle of Fort Magruder, took place on May 5, 1862, in York County, James City County, and Williamsburg, Virginia, as part of the Peninsula Campaign of the American Civil War. It was the first pitched battle of the Peninsula Campaign, in which nearly 41,000 Federals and 32,000 Confederates were engaged, fighting an inconclusive battle that ended with the Confederates continuing their withdrawal.

7. "J.E.B. Stuart, Peninsula" *Wikipedia*, last modified November 14, 2013, http://en.wikipedia.org/wiki/J.E.B._Stuart. During the Union's Peninsula Campaign, Gen. Robert E. Lee requested Stuart to determine whether the right flank

of the Union army was vulnerable. Stuart set out with 1,200 troopers on the morning of June 12 and, having determined that the flank was indeed vulnerable, took his men on a complete circumnavigation of the Union army, returning after 150 miles on July 15 with 165 captured Union soldiers, 260 horses and mules, and various quartermaster and ordnance supplies. His men met no serious opposition from the more decentralized Union cavalry, coincidentally commanded by his father-in-law, Col. Cooke.

8. "How did Robert E. Lee Become and American Icon" *National Endowment for the Humanities,* James C. Cobb, HUMANITIES, July/August 2011,Volume 32, Number 4, last accessed on December 8, 2013, http://www.neh.gov/humanities/2011/julyaugust/feature/how-did-robert-e-lee-become-american-icon. The referenced source addresses key Robert E. Lee professional and personal traits that distinguishes him from other military leaders. The article's author, Mr. James C. Cobb was commissioned by the federal government's National Endowment for the Humanities to produce an interesting read about Robert E. Lee.

9. "Civil War Summaries by Campaign, Peninsula Campaign [March-July 1862]," *National Park Service American Battlefield Protection Program,* last modified December 3, 2013, http://www.cr.nps.gov/hps/ABPP/battles/bycampgn.htm. The Union's Peninsula Campaign consist of fifteen battles fought in Virginia at Hampton Roads, Yorktown, Williamsburg, Eltham's Landing, Drewry's Bluff, Hanover Courthouse, Seven Pines, Oak Grove, Beaver Dam Creek, Gaines' Mill, Garnetts & Goldings Farm, Savage's Station, Glendale/White Oak Swamp (VA020) and Malvern Hill

10. "Seven Days Battles." *Wikipedia,* last modified November 14, 2013, http://en.wikipedia.org/wiki/Seven_Days_Battles#The_Seven_Days. The Seven Days Battles was a series of six major battles over the seven days from June 25 to

July 1, 1862, near Richmond, Virginia during the American
Civil War. Confederate General Robert E. Lee drove the
invading Union Army of the Potomac, commanded by Maj.
Gen. George B. McClellan, away from Richmond and into
a retreat down the Virginia Peninsula. The series of battles is
sometimes known erroneously as the Seven Days Campaign.
It was actually the completion of the Peninsula Campaign.

11. "Seven Days Battles." *Wikipedia*, last modified November
14,   2013,   http://en.wikipedia.org/wiki/Seven_Days_
Battles#The_Seven_Days. Numbers are only estimates.

BATTLE OF ANTIETAM

12. "Battle of Antietam," *National Park Service American
Battlefield Protection Program*, last modified December 3,
2013,   http://www.cr.nps.gov/hps/ABPP/battles/md003.
htm. Antietam (pronounced /ænˈtiːtəm/) also known in the
South as the Battle of Sharpsburg was fought on September
17, 1862, near Sharpsburg, Maryland, and Antietam Creek,
as part of the Confederate's Maryland Campaign. It was the
first major battle in the American Civil War to take place
on Northern soil. It was the bloodiest single-day battle in
American history, with over 23,000 casualties.

13. "Eyewitness to the Battle," *National Park Service*, last modified November 28, 2013, http://www.nps.gov/anti/history-
culture/eyewitness-to-battle.htm.

14. "The Bloodiest One Day Battle in American History,"
National Park Service, last modified November 28, 2013,
http://www.nps.gov/anti/index.htm. Over 23,000 soldiers
were killed, wounded or missing after twelve hours of savage combat on September 17, 1862. The Battle of Antietam
ended the Confederate Army of Northern Virginia's first
invasion into the North and led to Abraham Lincoln's issu-
ance of the preliminary Emancipation Proclamation. To bet-

ter understand what the soldiers and horses viewed as the ground truth, the author and his wife walked this battlefield on September 17, 2012.

BATTLE OF FREDERICKSBURG

15. "Battle of Fredericksburg," *National Park Service American Battlefield Protection Program*, last modified December 3, 2013, http://www.cr.nps.gov/hps/ABPP/battles/va028.htm. To better understand what the soldiers and horses ground truth, the author and his wife walked this battlefield on December 15, 2012.

GETTYSBURG FIELDS OF SORROW

16. "Battle of Brandy Station," *National Park Service American Battlefield Protection Program*, last modified December 7, 2013, http://www.nps.gov/frsp/brandy.htm. Over 11,000 Union men had massed on the other side of the Rappahannock River. Maj. Gen. Alfred Pleasonton, commanding the Cavalry Corps of the Army of the Potomac, had organized his combined-armed forces into two "wings," under Brig. Gens. John Buford and David McMurtrie Gregg, augmented by infantry brigades from the V Corps.

17. "Battle of Brandy Station," *National Park Service American Battlefield Protection Program*, last modified December 7, 2013, http://www.nps.gov/frsp/brandy.htm. Pleasonton launched a surprise dawn attack on Stuart's cavalry at Brandy Station, Virginia. After an all-day fight in which fortunes changed repeatedly, the Federals retired without discovering Gen. Robert E. Lee's infantry camped near Culpeper. This battle marked the end of the Confederate cavalry's lop-

sided dominance in the East. From this point in the war, the Federal cavalry gained strength and confidence.

18. "Gettysburg," *National Park Service American Battlefield Protection Program*, last modified December 3, 2013, http://www.cr.nps.gov/hps/ABPP/battles/pa002.htm. To better understand what the soldiers and horses viewed as the ground truth, the author and his wife walked this battlefield on July 1, 2012.

19. "The Battle of Yellow Tavern," *National Park Service*, last modified December 7, 2013, Source: http://www.nps.gov/anti/index.htm. The Battle of Yellow Tavern occurred on May 11, at an abandoned inn located six miles (10 km) north of Richmond. The Confederate troopers tenaciously resisted from the low ridgeline bordering the road to Richmond, fighting for over three hours. The Federal horsemen punctured Lomax's brigade and pushed the Confederate let flank backwards. General Stuart rushed among his men and tried to rally them. Some of Custer's men swirled past Stuart, but a timely counterattack by a portion of the 1st Virginia Cavalry stopped their progress and drove them back. As the Federals withdrew, Private John A. Huff of the 5th Michigan Cavalry hurriedly fired his pistol into a group of mounted Confederates by the Telegraph Road. J.E.B. Stuart clutched his side. His head dipped and the general's plumed hat fell in the dust. He calmly whispered, "I am shot." A trooper supported Stuart while another led his horse to the rear.

TEMPORARY DUTY

20. Dr. William Glenn Robertson and others, *Staff Ride Handbook for the Battle of* Chickamauga, 18-20 1863, (Combat Studies Institute U.S. Army Command and General Staff College 1992), 46.

21. "William T. Sutherland." *Wikipedia*, last modified October 27, 2013, http://en.wikipedia.org/wiki/William_T._Sutherlin. William Thomas Sutherlin (1822—1893) was a 19th Century tobacco entrepreneur most famous for opening his Danville, Virginia, home to the President of the Confederate States of America Jefferson Davis and his Cabinet during the week before Gen. Robert E. Lee surrendered the Army of Northern Virginia at Appomattox Courthouse (April 3—April 10, 1865). Before the Civil War, Sutherlin operated the second largest tobacco factory in the state of Virginia and was the first Virginian to apply steam power to hydraulic tobacco presses. Sutherlin also founded and served as the first president of the Bank of Danville. In 1855, Sutherlin was elected as Danville's mayor and served for six years in this capacity.

HOME HAS CHANGED

22. "Andersonville," *National Park Service*, last modified December 7, 2013, http://www.nps.gov/ande/planyourvisit/special.htm. Andersonville National Historic Site began as a stockade built about 18 months before the end of the U.S. Civil War to hold Union Army prisoners captured by Confederate soldiers. Located deep behind Confederate lines, the 26.5-acre Camp Sumter (named for the southern Georgia county it occupied) was designed for a maximum of 10,000 prisoners. At its most crowded, it held more than 32,000 men, many of them wounded and starving, in horrific conditions with rampant disease, contaminated water, and only minimal shelter from the blazing sun and the chilling winter rain. In the prison's 14 months of existence, some 45,000 Union prisoners arrived here; of those, 12,920 died and were buried in a cemetery created just outside the prison walls.
23. "Reading 1: Andersonville Prison," *National Park Service*, last modified December 8, 2013, http://www.nps.gov/ande/plan-

yourvisit/special.htm. Along the interior of the stockade, 19 feet from the stockade wall, was a line of small wooden posts with a wood rail on top. This was the "deadline." Any prisoner who crossed the deadline could be shot by guards stationed in the sentry boxes.

24. "Wade Hampton," *National Park Service*, last modified December 8, 2013, http://www.nps.gov/ande/planyourvisit/special.htm. Born in 1818 in South Carolina, Wade Hampton was the son of wealthy planters. He ran his plantations in South Carolina and the lower Mississippi Valley and held several public offices before the war. At the start of the war he personally raised and mostly equipped the Hampton Legion, a force of infantry, cavalry and artillery. Hampton fought at First Manassas and participated in the Peninsula, Antietam and Gettysburg Campaigns. The last two as a cavalry commander. In September 1863 he became a major general and with Gen. Jeb Stuart's (CSA) death in May, 1864 he takes command of the cavalry corps during the siege. During the siege of Petersburg he was involved in the Beefsteak Raid, Reams Station and Burgess Mill. He was twice elected governor of South Carolina after the war and served as a U.S. Senator until 1891.

LEE'S SURRENDER AND GRANT'S VICTORY

25. "Black Soldiers on the Appomattox Campaign," *National Park Service*, last modified December 8, 2013, http://www.nps.gov/ande/planyourvisit/special.htm. On August 25, 1862, Secretary of War Edwin Stanton authorized the enlistment of black troops into the Federal Army. Although enlistments began in 1862, it was not until 1864 that recruitment of blacks gathered momentum. Eventually, 178,982 men served in 166 regiments in the Union Army. These regiments, designated United States Colored Troops (U.S.C.T.), saw

service throughout the South; however, the largest number in any one theater fought in the campaigns against the Army of Northern Virginia.

26. "The Civil War, Soldiers and Sailors Database," *National Park Service*, last modified November 24, 2013, http://www.nps. gov/civilwar/people.htm. According to the NPS Soldiers and Sailors Database, R.W. Goodwin was never assigned to the Confederate States of America 7th Regiment South Carolina.

27. "Petersburg, The Siege of Petersburg: The Longest Military Event of the Civil War," *National Park Service*, last modified November 30, 2013, http://www.nps.gov/pete/index.htm.

LEE'S SURRENDER AND GRANT'S VICTORY

28. "Thomas Smith," Index of /va/fauquier/census/1850, last accessed December 8, 2013, http://files.usgwarchives.org/va/ fauquier/census/1850/pg0273b.txt.

29. "Opie Norris," *USGenWeb Archives, Lancaster County Virginia 1850*, last accessed December 8, 2013, http://www.usgwcen- sus.org/cenfiles/va/lancaster/1850/1850cena.txt.

30. "Henry Steer," Index of /va/loudoun/census/1850, last accessed December 8, 2013, http://files.usgwarchives.net/va/ loudoun/census/1850/pg0290a.txt.